To Rick

GINGERBREAD MAN

A Nursery Rhyme Suspense
By Lee Strauss

Enjoy!

Lea Strauss

Lee Strauss

Gingerbread Man
By Lee Strauss
Cover by Steven Novak Illustrations
Copyright © 2015
ISBN: 9781927547762

PART ONE
Chapter 1

Teagan

CLAY FROM HER SCULPTING class remained stubbornly under her nails. Teagan let her messy blond locks fall over her eyes and returned to the vigorous scrubbing of her hands. She swallowed a lump. Sage was leaving her to go out for drinks with a bunch of math brainiacs. It was nice of Sage to invite her, but Teagan didn't like to meet new people in that kind of setting. It was too loud to have a decent conversation and too crowded. All the noise and the bodies overwhelmed her. Besides, Teagan had nothing in common with Sage's friends, and she'd just end up looking like a dork with no one to talk to.

Sage leaned her dark head against the open bathroom door. "Teagan, are you sure you don't want to come?"

"Nah, I'm really tired," Teagan said, avoiding Sage's eyes. "And I've got a lot of reading to do."

"You're sure?"

Teagan glanced up at her then, since refusing would just make Sage persist. She forced a small smile. "I'm sure.

Go have fun."

Sage left and Teagan actually felt relieved. She enjoyed solitude and quiet. She finished her homework and required reading for the night and eventually found herself playing on the campus's Facefacts sites. She joined the student chat forums thinking she could hang out virtually. It was quieter and safer, socially speaking. She didn't have to worry if she was wearing the right thing or if she laughed at the wrong moment.

Rain began to pelt the windows, the first weather change since college started, and Teagan saw a huge bolt of lightning stretch across the emerald sky. The lights in the room flickered, and a sizzling electric shock zapped her fingers through the keyboard.

"Ow!" She rubbed her fingertips. Not that it hurt so much. It just surprised her. Nothing like that had ever happened before. A quick look around the room confirmed that the lights and electricity continued to function normally. Teagan tentatively lowered her fingers to the keyboard and let out a short breath. She examined her laptop and both the hardware and software programs seemed to be fine. She shook it off as a random freak event.

It was a slow night in the chat forums

because everyone was out socializing in real life) and not many people were signed on. Teagan randomly picked a person: averagegeek99. She considered herself an art geek and just a geek in general, so she felt a measure of confidence that averagegeek99 and she could be friends.

@art4ever to @averagegeek99: Hi

Teagan waited, but averagegeek99 didn't respond. Maybe he or she was shy? Or away from their desk? Or just forgot to log off. It was entirely possible that she was the only student at Detroit University who remained in her dorm room on a Friday night.

She almost shut her laptop when she heard the beep indicating a response to her salutation.

@averagegeek99: Hi, @art4ever.

Now what? Teagan didn't even know if this was a guy or girl, and it was hard to tell by their poorly chosen blurry profile picture. Best just to ask.

@art4ever: I hope you aren't offended by my next question, but might you be MR. averagegeek99 or MS averagegeek99?

@averagegeek99: Most definitely Mr. I assume you are a student, Ms. art4ever. Your profile pic makes your gender clear. Note to self: must change my profile pic pronto!

@art4ever: I am. In the arts program. Freshman. You?

Oh, this was fun! And worry free. If the conversation got weird she'd just say goodbye and log out. No awkward conversational dead spaces where you didn't know where to look exactly, or inner debates on whether it was socially acceptable to excuse oneself after fifteen minutes at a party (or worse, a date—not that she'd know) and how to go about a successful extraction.

@averagegeek99: I'm in the science program, so not likely to share any classes. Unfortunately.

Frankly, Teagan was glad about that. For what it was, she liked to keep her online social life separate from her real-life social life. It was neater that way.

@averagegeek99: Also Freshman. Do you hail from Detroit?

@art4ever: No. I'm an import from Illinois.

@averagegeek99: A worthy state.

@art4ever: I think so. Detroit is lovely though.

@averagegeek99: lol

Teagan was a little confused as to why he thought that was funny. She chalked it up to the lack of emotional signals that one gets through vocal expression, certain nuances that can be missed when typing a conversation.

@art4ever: I take it you are also spending this fine Friday evening in your dorm room?

@art4ever: Not that there's anything wrong with that.

@art4ever: Obviously. As I am also, clearly, not out.

Oh, God. She was wrong about not being a social misfit online. She sounded like a loser.

@averagegeek99: Friday nights out on the town are hugely overrated.

@averagegeek99: In my humble opinion

She liked this guy!

@art4ever: I couldn't agree more. Besides chatting with perfect strangers not IRL, what else do you like to do? Do you like music?

Mr. averagegeek99 proceeded to fill her feed with a long list of his favorite bands. Teagan was happy to see they were a mix of mostly indie and many she hadn't heard of. She was rewarded with a couple links and took a listen.

@art4ever: You have good taste in music. I like it very much.

Before she knew it, midnight had come and gone. She'd spent three hours talking to a perfect stranger whose face she couldn't imagine.

@art4ever: Would you like to chat again tomorrow?

It was a brazen post and Teagan immediately regretted it. What was she thinking? How pathetic must he think she was now?

Worse, he didn't respond right away, and when he did Teagan's cheeks blushed with embarrassment. She was so thankful he couldn't see her.

@averagegeek99: I'm sorry. I have something on tomorrow night.

She typed quickly.

@art4ever: Of course. Actually, I do too.

Completely forgot. I can be such a dunce sometimes.

There. He was off the hook. This was just a one-time thing. No biggie. Whatever.

@averagegeek99: How about the day after next?

Oh. He did want to meet her again. She felt her lips purse into a smile.

@art4ever: Okay. Sure. Same time?

@averagegeek99: Same time. See you then!

Teagan didn't know why this made her happy. She had no idea who averagegeek99 was or even what he looked like. But he had a very nice online personality. A little warning flag niggled at the back of her brain about the dangers of online dating, but it wasn't like their meeting online Sunday night was a date. He was a friend. Not even a friend. Faceless and nameless.

Nothing to worry about.

Chapter 2

Sage

I PROPPED against soft pillows on my narrow bed, my laptop comfortably resting on my legs, and adjusted the lenses on my face. I had a collection of nonprescription glasses and today I wore the purple plastic frames. Lots of people wore them as a fashion accessory, which had become the trend since prescription lenses became a thing of the past, but I liked to wear them because they detracted from my nose. It had a notable bridge, and I was always self-conscious about it. Teagan said it made me look refined and sophisticated, but that was easy to say when you had a cute little ski-slope for a nose.

My eyes zeroed in on the campus website's front page. "Did you see these special bulletins warning girls not to walk alone after dark?" I said to Teagan. "There's even a free self-defense class offered."

Teagan glanced up from her tablet and frowned.

"This campus is safe, right? Those announcements are just the administration doing its due diligence. Right?" She stroked the blue streak in her hair. "There hasn't been a serious crime committed against a student at Detroit University in over fifteen years."

"I'm sure it's perfectly safe," I responded, fully aware of her OCD process when it came to sending out college applications. "But it's always good to be on alert, no?"

Teagan nodded, her shoulders relaxing, and her attention returned to her tablet. She twisted the blue streak in her hair around her fingers. The splash of color was a new addition, a move of passive rebellion against her controlling mother.

Teagan and I became best friends the day I moved into the house next door to hers, back in fifth grade. She ran over to say hi, a bubbly wide smile on her round babyface. Her mother followed quickly wearing a body-fitting dress and high heels. I remembered, even at that young age, that she didn't look like any mom I'd ever known, and certainly not like my mother who wore loose jeans and an oversized sweater with sneakers on her feet most days.

Mrs. Lake introduced herself politely, but I didn't miss her look of disapproval. She apologized for interrupting us since we were obviously very busy moving, and then pulled Teagan away by her skinny arms. I thought that would be the last I'd see of Teagan, but we had to ride the bus together and ended up in the same class. Mrs. Lake couldn't stop us from being friends and eventually she just accepted that I was going to be a part of her life like an annoying stray dog. After a few years she began to soften toward me and now I believed she actually liked me a little bit.

"Did you know Van Gogh went crazy?" Teagan said. "Died before he saw any success. Makes me wonder once again about the wisdom of going for an arts degree."

"Because you're a fantastic artist," I said. Only a few weeks into the first semester and Teagan had already decorated our room with her art projects. They made the small space feel warm and cozy.

She flashed me an appreciative grin. "*And* I'm crazy."

"You're not crazy. I couldn't imagine you doing anything else."

"Ah, thanks besty."

I laughed at her. "You know it's true."

I checked the time and took a deep breath. If Teagan had her way, we'd stay in every night, just the two of us, watching streaming TV or listening to music while doing homework. I needed more. I needed different. I also didn't want to hurt Teagan's feelings by leaving her out, so I extended another offer. "A few of us are meeting for drinks soon. You should come this time."

Teagan let her tablet fall to her lap. "Again? What the hay? You're not even old enough to drink."

"They serve soda, ya know. It's just a social thing. It's not about getting drunk. Teagan, come with me! You're acting like an old lady staying home all weekend alone. All you need are a couple cats."

Teagan's face fell and I steeled myself for another rejection, a repeat of her mini lecture on how she preferred small social groups of two, three tops, but she surprised me by saying, "Fine. I'll go."

"Great!" I bounced a little on my bed, but restrained myself from showing too much enthusiasm.

I didn't want to scare her off. "It'll be fun, you'll see."

I winked. "Maybe you'll meet your 'cute, well-rounded, thoughtful guy.'"

She threw a pillow at me. "I so regret telling you that!"

I chuckled. Teagan had made it through high school without a boyfriend.

She claimed to be too busy with her art projects and working on getting the best grades she could. Dating took up too much time. She claimed she was waiting for a cute, well-rounded, thoughtful guy.

I often accused her of being too picky. She said she wanted a romantic, mature guy who didn't think burping the alphabet while drunk on beer was the epitome of modern culture.

She had a point. I'd dated enough immature guys to know.

Plus there was her mother. I didn't blame Teagan

for not wanting to bring guys home with her there. For many reasons.

I pushed my laptop aside and began to dress. I searched for my cleanest jeans and a long-sleeved blouse. Almost time to make a trip to the laundry again.

Teagan stared at the pile of clothes that cascaded out over her open dresser drawers. "What should I wear?" she asked. "Is this a cute-little-dress function or a jeans-and-pretty-blouse affair?"

"Jeans," I said. "Do you have heels with you? That'll dress them up."

Teagan didn't often wear heels because she was already quite tall and I knew she hated feeling like she was towering over everyone. She tended to slouch to compensate.

She sifted through an assortment of scarves lifting a red one with white polka dots in one hand and a purple and yellow paisley print in the other. "Which one?"

"Purple. It brings out the green flecks in your eyes." She folded the scarf until it was a narrow band, wrapped it over her head and made a knot at the base of her neck.

Now that Teagan had agreed to come, she was taking her time getting ready, a typical stall tactic. I'd already dressed, applied makeup, and did my hair while she was still messing around. I grabbed the handle of our door with one hand and tapped my foot. "Almost done?"

I hated to be late to anything, even when it was just meeting up casually with friends. Teagan was almost always late. She rushed around under my scrutiny, grabbed her jacket and threw her phone into her purse.

She flashed a careful smile. "As ready as I'll ever be."

Chapter 3

A WRY SMILE tugged up one side of his face as he counted all the pretty blond heads at the campus bar. He felt like a lion at a gazelle convention. He'd developed a taste for feisty blonds at fifteen when he cornered unsuspecting little Lola Fenster at a party.

That party happened on a Saturday night, forty-five minutes after his old man had used him as a punching bag. His mother, with her perfectly coifed blond hair winced as her son took each blow, but did nothing to stop it. Nothing. He hated her.

Lola and Doug Fenster's parents had left for the weekend, giving Doug a long-awaited opportunity to throw the biggest party of the year. Doug was supposed to be watching his twelve-year-old sister, but he'd gotten so stupidly drunk that night he had trouble locating the bathroom, much less paying attention to her.

Smug little Lola reminded him of his mother, the way she twisted her blond hair around her finger and ignored him with a cocky superiority.

He was still tense and riled up, adrenaline rushing from the pain his father had inflicted to his torso. The bastard never struck his face where he might leave evidence of his brutality; his bruising ran from the neck down. He needed a way to find a release. Something.

That was when Lola strutted past him dressed like she was an eighteen-year-old hooker without even a nod of acknowledgment, as if he were yesterday's trash. He knew the layout of Doug's house, having been invited over once before. He knew about the guest room.

He sprinted up the stairs and reached Lola just as she walked past the bedroom door. He grabbed her by the arm, pushed her into the darkened room and slapped a hand over her mouth, stifling her screams. The way she fought back just excited him more. The loud music from the floor below drowned out her muffled cries. He took what he wanted and threatened to kill her and her family if she told anyone about it.

He zipped his pants and headed out through the party like he was just stepping outside for a smoke. No one looked at him like they could tell what he'd just done. He kept walking until he was alone on the street. He felt powerful, awash with a sense of euphoria.

There had been a couple other girls since, but they'd been passed out from the date rape drug he'd put in their drinks, and those ones hadn't been very satisfying. He liked it better when they fought back. Screamed a little. Their eyes glassy with fear and awash with pain, dulling finally with resignation.

He hated when they cried but there was nothing he could do about that. Unless he shut them up for good.

He ordered a beer.

"Welcome to Detroit University," the server said after ascertaining that he was new to the city. "Have a good time."

"Thanks," he returned with a warm smile. "I think it's going to be a great year."

Chapter 4

Teagan

THE CLUB WAS a trendy place on the perimeter of the university grounds. Energy-efficient cars moved quietly along tree-lined roads. Pop music played loudly through a speaker system and the air smelled like beer and savory food. French fries and nachos. Someone waved from a table in the center of the room and Sage waved back as she and Teagan wove their way through the crowd.

"Hey, everyone!" Sage said while taking an empty seat. "This is Teagan." Teagan took the last chair beside her and waved limply. "Teagan, this is everyone."

Teagan smiled but wished that Sage had taken the trouble to tell her actual names. Teagan covertly examined each face, giving the guys an extra moment as she tried to discern if any of them could be averagegeek99. She stared when they looked off to the side, but even their profiles didn't give her enough clues.

Hmm. It occurred to her that averagegeek99 knew what she looked like by her profile pic, but there would be no way she could pick him out in a crowd based on his. She'd have to rely on him recognizing her and making introductions.

Sage whispered in her ear. "Why are you staring like that?"

"I'm staring?"

"Yes. It's weird."

"Sorry. I'll stop."

Teagan reverted to gazing at her hands. Finally, a server came and she ordered a coke. The conversation at the table moved from math to movies to sports. Two of the math whizzes also played hockey for the university team. Full scholarships. Teagan knew this because one of the guys, Chet (Sage had addressed him as such), told them. Twice, in case they missed it the first time. His dark eyes kept cutting to Teagan and shifting away when she caught him looking.

"Teagan Lake, right?"

Teagan's head popped up at the mention of her name. "What?"

The guy next to her waved a hand in front of her face, and his mouth pulled up into an amused smile. "Over here."

She glanced at him cautiously. "How do you know my last name?"

"I'm in your philosophy class. I sit behind you. I'm Jake Wentworth."

He held out his hand and Teagan stared at it for a second before it clicked that he wanted her to shake it. "Oh, hi."

She couldn't help the little giggle that escaped her lips. Jake was attractive, and he smelled good. Maybe *he* was her cute, well-rounded, thoughtful guy. They talked a little about the class and how much they liked Professor Madsen, but then his attention went back to the other guys at the table and the subject of hockey, which she knew nothing about and therefore was ill-equipped to contribute to the conversation further.

Teagan found herself searching the sea of faces beyond their table, wondering if one of them belonged to averagegeek99. She waited for some sign of recognition. A connected gaze that lasted a moment longer than necessary, but alas, there was nothing so romantic as that.

Jake nudged her arm and she spent the rest of the evening chatting with him about mundane things. The experience was surprisingly pleasant until Chet threw a peanut at Jake to get his attention. It ricocheted off the table and hit her in the forehead.

"Ow!"

"Jerkwad!" Jake said. Then to Teagan, "Are you okay?"

She pressed two fingers against her forehead and forced a small laugh. "Yeah, it's nothing. Just an accident."

She glanced up across the table at Chet, expecting to see an expression of surprise and remorse. Instead, his dark gaze narrowed before he quickly looked away.

What was *his* problem?

Teagan turned to Sage and pleaded with her eyes to please go home. Sage stiffened under her less than subtle stare.

"Okay, fine," she finally said. "We'll go."

Chapter 5

Marlow

FOR SOME REASON some reason I couldn't stop thinking about art4ever. Her profile picture was cute, but you couldn't trust those. For all I knew, she pulled the photo offline and she didn't look like that at all. But I couldn't complain since mine wasn't even gender-definable, apparently. I needed to change it, but the God-honest truth? I was afraid she wouldn't show up for our meeting tonight if she knew what I really looked like.

I took a selfie without my glasses, but had to put them on to see what the photo looked like. Okay, I guess, but not handsome by any stretch of the imagination.

Hiding my unremarkable mug behind black plastic frames wasn't a bad idea. I took another selfie with the glasses on, purposefully making a funny face. I might look like a joker, but at least I now looked like a guy.

We weren't meeting up until 8:00, so I spent time in the library studying the plasma membrane of animal cells and drank more coffee than was good for me. I made it home three minutes after the hour which was fine. I didn't want to appear too eager. I'd learned from experience that girls fled the scene if a guy came on too strong.

Actually, they fled any scene I was in as if they had geek alert apps embedded in their brains. This girl seemed different. She was already aware by my handle that I was a self-proclaimed geek, and *she* had contacted me first.

One could always hope.

@averagegeek99 to @art4ever: Are you there?"

@art4ever: I'm here. You changed your profile pic! Nice glasses!

I chuckled. This chick was cool.

@averagegeek99: Thanks. They complement my nose. At least that's what I'm told.

@art4ever: My roommate wears frames for fun, too. She's also self-conscious of her nose.

@averagegeek99: I can't say I find wearing them fun, but they do the trick. How was your weekend?

@art4ever: Good. We went to a pub with friends.

@averagegeek99: We?

She never mentioned a boyfriend, but that didn't mean there wasn't one.

@art4ever: My roommate and me. She studies math and technology, so I generally find the conversation she has with her other friends hard to follow. Mostly, the talk was about the Bluewings.

That made me laugh.

@averagegeek99: It's the Redwings. Honest mistake since you're not from here. Nor, apparently, a sports fan.

@art4ever: I suck at sports. But I'm pretty sure they called the hockey team the Bluewings.

Okay. Certainly not a point to get into an argument over.

@averagegeek99: So @art4ever, tell me about yourself. Besides the fact that you are an art student from Illinois.

@art4ever: I feel like we're speed dating. Lol. Okay. Um. I'm an only child, so yes, my parents are overprotective and have given me every advantage. But, I'm not spoiled. Unless I am. It depends who you're talking to. I like maple walnut ice cream, the color pink and the way wet clay feels in my hands as I shape it into something incredible.

@art4ever: Your turn.

@averagegeek99: I also am an only child, raised by a single mom. I dislike ice cream—too sweet—but love any flavor of potato chip. Even the

weird ones like ketchup.

@art4ever: Ketchup-flavored potato chips?

@averagegeek99: Yeah. They ship them in from Canada. You'll have to try them someday.

@art4ever: I'll try anything once.

@averagegeek99: Anything?

@art4ever: Well, within reason. I won't try plastic surgery. What if my new nose turned out worse than my old one? Or suicide. Obviously.

Obviously.

@averagegeek99: What's your favorite book?

@art4ever: Harry Potter

@averagegeek99: That's a series, not a single book.

@art4ever: I like to think about it as one long book. What's yours?

@averagegeek99: *One Who Flew Over the Cuckoo's Nest*.

@art4ever: I couldn't finish that book. Can we still be friends?

I chortled and felt strangely warmed. She thought of me as a friend.

@averagegeek99: Lol. Of course. And since we're friends, is it okay if I ask you your first name? Mine is Marlow.

I figured first-name basis should be okay, but when she didn't respond right away, I worried I'd overstepped. But then she finally answered.

@art4ever: Teagan. Nice to meet you, Marlow.

@averagegeek99: Nice name.

@art4ever: Thanks. Anyway, I should go. Busy week ahead and I still have homework to do.

@averagegeek99: Me too. See you around?

@averagegeek99: In cyberspace, I mean.

@art4ever: ☺ I'm here most evenings.

@averagegeek99: Great. Have a good rest of your evening. Marlow out.

We were on first-name basis. She saw my mug shot and still wanted to chat again. Things were definitely looking up.

The days were at best ordinary and crawled by. That was life when you took sleeper classes and hung out with dull people. The highlight of each day was my evening chat with Teagan. My dorm mates were starting to give me grief over it and called her my Virtual Girl.

I pushed my glasses up the bridge of my nose and squinted. So much monitor work was making me blind. My inbox announced a college social—no way was I going to that. I already knew most of the nerds here, anyway. We'd lived in the same Detroit neighborhood, gone to the same schools, ran from the same bullies.

For amusement our geek gang had hung out in a rather large selection of abandoned houses and factories. My buddies and I would discuss molecular science as we balanced along cement ridges, watching the cool guys from a distance with a mix of envy and revulsion as they got high and groped girls.

I didn't have brothers or a dad to guide me. My friend and roommate Zed Zabinski (born Arnold, but insisted everyone called him Zed. Not Zee. The Zabinski family originated from some small town across the border and Zed was a nod to his Canadian roots) wasn't exactly a manly-man role model either. We were the blind leading the blind, both figuratively and literally. I pushed my glasses up the bridge of my nose again. I hated humidity.

It wasn't that I was bitter.

Okay, maybe a little. Zed and I had gotten the short stick, no question about it. We lacked conventionally attractive looks. We were too skinny, too smart and socially challenged. Plus we were poor. If not for my scholarship, I'd be flipping burgers somewhere.

I was a freshman in college and had never been with a girl. And no, I don't count that sloppy encounter with Reba Jones for Seven Minutes of Heaven in Brendon Herbert's basement closet in sixth grade.

Detroit University had a student Facebook page. I didn't really see the point in "liking" it. So far it only announced weekend keggers and jock practice times. "Come cheer on your team!"

I planned to keep my nose to the grindstone and graduate in four years—if I could survive college life, that was.

Zed entered our dorm room with a couple Cokes in hand. "It's crazy out there, but I think, you know, maybe not as bad as we thought."

Zed was the cautious optimist of our duo. I accepted the soda with a doubtful glance. "I hope you're not suggesting we go to the fall social."

He sat at his desk hitting the edge with his knobby knees, and spilled Coke on his crotch. "Dang! And of course not. Guys who go to events like that eat guys like us alive."

An optimist with a healthy dose of reality. I averted my eyes as Zed removed his soiled jeans and awkwardly hopped into a pair of sweats. He made this ordinary task seem difficult and it was hard to watch. I closed my eyes. "Okay, Marlow Henry," I thought to myself, "this is your new reality. Let's make the most of it."

"Gotta head out," I said. I stuffed my wallet into my pocket. "Outta supplies."

Zed snorted. "You buying toilet paper?"

"Among other things. Like food."

"Bring me back something."

I stared at him over my glasses. "Show me the money."

Zed scooped some change from the top of his desk and filled my palm. "No tomatoes."

I returned a while later with grub. I threw the TP into the bathroom. We moved to the common lounge to eat. Our room was so small Zed and I would practically knock elbows if we ate in there.

We were halfway through our sandwiches when Paul and Steve, fellow dorm nerds we met on the first night we moved in, blew into the common room all excited.

"We were just leaving the library when a couple cop cars pulled up," Paul said.

I sat up. "What happened?"

"A girl was raped in a the park behind the library. The university is under investigation."

"That's terrible." I checked my watch. Teagan time. I returned to my dorm room, logged into the chat room and waited. I grew antsy. Where was she? She was usually there this time of night. She hadn't gone to the library this afternoon, had she?

@averagegeek99 to @art4ever: Are you there?

CHAPTER 6

Teagan

THE EARLY MORNING sky was a wonderful wash of green—lime to moss—dotted with happy fluffy tangerine clouds: a great midweek day in Detroit City! Teagan said good-bye to Sage, who forked off into the direction of the math and tech classes, and strolled to her philosophy class feeling light-hearted and optimistic. She thought about Marlow. They had chatted together the last three nights. Maybe *he* was her cute, thoughtful, well-rounded guy? It didn't matter that they met online. Lots of people did.

Slow down, Teag, you're getting ahead of yourself again.

Jake Wentworth startled her when he slipped into the gray plastic chair beside hers.

"Good morning," he said with a twisted grin. "You don't mind if I sit with you, do you?"

Teagan sat with a straight back, the way her mother taught her, and smiled. "Not at all." Now in the bright light of the lecture room she could see that Jake's hair was a lighter blond than she'd first thought. His eyes were also a deeper blue. She inhaled his musky aftershave.

Teagan could tell her eyelashes were blinking too quickly and a shiver of nerves ran down her spine. She'd never been pursued, if that's what that was. She'd seen Jake before, he was kind of hard to miss, but had never given him a second thought. Guys like him didn't usually pay attention to girls like her. Teagan's mouth suddenly felt dry. She swallowed.

Professor Madsen entered the hall and placed an old leather satchel on his desk. The class quieted while he took his usual stoic stance at the front of the room. He was young for a professor—she guessed late twenties. He moved stiffly like he needed oil for his knees. Except when he got excited about something Kierkegaard or Hegel said, then his body seemed to float across the platform. He oozed intellectualism and an odd sort of charisma, catching the eye of most of the girls and some of the guys too.

Today, for the first time, the teacher's aid desk was occupied. A male student with short dark hair wearing jeans and a black cardigan over a white T-shirt sat in the wooden chair. His fingers were propped over an open laptop, ready to take notes.

Professor Madsen tilted his head forward, long dirty-blond curls falling over closed eyes and spoke.

"What does it mean to be human?" He proceeded to elaborate on the evolving ideals regarding existence, fascinating stuff, but not enough to keep Teagan's mind from wandering. Her eyelids grew heavy and she had the strongest impulse to lay her head on the table. Clearly, she'd been getting to sleep too late at night. Her nightly chats with Marlow had cut into her study time, forcing her to stay up later than normal. She'd have to tell him gently tonight that she couldn't chat long. That was if he showed up. Teagan frowned a little at the thought that he might not. He couldn't meet up every night, right? Already she was married to their routine. Marlow was fun. And safe.

Teagan jumped at the sensation of a finger poke in her side. Jake whispered in her ear, "Wake up, sleepyhead."

Oh, God. How embarrassing. She almost fell asleep in Madsen's class and in front of Jake! What if she'd started drooling, or worse, snoring? She reddened with the mortification of what could've been.

After class, Jake surprised her by asking if she wanted to meet him for coffee later on. "You look like you could use a cup."

Teagan's eyelids fluttered and she stared at the floor, hoping Jake didn't notice.

"I really should study."

He nudged her shoulder, causing her to look up. "So should I. We can study at the coffee shop." Then he added his megawatt smile. "Come on. My treat."

It was hard to say no to those puppy dog eyes. "Okay." He recited the time and place, The Literary Latté near the library, and Teagan agreed to meet him there.

She had some time before her next class so she decided to go back to her dorm. She told herself it was so she could prepare and go over her notes, but the truth was, she was thinking about a teeny, tiny nap.

Sage was out as Teagan expected, and she sighed happily at being alone. She opened her laptop and was surprised to see a message there from Marlow. It was only midafternoon. She paused before clicking the message icon.

@averagegeek99: Are you there?

@averagegeek99: You probably heard about the rape. Just be careful. Okay?

Oh, God! A rape? Teagan couldn't believe it! Not at Detroit University. Her heart bounced around as she surfed the university website for news. She couldn't believe she hadn't heard about this. Was this not noteworthy enough for students to engage in discussion? Surely, the female students would be outraged.

Teagan clicked through all the recent news bulletins. There was nothing more than an innocuous warning that bad weather might disturb the football practice.

What was Marlow talking about then?

@art4ever: Did you mean on campus? Or elsewhere? Thanks for the warning, anyway. I'm

always very cautious.

Teagan lay down and closed her eyes but her heart beat too strongly for sleep to come. Even though it was a false alarm, it got her adrenaline going. It made her think twice about meeting up with Jake. It was starting to get dark earlier now and maybe it just wasn't safe.

No. That was dumb. Jake was a nice guy. Not a stranger, like Marlow was. Jake was in her philosophy class. He had friends. Played on the hockey team. Besides, it was a false alarm. Detroit University was one of the safest colleges in America. It was the home of the grand car factories where most of the world's supply of green autos were made. The rich had homes along the shores of Lake Erie and Lake St. Clair and along the banks of Detroit River. There were a lot of wealthy people here. The city had one of the lowest crime rates in America.

She would meet Jake as planned. But first she better set off to her art history class, otherwise she was going to be late. She grabbed a cream-colored corduroy fall jacket and wrapped a blue and pink scarf around her neck. She slipped into low-heeled brown faux-leather boots and slung the strap of her book bag over her shoulder, preparing to speed-walk all the way to class.

Later on, Teagan ran into Sage on one of the many pedestrian paths. The leaves on the trees that arched overhead had started to turn and the bluish grass was dotted with yellow from the ones that had fallen.

Sage shifted the bundle of books in her arms. She puffed a breath through her lips to blow the dark bangs over her eyes. "Where are you off to?"

"I'm meeting Jake for coffee," Teagan said. "And to study."

Sage's eyebrows bounced. "Jake Wentworth? He's cute!"

Teagan nibbled her lip. "Yeah, I noticed. But it's just coffee."

"Ha! It's never just coffee. He doesn't have to sit with you to drink coffee." Sage poked her arm. "He likes you!"

"He hardly knows me enough to like me. We're studying together, that's all."

Sage winked. "If you say so. Have fun! I can't wait to hear all about it!"

Teagan bit the inside of her cheek to keep herself from breaking out in a huge idiotic smile.

Jake was already there when she arrived. The Literary Latté wasn't large and most of the tables were full of students, either hoping to study or just hanging out. Music pumped quietly in the background, and the aggressive sound of the espresso machine went off in intervals. Jake waved her over. "I'm glad you came. I wasn't sure that you would."

"I said that I would."

"You did. What can I get you? Remember, I said my treat."

"I'd like a London Fog."

"Tea?"

"That's okay isn't it? I know this is a coffee shop."

"Just giving you a hard time. I'll be right back."

Teagan pulled out her books while waiting for Jake to return. She recalled the rape Marlow had mentioned and wished now she'd thought to ask Sage about it. A glance around the space proved that she didn't know anyone there. She didn't overhear any talk of an assault. Marlow must've been mistaken.

Jake returned with hot drinks in his hands. "A London Fog for the lady," he said, handing her the drink. She blew on it carefully before taking a sip.

"Yum. Perfect."

"So, you're an art major?" he asked.

She nodded. "And you?"

"Economics. Here on a hockey scholarship."

"I heard that. At the club the other night. That Chet guy is your friend?"

"Nah, not really. We just met when I got here. He's a dip personality-wise, but he knows his way around the ice."

"I don't know anything about hockey."

"The object of the game is pretty simple. Your team has to get the puck in the net of the opposing team. Each goal is one point. Whoever has the most goals after three periods wins."

"I imagine the skating thing makes it more difficult."

"Only if you can't skate. Do you skate?"

"I've done it a few times, but I'm certainly not graceful."

"There's a nice outdoor rink nearby that opens up in winter. I'll take you when it's cold enough."

Teagan smiled and nodded and wondered if he'd just asked her on another date. Though winter was still another month away, so maybe not. She flipped through the pages of her textbook and tried to concentrate.

They talked more about Professor Madsen, Jake filling her in on some of what she'd missed by dozing off, and she tried to make sense of it. Her brain worked better with tangible things like clay and paint. When it came to words and theories and deep philosophical concepts, her synapses wanted to shut down.

Teagan just happened to look toward the front of the shop when she saw the strap of a girl's handbag snag a display case, knocking coffee packages over the floor. She immediately felt sorry for her. How embarrassing.

Jake jumped up to help and Teagan watched as they worked together to restore the display. She would've helped too, but the area was tight, and a third person would've gotten in the way. The girl had short, blond hair held back with a black headband. Teagan recognized her now, from her art history class.

Vanessa something. She felt a strange tug in her gut as she watched Jake help her. Teagan could hear his words of reassurance from where she sat and the girl's repeated responses of gratitude.

Once everything was cleaned up, Vanessa thanked Jake again before leaving. Jake slid back into his chair.

"That was very kind of you," Teagan said.

"Oh, that? It was nothing."

Jake slurped the last of his coffee and checked the time on his phone. "Oh, damn. I gotta go. Coach will kill me if I'm late for practice. I'm sorry. Will you be okay getting back to your dorm? Normally, I would walk you."

"No, I'm fine. Go. I still have some studying I want to do anyway."

Jake shoved all his books into his backpack. "I'll see you in class tomorrow."

"Sure."

He left the coffee shop like a thunderstorm. The room seemed quieter and calmer just by his absence and Teagan forced herself to stop thinking of him and to focus on her homework. Her mother was right. Boys were a big distraction from studies.

Teagan worked on an essay for about forty-five minutes before sirens broke through the background clatter. She wondered what that could be about, since she'd never heard sirens on campus before. It was time she left anyway, so she packed up her things.

—

Before she could leave, a girl Teagan didn't know blew into the café and screeched to a group of girls at a booth across the room. "You won't believe this! Someone was just raped in the park behind the library!"

Teagan's blood cooled, pooling at her knees and she slid into a nearby chair. She grabbed at her chest and swallowed dryly, trying to process what she'd heard. Someone was just raped. So, how did Marlow know? How could he possibly know about something before it happened?

Unless? Teagan could barely cope with the next thought. Unless he had planned to commit the crime himself? Blood rushed from her head and she felt faint at the thought.

Teagan ran home and locked the door to her dorm behind her. She would remove herself from the chat forums and never talk to Marlow again. Oh, God, how she wished now that she'd never given averagegeek99 her name!

Chapter 7

Marlow

TEAGAN DIDN'T SHOW up for our meeting last night. She didn't respond to any of my messages. I tried to think of what I'd said to turn her off. Maybe she was just sick of my ugly mug or my corny jokes. Maybe she met an IRL guy and no longer had time to mess around with the likes of me.

Fine. Whatever.

It wasn't like I didn't have a life. Look at me now, sitting in the guys' stinky lounge playing video games with other geeks. Zed was with me, as per usual, along with Paul and Steve. We were the only four dudes to *not* go to some kind of fall event.

Paul shot my guy in the back and shouted, "Oh, yeah, loser!"

"Who are you calling a loser, loser?" I retorted. My virtual guy magically recovered and I lobbied a grenade into Paul's virtual Jeep. "Kaboom!"

Zed chugged a soda and let out an impressive belch. I catapulted a stained cushion at him from the sagging couch. It might have been orange at one time, but now, I would definitely call it brown. Steve called time-out to take a piss.

I stared outside and saw the sun peeking out from under gray clouds as it slunk lower on the horizon. My legs twitched with nervous energy and I jumped up.

"I'm heading out."

Zed glanced up with a surprised stare. "Out where?"

"Dunno. Need some vitamin D. I'm as pale as a vamp."

"You should buy a green smoothie, man," he said. Zed swore by his green breakfast smoothies. I just chalked the weird habit up to one of many idiosyncrasies he had.

"Too gross for my sophisticated palate," I said as I grabbed my hoodie. I shrugged it on as I skipped down the steps, pushing the exterior doors open with a two-handed thrust.

I didn't know how a girl I'd met online and had only chatted with for a few days could make me so agitated. For an intelligent guy I could be really stupid sometimes. All I knew of her appearance was from her profile pic. Blond hair, friendly eyes, a cute little rosebud mouth.

She was here, somewhere on this campus. I couldn't stop myself from scouring the grounds. I sat on the top of a short brick wall, balancing myself against the lamppost that jutted skyward. The automatic lamp flickered on, signaling nightfall. Leaves dropped as the cool breeze picked up and floated downward to join the paper litter along the curb. Students milled about, some at a leisurely pace and others with quick determined strides—destinations and deadlines looming.

I sorted through all the female heads looking for blonds.

Blond, blond, another blond. All the pretty faces made my skin tingle. There were a lot of attractive girls around—with every hair color—just none for me, apparently.

I was about to head back when I spotted her. At least, I thought it was her. She wore a short, fall jacket with a scarf around her neck. I leaned forward and squinted. Was it her? She was with a guy.

Of course she was. A jock. That should've been enough to keep me from shouting out, but my stupid mouth moved before my brain could check it. "Teagan!"

She stopped and looked in my direction. I shimmied off the wall and strode toward her. "Teagan? It's me, Marlow."

She blinked a few times and tilted her head. "Who?"

"Marlow. You know, averagegeek99?"

The guy beside her smirked at my handle. I ignored him and focused on Teagan.

"You *are* Teagan, right?"

She nodded warily. I opened my palms and waved them as though that would jog her memory.

"Where do I know you from?" she asked.

"The chat forums. We talked this week. A few nights in a row."

That brought a scowl to the face of the jock. Teagan glanced up at him with wide eyes. She turned to me and said politely, "You have me mistaken for someone else."

And then the kicker. She grabbed the jock's hand and walked away leaving me standing in their wake like a complete idiot.

Chapter 8

Sage

"I JUST CAN'T BELIEVE IT," Teagan said again for the millionth time. She sat on her bed, a mirror image of mine, with blankets pulled over her soft tummy. She continued, "The thought that someone has been attacked is unfathomable. Not at Detroit University!"

I wrapped my arms around my knees, awash with the same kind of dread and disbelief. The crime was horrifying, and made us all feel so vulnerable. "It wasn't even that dark yet. It's just crazy."

My new friend Nora O'Shea sprawled across the foot of my bed, red hair falling off the edge like a crimson waterfall. She made mew noises. "I cut across that park all the time. There are a lot of trees and bushes."

"I want to go home to the safety of my pink princess room," Teagan whined, "and the overprotective embrace of my mother."

"Teag," I said. "You can't let one maniac control where and how you live." *Or your mother*, I thought, but didn't say that aloud.

Her big eyes implored me. "What can we do to protect ourselves?"

I was asking myself the same question. I rubbed my forehead. "Safety in numbers."

"Carry a whistle," Nora added. "Though that won't help if you get jumped from behind."

I wanted to kick Nora. She didn't know Teagan like I did. I could see her trembling from across the room.

"Call before you leave a place, and if you don't arrive in time, we'll call for help," I said, trying to be encouraging.

Teagan flicked a hand toward me. "By then the damage will be done."

A thick silence descended, and Teagan curled into a tighter ball, yoga pant-covered legs clutching a body pillow. My gaze drifted along the room. Clutter littered Teagan's side, clothes strewn casually on the floor, makeup scattered across her dresser. In contrast, my side was neat and tidy. My closet and drawers were closed. My makeup was lined up on my dresser in the order I applied them. A poster of Einstein with the quote "Anyone who has never made a mistake has never tried anything new," hung above my bed.

"I met this guy," Teagan said quietly. "He said something that kind of creeped me out."

I blinked several times as I processed this and twisted to face her. "You're online dating?"

She shot me a horrified look. "No! It's not a dating site. It's a campus chat room."

Nora swung her legs around and returned to a sitting position. "What'd he say?"

"Well," Teagan began, "he told me that there had been a rape and that I should be careful."

I didn't get it. "Why does that creep you out?"

"Because he told me about the rape before it happened."

What? Nora and I chimed in together. "*Before?*"

I leaned forward and asked, "He predicted the rape? How?"

Teagan shrugged. "Maybe he's psychic?"

"Or," Nora began, "he did it. His way of playing with your head."

Teagan paled. I skittered over to her side of the bed. "What's his name?"

"Marlow. I don't know his last name."

"He'll be listed in the student directory," Nora offered.

"Good idea," Teagan said. She opened her laptop and brought up the student directory. "He said he was a freshman, so that narrows it down." She scanned the faces and names, and a frown tugged on her lips. "Still, there are hundreds."

Nora and I waited as Teagan squinted at her screen. I was dying to see what this guy looked like. After all my failed attempts at trying to set Teagan up, she chose to hang out with a guy online.

"That's him."

Nora and I jumped up and peered over Teagan's shoulder. She pointed. "Marlow Henry."

"In the science program," I said. "He's probably in some of my math classes."

"He's nerdy-looking," Nora said.

Teagan pulled her laptop away with barely veiled irritation. "I think he's kind of cute, but that's not the point here."

A pit weighted in my stomach as I settled back onto my own bed. "Have you told anyone?"

"I didn't see a reason to," Teagan answered. "Until now. Besides this isn't proof of anything."

Nora thumbed through messages on her phone. "People are saying the victim was a freshman. Vanessa Rothman."

Teagan's eyes popped open and she shot upright. "No way! She's in my art history class. I just saw her at The Literary Latté where I was studying with Jake. She'd knocked over a display before she left."

Teagan covered her mouth with her hand. "Jake helped her clean it up," she said with a hushed voice. "And followed her out."

Nora arched a brow. "So, you think Jake Wentworth's the rapist now?"

"No. I don't know," Teagan answered. "But isn't it weird that Vanessa leaves just before Jake leaves."

My heart went out to Teagan. She was so freaked out. "I'd call that a *coincidence*," I said gently.

Just then Teagan's phone rang and she yelped when she saw the caller ID.

"Who is it?" I asked.

"You won't believe it," she said. "It's Jake Wentworth."

Another coincidence?

Her ringtone continued. "Aren't you going to answer it?" I asked.

Teagan tapped the respond button and put it on speakerphone. "Hello."

"Hey, Teagan, Jake here. I was just wondering, would you like to grab a burger and then come hang out at my hockey practice? Lots of people come and you could learn a bit more about the game that way."

Teagan hesitated then said, "Can you hang on a moment?" She covered the receiver.

I widened my eyes. "What's wrong?"

"Nothing, just, do you guys feel like going for a burger and then watching a hockey practice after?"

"You want us to come with you?" I asked. "Why?"

"It feels too much like a date with just the two of us. I'm not ready."

I smirked. "Chicken. Yeah, sure. We'll come as your support team, won't we Nora?"

Nora grinned. "Watching a bunch of hot hockey players sounds like a good way to spend the evening to me."

Chapter 9

Teagan

TEAGAN SAID YES to Jake but she still felt nervous. What did she really know about this guy? And what did he see in her anyway? There were a lot of prettier girls on campus and more athletic ones, too.

She pushed herself off her bed and fished through the clothes piled on her floor and hanging out of her drawers. She settled on a pair of jeans, sucking in a little to get the button done, and a mint green wool sweater thinking it would be cold in the hockey rink. She tucked a wool cap and scarf into her purse. Her hair was already a mess so she just pulled it into a sloppy updo, slipping the blue streak behind her ear. Teagan examined her image in the mirror critically. She was soft. She had curves. Not athletic or lean in the slightest.

She spun to face Sage and Nora. "What do you think?"

"Makeup," Sage said.

Right. Teagan quickly put on mascara and lip gloss. She added a stroke of black pencil eyeliner to her lids at the last minute.

Sage and Nora had gotten ready at the same time, and both looked too good to take out on a "date" with Jake. What *was* she thinking?

"Ready?" Sage said.

Teagan put on a smile. "Yup."

She let Sage and Nora carry the conversation as they walked under violet skies. She'd met a total of two guys since she'd arrived (*met* used figuratively in Marlow's case) and had accused both of them of being capable of something as evil and devious as rape. Maybe she was the one with the problem. Jake was a nice, decent guy. Marlow probably was too. She was just paranoid.

Still, Teagan was glad Sage and Nora had agreed to come along.

They arrived at the burger joint just off campus near the arena before Jake did. Sage and Nora took one side of the table while Teagan sat alone on the other side. Of course Sage wouldn't sit beside her like she usually did. Jake was coming and it would be weird if he had to sit beside someone else.

They ordered sodas, which arrived just as Jake blew in.

"Sorry I'm late." He looked at Sage and Nora. "Company. Cool. Hi Sage." He reached for Nora's hand. "Hi, I'm Jake."

"Nora."

Teagan swore she blushed. Or maybe it was just the reflection of her red hair off the neon lights.

They talked about sports and politics, music and movies. Everything but the attack. Actually, Sage and Nora and Jake did most of the talking. Sitting so close to Jake and knowing he'd invited her personally made Teagan feel shy and nervous. She was happy to let the girls carry the conversation.

In fact, Nora and Jake seemed to have a lot to say to each other. They were both from Michigan, they both liked to cross-country ski, they both had an annoying little brother that they loved to death. They were both athletic.

Jake flicked his wrist and stared at his watch. "Oh, I gotta go." He turned to Teagan. "Are you ready?"

"Sage and Nora are coming too. We'll meet you there."

His mouth turned into a half grin as his eyes flicked to the opposite side of the table. Nora's eyelashes fluttered.

"Cool," Jake said. He dropped enough bills on the table to cover his and my burger before leaving.

"He's nice," Nora said, not catching Teagan's eye. "Have you been dating long?"

Teagan was pretty sure she said this was their first date back in their dorm when she begged them to join her. "We're not really dating."

Her gaze remained cool. "Oh."

Watching the hockey practice was fun only because Sage and Nora had come along to keep Teagan company. Mainly it was cold. Teagan waved good-bye to Jake when it was time for them to leave. They were keeping their pact to not walk alone after dark and Sage wanted to get back to study.

By morning the news feeds were buzzing. The rapist had been caught. Apparently the son of a senator had been arrested.

Such a huge relief. They could breathe easy and go on with their lives.

Teagan sighed. Now she felt bad for ignoring Marlow Henry all week. Was it too late to check in and say, "Hello"?

CHAPTER 10

HE FOLDED HIS LIPS in as he read the news feed on his tablet and kept his face blank. He sat inconspicuously at a corner table by himself in a coffee shop and he didn't want to risk being noticed by laughing out loud, or smiling like he'd just won the lottery.

He sipped his brew and took a moment to relish the warmth that swirled in his being. "Rapist arrested," the headlines read. His lips twitched at the absurdity. The ineptness of the law enforcement in this town was unbelievable.

He wouldn't let a wussy senator's son take credit, not for long. There was only one way to set the record straight, but he'd have to bide his time. Find the right place and the right moment. The right blond.

"Excuse me." A female voice pulled him from his reverie. "Is anyone using this chair?" The girl smiled and blew wheat-colored bangs out of her eyes. She wore a black bomber jacket and snug jeans. A collection of beaded necklaces hung exuberantly over swollen breasts. "It's just really busy and we need one more," she added when he failed to respond.

He suddenly believed in providence. "Help yourself," he said.

She smiled again and dragged the chair to the table next to his and joined her friends. He was careful not to stare, casting occasional glances out of the corner of his eye. He ordered a refill and a glazed donut.

When the girls left, he waited ten seconds, then followed.

Chapter 11

Marlow

SERIOUSLY? I got that maybe she didn't want her boyfriend to know she'd been chatting with another guy, but to outright pretend that she didn't know me? That was rude. Obnoxious. Crazy.

Her acting skills were pretty decent. I had to give her that.

The knot in my chest tightened. Teagan was prettier in real life than her profile picture let on. Maybe that was it. I was too geeky. Too skinny. Maybe she was embarrassed to be connected to someone like me.

Fine. She and her jock boyfriend could shove it.

I arrived for class with just minutes to spare, not my usual MO. I shifted my pack off my shoulder when I found my seat and pushed up my glasses. I heard a ruckus behind me as I pulled out my math textbooks. I stopped mid-retrieval and stared.

Teagan's jock. His face was in a wide guffaw—apparently his fellow jock friend had said something funny.

An oily spot of dislike filled my chest. I didn't know he was in this class. He bumped into my table as he strutted by, giving me the briefest glance. He didn't even seem to recognize me from the "incident." Was it possible that nerds accosted his girlfriend on a regular basis and my face just blended in with scores of others?

I was determined to shake off the whole dumb scenario and diligently took notes as the professor scratched equations on the board. Who was this Teagan chick to me anyway? Nothing. I would forget about her. She was forgotten.

This was the lie I told myself. The lie that was blown all to hell when I got back to my room and found a message from her waiting for me in the chat forums.

What did she want? To apologize? Ha! I chugged back my soda and let out a loud belch, letting the universe know just what I thought of that. Just delete it, man, I told myself.

I went to the bathroom, then checked out the dorm fridge and drank old orange juice from the carton. I did twenty push-ups. Okay, maybe just ten. I had a cold shower.

Turned out I was a bigger loser than even I would've pegged myself for because not only could I not delete it, I also couldn't ignore it. After thirty-five itchy minutes, I clicked on her name.

@art4ever to @averagegeek99: Hey! I know it's been a while, but I've just been crazy busy, settling in, getting lost on campus, homework, all those freshman excuses. How has your week been?

I jerked back, unbelieving. Was she on drugs? She was just going to pretend like her whole "I don't know you," schtick never happened?

@averagegeek99: So you know who I am now?

@art4ever: Well, since we haven't met IRL, I don't really know you.

This girl was a piece of work.

@averagegeek99: Why didn't you tell me you had a boyfriend?

@art4ever: I don't have a boyfriend.

@averagegeek99: You just go around holding random guys' hands?

@art4ever: No. What are you talking about???

@averagegeek99: Yesterday. When I talked to you in the square. You were with some jock. You pretended not to know who I was.

@art4ever: I'm sorry. I really don't know what you're talking about. I never saw you or spoke to you. I think that's something I'd remember.

I removed my glasses and cleaned them with the hem of my T-shirt. What was this chick on? Did she have an identical twin? I thought she said she was an only child. Plus, the blond with the jock admitted her name was Teagan. Teagan wasn't a common name. What were the chances of there being another girl who looked like Teagan and had the same name? The odds against that scenario were enormous.

@averagegeek99: I'm not a game player.

@art4ever: Neither am I. I'm starting to regret contacting you again.

Damn. I hadn't meant to piss her off. Despite her blow off, I did like chatting with her. It wasn't like I had a ton of girls lining up to talk to me.

@averagegeek99: Sorry. I must've mistaken you for someone else. Can we start over?

@art4ever: I guess so.

@averagegeek99: How was your day?

@art4ever: Fine.

I imagined that to sound like *fine,* as in you're an asshole fine, rather than a sweet, everything's fine. Time to lighten things up.

@averagegeek99: Knock, knock.

@art4ever: ???

@averagegeek99: You're supposed to say, "Who's there?"

@art4ever: You're telling me a knock-knock joke?

@averagegeek99: You're surprised? My handle does have the word *geek* in it.

@art4ever: ☺ Who's there?

Yes! A happy face emoticon!

@averagegeek99: Broken pencil.

@art4ever: Broken pencil who?

@averagegeek99: Never mind. It's a pointless joke.

I expected a raging LOL, but instead there was no response. Oh, God. Don't tell me she didn't get it? But then:

@art4ever: Knock, knock.

I smirked and wondered if she actually knew a knock-knock joke or quickly looked one up. Either way, she was game to play, which meant we were back on some kind of friendship track.

@averagegeek99: Who's there?

@art4ever: Madam.

@averagegeek99: Madam who?

@art4ever: Madam foot is caught in the door!

I couldn't stop a soft chuckle from escaping. I gave in with an LOL. We fell into an easy rhythm of lightweight topics after that. She sent me a picture of one of her paintings, but for some reason I couldn't receive it. She said she'd show it to me in person some time, and a lava flow of

heat spread through my gut. She wanted to see me again. I was cool with that.

@art4ever: Is there anything you're afraid of?
Going deeper?

@averagegeek99: What do you mean? Like the dark? Monsters under the bed?

@art4ever: Yeah. If that's what you're afraid of. What fears show up in your nightmares?

@averagegeek99: Um. I don't like snakes. I have a lot of dreams where I find a garter snake under my pillow, or in my closet, or somewhere I'm

not expecting to find one. I always scream myself awake.

@averagegeek99: What about you?

@art4ever: I often have dreams that I'm being chased.

@averagegeek99: By whom?

@art4ever: I don't know. Just a random person. I never see a face. I'm running for my life in dark alleys usually. I'm always exhausted and sweating when I wake with a start just before I'm caught.

@averagegeek99: I think that's a pretty common nightmare. Probably stress induced.

@art4ever: Yeah, probably. I'm also afraid of storms. And that's when I'm awake.

@averagegeek99: Maybe we need to face our fears to beat them.

@art4ever: Yeah? How about this? You go to the science lab and hold a snake or at least feed one, and the next time it storms I won't hide under the bed.

@averagegeek99: You hide under the bed? Really?

@art4ever: Don't change the subject.

My skin prickled at the thought of seeking out a snake. I didn't want to look at one much less feed one.

@averagegeek99: Not fair. Who knows when the next storm will be?

@art4ever: I looked it up. Weather's changing. Storm is in the forecast.

It wouldn't kill me to throw road kill into a snake pit, would it? And maybe this would help Teagan in some small way.

@averagegeek99: And when it storms you won't go under the bed. So where will you go?

@art4ever: Your dorm?

I sprung to my feet with surprise and nervous shock. She wanted to come here? My eyes took in the pigsty Zed and I lived in. It wasn't often a girl invited herself to my room, like as in never. She'd be worth cleaning it up for. I bent over and typed without sitting back down.

@averagegeek99: Okay, deal.

@art4ever: Deal.

Chapter 12

Teagan

TEAGAN HEARD his laugh before she spotted him. Jake Wentworth had a distinctive, happy-seal-like bellow. You couldn't help but smile and chuckle along even if you didn't quite get the joke. Mostly she never got his jokes. Maybe that was why she hadn't heard from him in a few days.

Now he was walking along the leaf-strewn path between the math and economics building. He was with that Chet guy again. Teagan had entered the path behind them, so Jake didn't know she was following. He turned to Chet and pounded his chest like an ape and burst out laughing again. Teagan wished she were close enough to hear what on earth they were talking about.

Jake was so boisterous and alive and just... out there. Teagan could feel the heat of his extroversion from here. She almost found herself ducking.

The contrast between Jake's personality and Marlow's was undeniable. She'd never met Marlow in real life, but somehow she couldn't imagine him puffing out his chest and beating on it in public.

She could be wrong. People often presented a version of themselves online that wasn't accurate.

Marlow seemed authentic. Teagan enjoyed their banter and even the juvenile knock-knock jokes. They'd become comfortable enough with their social-network friendship, meeting practically every night, that their conversation sometimes slipped into flirting.

At least it felt like flirting to her.

He still hadn't approached a snake, and Teagan had a lot of fun teasing him about that. She had yet to face a storm. The aqua-blue sky above was brandished with orange bruises. Sign of a possible storm, but who knew? It could shift away in the other direction from DU. Storms were unpredictable like that. It was one of the reasons she didn't like them. They weren't trustworthy.

Teagan's cheeks heated up when she recalled her impulsive offer to wait out the next storm in Marlow's room. It was momentary insanity. She hadn't even *met* this guy. Another reason she hoped the storm would redirect and pass by.

Nora had appeared from out of nowhere and suddenly she was walking beside Jake and Chet. Her giggle filtered back to Teagan and she slowed her pace, staring. Jake smiled down at Nora in a way that was just a little too friendly. Teagan suffered a sudden bout of heartburn. Jealousy? She had no right to be jealous. It wasn't like Jake was her boyfriend or anything. Nora petted his arm and beamed up at him with a too-wide smile. Her ginger hair glistened in the sun as if its rays were directed only to her. She scooped it behind one ear and stared up at Jake through thick eyelashes.

Teagan was so taken by this interaction she didn't pay proper attention to where she was going. She felt the jarring thump of a body and dropped her books.

"Pardon me," she said.

"No problem," a male voice said. Her head jerked up and for a split second she thought it might be Marlow. Wouldn't that be just the craziest coincidence?

But it wasn't. The guy had a wider jaw and thicker brow. He bent down to help Teagan pick up her belongings.

"I zoned out there," she said. The guy's gaze never left her face, and she grew heated with embarrassment.

"It's a busy campus." He stood and cocked his head. He flashed her a half-smile producing a dimple that was rather cute. His arm reached out and she thought he was going to touch her or something, but then he let it drop to his side. "I like the blue in your hair."

Teagan's hand automatically stroked the strand. "Thanks."

The guy stepped backwards and gave her a little wave. "See you around."

"Sure." Belatedly, she wished she'd offered her name.

At any rate, knocking into a good-looking stranger just reminded her that there were plenty of guys out there. It wasn't like Jake was her only choice for a future boyfriend.

Jake was no longer in sight and neither, thankfully, was Nora. Teagan squeezed her books to her chest and continued on.

Then she saw him. Marlow Henry stood in a corner with another, taller guy who had a short-cropped beard. Teagan squinted. It *was* him, wasn't it? He sure looked like Marlow's profile pic. She almost called out but the way he was talking to the other guy made her pause. They were standing face-to-face, closer than most guys do with each other. She swore she saw a brushing of their fingertips before they split and went opposite ways.

Oh, God. Was Marlow Henry gay? Teagan pinched the base of her nose and shut her eyes. She was such an idiot.

Chapter 13

Marlow

SOMETIMES I FELT LIKE A LITTLE KID. It wasn't like the snake was going to jump through its glass case and bite me.

I even brought Zed for moral support, though I told him I needed him to be my photographer. I had to get a picture for proof.

He'd scoffed when I'd first suggested it. "Take a selfie."

"Dude. I don't plan on getting that close. C'mon. What do you have on your busy schedule anyway? A hot date?"

He huffed and puffed but relented and now he stood with me in the sterile-looking, eerily empty lab holding up his phone. "Tell me when you're ready."

I didn't know how long we'd be alone, and I didn't want an audience. It was bad enough that Zed had to witness the shimmer of sweat that had formed on my brow. A big, fat, yellowish boa constrictor was curled up in the bin, its scaly self pressed up against the glass.

"Anytime now would be good," Zed said with a straight face. "Before, you know, my arm falls off or hell freezes over."

"'K, I got this."

I'd done my research. Asked questions. There were dead rats in the freezer in the corner. The prof even gave me permission to visit the reptile but I didn't know if it had been fed already and I didn't want to get in trouble by overfeeding it and maybe making it sick. My plan was just to hold up the rodent over top of the cage for the photo.

And honestly? Dead rats weren't really my thing, either.

"Marlow."

"Yeah, yeah. Hold onto your shorts." I opened the freezer and identified the frozen food section. The ropy tail of a frost-covered furry creature was front and center.

"Why are you doing this again?" Zed asked.

"I told you."

"Oh, right. To impress Virtual Girl. Someone you haven't even met."

That wasn't exactly true. I'd met her before.

Whatever.

I grabbed the cold tail and grimaced. I quickly made my way to the snake and held it over the case, hoping the fear I felt wasn't all over my face. The snake moved.

"Take it!"

Zed laughed. "Got it, scaredy-cat."

"You're one to talk. I don't see you over here posing as snake bait." I tossed the rat back into the freezer and washed my hands in the sink. With extra soap.

Zed cocked a bushy eyebrow. "We done here?"

I slapped my hands together. "We are so done here."

Zed sent me the pic and I studied it on my laptop. The expression on my face wasn't exactly cool. I looked like I was trying to hold in a fart. If Teagan wasn't convinced that I was a dork of the highest order by now, she would be when I sent her this. But I had to. I promised.

@averagegeek99: Snake pic delivered. Fear faced. Your turn next.

@art4ever: What pic?

I was surprised by her rapid response. I didn't think she'd get this until later.

@averagegeek99: Me and snake with cold dead rat.

@art4ever: I didn't get it. Send again.

I uploaded the photo again. Confirmed it was delivered.

@averagegeek99: Got it now?

@art4ever: Nope.

This was really strange. Unless she was fibbing. But why would she do that? That picture was sure to rock her world!

At least make her laugh a little.

I sent it again, but she still said she didn't get it.

@averagegeek99: Don't know why it's not working. You should've gotten it. But trust me, it happened! I have a witness.

@art4ever: Oh? Who would that be?

@averagegeek99: My roommate, Zed.

@art4ever: Zed?

@averagegeek99: Like Zee, but with a Canadian accent.

@art4ever: Does he have a beard?

Why would she ask that? Did she have a thing for beards? I scrubbed my chin. I supposed I could grow one. Last time I tried it was pretty patchy.

@averagegeek99: Yeah, actually. He's quite hairy. Like a tall, skinny gorilla. Why? Do you like bearded men?

@art4ever: Can I ask you a question?

Didn't I just ask one? Did she like bearded guys? Did she like tall, skinny gorillas?

@averagegeek99: Shoot.

@art4ever: Are you gay? I mean, it's not my business, but I don't think it's right for us to spend this much time chatting if you have a boyfriend.

My ears exploded with the sound of my chair screeching across the floor as I impulsively pushed away from my desk. Did the earth just split? Did she seriously just ask me *that?*

@averagegeek99: God, no! Why would you ask me that? Did I say something that sounded gay? Believe me, I wouldn't be chatting this much with you every night if I wasn't into girls.

@art4ever: I'm sorry. It's just that I thought I saw you with someone today. Someone whose description matches Zed's. By the econ building.

@averagegeek99: I was with Zed, but we were in the science complex at one of the labs. Taking snake pictures. Trust me, it was anything but romantic.

@art4ever: Ugh. I feel like such an idiot.

I didn't feel that great either. There was only one way to settle this.

@averagegeek99: Do you want to meet in person? I mean, before the big storm and you're alone with me in my dorm. Let's meet for coffee.

@art4ever: That's a good idea. We're both students here, and I feel like I know you, more or less, already. The one by the library?

We set a time for the next afternoon.

@averagegeek99: See you then!

I went to the mirror and studied my image. Did I really have a doppleganger out there? Surely one Marlow Henry in the world was enough. I coughed nervously into my hand. Soon I'd be meeting the lovely Teagan in person. I just hoped I wasn't a huge disappointment.

Chapter 14

Teagan

"MOM, EVERYTHING is fine." Teagan blew bangs out of her eyes as she waited for her mother's maternal worry rant to end. "Yes," she promised her. "They've beefed up security."

Teagan cyber-visited with her mom once a week. It was the deal she made to prevent her from calling Teagan. Every. Single. Day. After Vanessa Rothman's rape, her mom had gone ballistic and threatened to pull her out of college. Teagan managed to calm her down but her concerns came up at the end of their sessions, regardless.

"Never walk alone, especially at night!"

"Of course not, Mom. I have Sage, too."

Her mom was an older version of Teagan, but more beautiful. Striking, really. Teagan had seen guys of all ages stare at her mother as she walked by. She couldn't count how many times she'd heard that they looked like sisters.

"That attack was a one-time thing," Teagan said. "They caught the guy. It's perfectly safe here now."

"Speaking of guys." Her mom drew out her sentence with a wink. "Anyone interesting?"

"There are a lot of cute guys at DU, Mom."

"No one special yet?"

Teagan sighed. Jake seemed to have moved on to Nora already and her mother would freak if she told her how much time she spent chatting online with someone she hadn't even met. "No. No one special yet."

The glimmer left her mother's eyes. "That's good. You have lots of time before you get entangled with anyone. *Lots of time.*"

"Yes, I know, Mom." They'd had variations of the conversation countless times.

Her mom's eyes darted downward repeatedly, like she was checking the time or something. "Do you have to be somewhere?" Teagan asked.

Her gaze met Teagan's and the earlier shimmer of excitement in her eyes seeped out. "Yes, I have an appointment. I hate to run, sweetie." Her mouth stretched out into a smile but it seemed forced. "You have a great day."

"You too, Mom. Talk to you next week."

Her mom's arm filled the screen as she reached over to disconnect their call. A tiny black knot of worry worked itself in Teagan's gut. She couldn't shake the feeling that something was wrong with her mom. She couldn't pinpoint when her concern started, years ago maybe, a slow gradual awareness that her mother might be keeping something from her and her dad, the way she swung from happiness to melancholy on a dime. Teagan asked her father about her once and he only shrugged, saying that was just the way she was. Teagan thought she heard him mumble the word "hormones."

Teagan suspected her mother's appointment was with a shrink. Every time she'd tried probing in the past about where her mom was or what she was doing, she always blew Teagan off. Teagan finally stopped asking. It wasn't her business, anyway, she supposed.

Teagan's laptop chimed and she grinned like a silly school girl when she saw Marlow's handle pop up on her chat screen. They would be meeting in person in less than two hours. She ran a hand through her messy locks, feeling a sudden urgency to clean up and look good for Marlow. But first she had to see what he wanted. She hoped he wasn't canceling.

@averagegeek99: In case you don't recognize me, I'll be the one with a nerdy knitted sweater and eating an oatmeal raisin cookie.

A swoosh of relief flooded her. Their "date" was still on. She tapped rapidly on the keys.

@art4ever: Raisins?

@averagegeek99: Don't tell me you're one of those.

@art4ever: One of what?

@averagegeek99: A raisin hater—that's fruit discrimination.

Teagan couldn't help but laugh. She shook her head.

@art4ever: It's dried fruit discrimination. Totally allowed.

@averagegeek99: Ah, I think I missed that memo.

@art4ever: You have to get up early to keep up.

@averagegeek99: But what of my beauty sleep?

@art4ever: It's the price you have to pay.

Teagan didn't know how it happened, but time just seemed to fly by whenever she was online with Marlow.

Chatting with him was just so natural and easy. Before she knew it she was down to less than an hour before they were supposed to meet, and she didn't even have her face on!

@art4ever: Gotta run but see you soon.
@averagegeek99: Can't wait.

She spent the next twenty minutes rifling through her clothes, the piles on the floor and the ones poking out from her drawers. She didn't know why she felt so nervous, but she wanted to look just right. Not too stuffy, or too shabby. Teagan finally settled on a pair of skinny jeans and a red button-down blouse. She decided to let her hair hang loose, borrowing Sage's iron to straighten her locks. The heat of the iron made the blue streak shimmer.

She put on a tan faux-leather bomber jacket, adding a cream-colored woolen scarf around her neck and black knee-high boots with a one-inch heel zipped up over her jeans.

Sage entered just as she was about to leave. She scanned Teagan with her dark, insightful eyes. "Where are you off to in a hurry."

"Nowhere." Sage squinted hard and Teagan knew she could tell she was lying. "I mean, I'm meeting a friend for coffee."

Sage placed a hand on her skinny hip. "Dressed like that I'd guess a *male* friend?"

Teagan mimicked her by propping out a hip and cupping it with her hand. "*Maybe*."

Sage grinned. "You look good. Knock him dead and be prepared to tell me all about it when you get back. I'd grill you now but I'm in a hurry. I promised Nora I'd go into the city with her."

Hearing about Sage's plans with Nora put an instant damper on her mood. Sage and Teagan had spent years hanging out with just each other. They grew up as neighbors. It was time, as Sage repeatedly said, for them to spread their own wings.

Teagan flapped her arms as she walked down the hall to the exit. This was her, flying.

Arriving right on time, Teagan scanned the busy shop for Marlow who should be wearing a wool sweater and eating an oatmeal raisin cookie. Someone eyeing the door waiting for her. She searched each table, but no one matched his description.

Teagan pushed down the disappointment of having arrived first. Usually she was the late one. Marlow would blow through the door any minute. It would be easy to spot him when he did.

She ordered a hot tea and a chocolate chip oatmeal cookie—just to meet him halfway on the cookie selection. Then, before her order was complete, she ordered a coffee and an oatmeal raisin cookie for him. This first encounter could be her treat, and if that made him uncomfortable, he could pay her back. Either way, it would save them the awkward moments with her waiting at a table while he stood in line.

Minutes ticked by as Teagan picked at her cookie and sipped on her tea. Her phone lay on the table and she continually tapped it, checking the time. At fifteen minutes past the hour, her face tightened into a frown. By twenty after, her stomach juices started to swirl. Her neck grew hot, and she removed her scarf, scratching nervously at the exposed skin. She finally pulled up the chat forum on her phone and messaged him. The message bounced back, which was odd. She didn't know any other way to contact him.

Teagan stared at Marlow's untouched coffee and cookie. Was she seriously getting stood up?

She waited a full hour, feeling embarrassed as students passed by, eyeing the empty seat and one empty tea cup. People waited by the door searching for a place to sit. Teagan cleared her spot knowing her face was twisted in a scowl. The second she stepped away, her table was scooped up by a happy couple holding hands. She kept her eyes averted as she stormed out into the cool autumn evening.

Stupid tears ran down her face, and she swiped at them with the back of her hand. For once she was glad Sage was away. Teagan hated that she was expecting some kind of juicy story from her and once again she had nothing but bitter disappointment and humiliation to offer.

Sage was her best friend. She wouldn't make her feel bad. In fact, she'd come up with ten evil ways to retaliate. They'd laugh, knowing they'd never act on her ideas, and Teagan would promise never to chat with Marlow Henry again.

Teagan didn't think she'd fall asleep, but there was nothing like a good cry to wear a person out and dip them into la-la land. All fine except she had the dream again. The nightmare. It was dark and she was running, running, running, out of breath, lungs burning, heart beating in her ears. Her faceless pursuer was stronger than she was, and faster. He wanted her. He wanted to *hurt* her. Teagan pumped her arms and dodged through bushes and trees, branches scratching her face and arms. She couldn't out-maneuver him. He grabbed her ponytail, jerking her backward.

She awoke with a scream.

The next morning it was all over the campus news. Another girl had been raped. This time she didn't survive.

Her throat closed up as one shallow word escaped: Marlow.

Chapter 15

Marlow

@averagegeek99: Where were you?

@averagegeek99: You did say the coffee shop by the library, didn't you?

@averagegeek99: Is there more than one?

@averagegeek99: I don't know what happened, but I'm really sorry I missed you.

I wrote to Teagan in the morning before class. My knees jiggled as I sat in front of my laptop, waiting. I wanted to be pissed off and accuse her of playing mind games, but a female student had died off campus. Blond. Freshman. They weren't giving out her name until next of kin was identified.

What if it was her?

"Hey man," Zed said, sipping noisily on his green drink. "We're going to be late."

"Go ahead. I need a few more minutes."

Zed shrugged. "It's your funeral."

I hadn't told Zed about Teagan's no-show yet, and he hadn't asked. He knew me well enough to read my moods and kept his distance when things were sour. Right now my mood smelled like vomit.

I hiked up my heavy bag onto my shoulder, and once outside, I leaned into the wind and walked briskly.

"Hey, Marlow!" Paul and Steve fell into step beside me.

"Hey," I responded back without slowing.

"Where's Zed?" Steve asked.

"Dunno."

"We just thought," Paul said, "since you guys are always together."

I shot him a look. "Like you guys?"

Paul slapped his head. "Man, we gotta brings some chicks into our scene."

"Speaking of chicks," Steve said. "How'd it go with Virtual Girl last night?" His thick brows jumped. "Can we call her Reality Girl? Are you going to break the curse of girl-lessness?"

I groaned inwardly, wishing I hadn't told the guys I'd planned to meet her. My excitement had dimmed my senses. "I don't kiss and tell."

Why did I say *that?*

Paul grabbed my arm. "Seriously? You *kissed* her already?"

"Shut up. And no. And I'm not talking about it." I didn't want to tell them I was worried for Teagan, that maybe she was the victim of the campus attack. And if she wasn't then she stood me up and I didn't know why. I didn't want to tell them that, either. Thankfully, I arrived at the science lab. I gave them a quick chin nod. "See ya later."

I was the last to arrive, and I took a seat at the last empty table. There was an uneven number in this class, which meant I got to sit alone. I was glad. I didn't want to have to talk to anyone and force amiability.

Professor Garvin stood at the front of the class, rubbing his bald head with one hand, and told us to continue working on our hypotheses assignment.

I opened my files on my laptop and stared at my work. I pushed my glasses up the bridge of my nose as if that was a special trigger to help me focus. My working title beckoned me: A Singular Quantum Event.

I forced my brain to concentrate on quantum physics but it stubbornly skipped back to Teagan. I wouldn't be able to work until I knew she was okay.

I switched screens, logged onto the campus internet and re-read my messages.

@averagegeek99: Where were you?

@averagegeek99: You did say the coffee shop by the library didn't you?

@averagegeek99: Is there more than one?

@averagegeek99: I don't know what happened, but I'm really sorry I missed you.

She hadn't answered.

My nerves shot off, and I scratched my head with both hands, my mind going to the darkest place. What if it was her? What if the girl who had been raped and killed was Teagan?

If she were ignoring me, she'd be in class and not hanging out in chat forums. I forced myself to focus on my assignment.

When the hour and a half was up, everyone gathered their things and left. I returned to the forums and typed.

@averagegeek99: Teagan, I don't know why you didn't show. Maybe I said something to make you mad or turn you off, but can you please just let me know you're okay?

@art4ever: Stop writing to me.

My neck flushed with the pleasure of relief and the bitter pain of rejection.

@averagegeek99: Will you at least tell me what I said?

@art4ever: Just stop!

One exclamation mark had the sharp edge of a knife. She didn't want to talk to me anymore? Fine. At least she was safe. But I was still really, really pissed.

This was a load of bull. I didn't need her company anyway. I was busy. As it was I was going to be late for my advanced calculus class. I grabbed my coat and backpack and raced out.

Chapter 16

Sage

I EYED TEAGAN from across the room as she paced the narrow space between our beds. "What's the matter with you?" I asked.

"Nothing." She stopped and stared back at me. "What if it's Marlow?"

I squinted in question. "What if what's Marlow?"

"The killer?" She lowered herself onto the edge of her bed and whispered, "Marlow didn't show." She lifted her palms as if she didn't want to put words to the rest of her thoughts.

"What do you mean?" I asked, though I immediately knew what she was saying. "He stood you up last night?"

She shook her head, her face flushed with embarrassment.

"Oh my God, Teagan." Panic flushed through my chest. "You need to tell someone."

She sprung to her feet and paced some more. "He wrote me this morning. He acted like I was the one who didn't show."

"Do you think he's trying to establish an alibi?"

She flopped on her bed. "I don't know. I don't even know him. I've never seen him in person. He probably looks nothing like his profile picture, which would explain why he didn't show."

I didn't know if she was overreacting or if she was onto something.

Her scowl drew deeper. "Or maybe he did show! Sage? Maybe he was there the whole time watching me!"

My whole body broke into goose bumps. "You have to tell someone, Teag. Call the police."

"And tell them what? That I was stood up? That's hardly proof."

"Still, it's a tip. I'm sure they get lots of false ones before the real ones come in. No one who calls knows if theirs is the real tip or not." I walked across the room to her desk, grabbed her phone and tossed it to her on the bed. "You have nothing to lose and maybe you'll save a life."

Teagan made the call. We didn't have to wait long for her to make her report as the police were already canvassing the campus. Within half an hour two detectives showed up at our dorm.

"I'm Detective Kilroy," the female cop said. She had dark hair pulled back in a severe ponytail. She motioned to her partner, an African American male.

"And this is Detective Simpson."

Teagan told them everything.

"His name is Marlow Henry. He's a science student. I met him online." Teagan showed them their chatting transcripts. Her cheeks reddened when their flirty comments came up.

Detective Simpson asked, "So, you've never met him in person?"

"No."

"And you can't confirm his identity or whereabouts last night?"

"No."

The detectives shot each other a look, just short of an eye roll. Listening to Teagan talk, I could see how to them she sounded like a girl who was just angry and humiliated for being stood up."

Detective Kilroy spoke into a handset. "Marlow Henry. Science student. Check his alibi."

At least they'll get this Marlow guy's alibi and if he has one, they can scratch him off the suspect list.

Teagan slumped on her bed after they left and my heart went out to her.

"Teag," I said. "You did the right thing."

"He's only ever been nice to me and maybe he *had* gotten the café mixed up. I could've just implicated an innocent man."

"Well," I countered. "If his alibi checks out, then no harm done. They won't tell him they got their tip from you."

"He's smart," Teagan said. "He'll figure it out."

Her phone rang and she groaned. "It's my mother. She must've heard the news."

I smiled sympathetically. Mrs. Lake was beautiful, but a tough mother to manage. I admired Teagan's patience. Just being in the same room with Mrs. Lake made my anxiety levels soar. She was so intense and demanding, and she micromanaged Teagan's life with an iron fist. My mother wasn't always reasonable, but she was a walk in the park in comparison. I left for the lounge to get something to drink. I wanted to give Teagan privacy. I also didn't want to get sucked into their ongoing drama again.

Chapter 17

Teagan

THE WEEK PASSED by slowly. Everyone was on pins and needles waiting for an announcement that the killer had been caught. The senator's son who'd been arrested for the rape of Vanessa Rothman was released and charges dropped. His lawyers got him off on a technicality, but now with a second blond female student victim, the police were looking at a possible serial rapist.

It almost made Teagan want to dye her hair.

Her mom called her every night now, and she spent at least ten minutes reassuring her. She never walked alone or after dark. She was careful.

Despite this huge blight on the university, Teagan really enjoyed her professors and loved the art she was producing. It was too late in the year to transfer somewhere else. Besides, Thanksgiving was coming.

She'd be home then, and her mother could rest easy for a while.

Every day Teagan half expected to hear that Marlow Henry had been arrested, but his name was never mentioned

anywhere. Especially not in *this* dorm. Sage expertly avoided any discussion of him.

Another week passed without incident. The leaves dropped from the trees and covered the paths in yellow. Exposed branches stretched out like scratchy silhouettes across the teal green sky. Soon the snow would fall. Teagan deeply inhaled the crisp air.

Jake and Nora had become an official couple. They were well-suited to each other, better than she and Jake would've been. She couldn't help but wonder what he saw in her in the first place. Nora had thanked her more than once for being instrumental in their meeting. She gushed to Sage and Teagan about how she and Jake were soul mates. Teagan supposed that should make her feel good.

It didn't. It made her feel lonely and inadequate. Where was *her* soul mate?

Her mom kept telling her she had a lot of time to find *the one*. "Just focus on getting good grades," she said, "and find a way to support yourself so you never have to depend on a man."

It seemed like good advice.

Teagan was working on an art history project when she heard the ding of the chat room bell. It had been almost three weeks since she last chatted with

Marlow and she hadn't chatted with anyone else since.

It had to be him and she almost didn't look, but her curiosity got the best of her. She blinked a couple times as her mind registered the message. She had sense enough finally to experience a cool spread of fear.

@gingerbreadman to @art4ever: You're next.

Chapter 18

Marlow

I HAD THIS STUPID compulsion to time everything to the last minute. Class started at 4:00 pm. The physics department was a twelve-minute walk door to door. So naturally I waited until quarter to before I packed up my books, used the facilities and brushed my teeth—which I did at rapid speed to comply with my three-minute limit, and then I left at precisely twelve minutes to, my heart racing as I hopped down the three cement steps to the campus walkway.

Which would be fine, except that it didn't account for any unforeseen mishaps or events that could bite into the tight schedule and there was *always* an unforeseen mishap or event—I should know better by now.

The mishap happened on the steps, not two seconds after I exited the door. Another guy was coming in at the same moment, the both of us with our heads down watching our feet. I saw him at the last second, made an impressive dodge to the right and almost passed by unscathed except for the fact that one of my laces had come undone and the guy stood on it solidly while I tried to take my next step.

The tumble knocked the wind out of me as I exhaled with a painful, "Oof."

I became aware of a barely pubescent voice, "Dude, are you okay?"

I squinted one eye open to see a face almost as nerdy as mine peering down at me. The image blurred and I wondered if I'd hit my head, but then the guy offered me my glasses which I had apparently knocked off while trying to break my fall.

"Thanks," I said, feeling like a moron.

"Are you all right?" the guy asked again.

"Yeah." I pulled myself onto my feet. My right knee and elbow hurt, but other than my bruised ego, I was fine.

I broke into a gimpy jog. Professor Garvin was known to close and lock his doors before starting his lecture to discourage tardiness. The sky above was a bright blue, the sun sending warm yellow rays through bare tree branches, but the horizon to the north was a dark, eerie gray. The wind swished through the piles of leaves in mini whirlwinds. The energy in the air made the hair on my arms stand on end. A storm was coming.

The thought reminded me of Teagan and her fear of storms. If things had turned out, she'd probably be coming to see me tonight and I'd be the one to comfort her and ease her fears.

I snorted in frustration and picked up my pace. I needed to attend this lecture if I wanted to get a jump on the assignment. As it was I was going to be working on homework through the Thanksgiving weekend.

I puffed like an old dog, reaching the hallway just as Professor Garvin stretched an arm out to close the door.

"Wait!" I rasped out as loud as my burning lungs allowed.

The door stilled and Professor Garvin's bald head peeked out. "Mr. Henry. This is your lucky day. Perhaps in the future, you could budget a little more time to travel to my class."

"Thanks," I muttered, trying in vain to compose myself before being ushered inside. A dozen or more heads turned to watch me slide in. I refused to meet anyone eye to eye, keeping my gaze at table level, looking for an empty seat.

The last chair left was beside Blaine Tucker. I suppressed a groan. Blaine was everything I wasn't: tall, clean-shaven with neatly trimmed hair and what girls would call a strong jaw. He had no need for glasses and when he smiled, he produced two "adorable dimples," according to the girls in the room. I didn't think they realized how their voices carried over all the stainless steel.

And he was smart, otherwise he wouldn't be in this class.

Life wasn't fair.

"Hey, Marlow," he said.

"Hi. Where's Gina?" Gina was Blaine's pretty brunette girlfriend and his usual lab partner. If she'd been here, I'd get a table to myself, but Professor Garvin wanted everyone to have a partner when possible.

"Sick today."

"Oh." I unloaded my books, settled onto the stool and leaned forward as Professor Garvin started his lecture on quantum physics and the many theories regarding the possibilities of alternate realities and parallel universes.

"Time can be perceived like a fork with many tongs extending out in parallel realms. In many ways the same, but also different."

Blaine whispered from the side of his mouth, "This is a crock."

"They're just theories," I whispered back. "And there's a lot of supporting evidence."

Maybe in another universe Blaine was the dork and I was the cool, smart guy with the pretty girlfriend.

By the time the class ended, the storm outside had descended into a fury. I kept my chin tucked into the collar of my jacket and pinched my eyes against the sting of the wind. It hadn't started raining yet, but when it did, it would be a downpour. I walked as fast as I could, body pressed to the wind, eyes opened only slivers, just enough so I could make out where I was going and hopefully avoid another embarrassing tumble.

Once I made it back to the safety of my dorm room, I stripped my outer clothes and plopped onto my bed, exhausted. I folded my hands behind my head, closed my eyes and tried to relax. I imagined Teagan Lake with me, lying pressed against my side as I stroked her back and made comforting noises in her ear. Every time the wind whistled through the windows or a clap of thunder sounded in the distance, she'd whimper and press herself closer.

I didn't let my imagination go beyond that. Even in my daydreams I was a gentleman. I wondered what she was doing and who she was with. Probably that jock. My stomach muscles tensed at the thought. Maybe I should start going to the gym.

I huffed out loud at the absurdity. Me and my skinny arms pumping iron next to those hockey jerks? Not gonna happen.

Chapter 19

RUN, RUN, RUN, as fast as you can. You can't catch me. I'm the Gingerbread Man.

The nursery rhyme would forever remind him of his father and trigger frosty threads of fear that rippled through his veins even now.

It was the tune his old man would sing in a low, menacing whisper, late at night once his mother had passed out after her fourth shot of bourbon. His dad's massive frame would fill his bedroom door before he stepped into the glow of the Spiderman nightlight that cast a long ghostly shadow along the floor and cut sharply up the wall.

The tune was like a war siren to his young ears. His father would make just enough space for him to escape into the hallway and down the steps, and after singing through it for the third time, the chase would be on.

His little boy feet raced as fast as they could down the stairs, his heart thundering like a blow horn in his ears, his hand picking up slivers along the rough edges of the railing.

He didn't even feel the pinch of the short splinters. A far worse pain was in store for him. This was a certainty. The only question was how long he could delay the inevitable. And he'd learned from experience that if he didn't play the game, make the hunt exciting for his dad, the outcome would be even worse.

In those days, their house sat on the edge of town. The city had since sprawled, swallowing up their rural neighborhood with a cookie-cutter, boxy-house suburb, but in his youth, there was a forest beyond their wooden fence.

When the game first began, he'd sought out hiding places in the house—a linen closet, under the sofa, even downstairs in the absolutely terrifying dark, musky cellar. It didn't take him long to figure out that he had to get further than the walls of their house. The problem was the distance from the back door to the fence. His legs were too short and his father's stride too long. His heart pounded so hard he thought his ears were bleeding. His face grew wet with tears and snot, and he screamed every time his father caught him and wrapped a beefy palm over his face to suppress his cries, nearly suffocating him. His dad carried him under his arm like a sack of flour, back to the house and down the steps to the cellar.

That was where the belt would come off.

He hated the musky damp scent of old cold rooms. He hated his old man.

Eventually, he grew tall enough and fast enough to outrun his dad, losing him in the welcoming darkness of the forest, able to climb tall pines out of reach and out of sight.

It was there that he vowed to kill his dad one day.

He was still scared of the old bastard. Though they were now the same height, his father outweighed him by fifty pounds. He was big, strong and mean.

A liar and a cheater.

He wondered if his mother ever knew about the other woman? Maybe that was why she'd started drinking?

Didn't matter now.

He hadn't planned to kill the last girl. Not really, though he had played with the idea more than once. He'd just gotten carried away, but now he could see that the killing had been a dry run for his dad. Watching her gasp for breath, her eyes glossy with fear, and the awareness that the end of her existence was in *his* control gave him a sense of empowerment. He wasn't the weak, helpless little victim any more. He was the *Gingerbread Man*.

One day he'd kill his old man, but for now he had someone better. He'd made a fortuitous discovery. The whore's daughter was a student at Detroit University. He'd been watching her.

He grinned as he sipped the beer in his hand, his mind slowly tuning back into the bar noise and activity around him. This would be his first real hunt. He just had to think of a way to lure her to him.

Chapter 20

Teagan

TEAGAN SQUEEZED the plastic bottle of brown goo on her hair, unsure if her eyes were burning from the chemicals or from the emotional impact of watching her blue streak disappear. Her plastic-gloved fingers trembled against her scalp as she worked the solution into her roots and dragged the color along the blond strands until every last bit of yellow had disappeared.

You're next.

Those two words were a fiery stake to her heart. Whoever the hell gingerbreadman was scared the bejeebers out of her.

Her first impulse was to delete, delete, delete. Then she'd curled up into a little ball on her bed and moaned softly into her pillow. That was how Sage found her.

She had to pull the message out of her trash bin on her laptop, but thankfully it was still there. Proof she wasn't going crazy. Sage insisted that she call the detectives who'd questioned them before.

She did, and they followed up, but gingerbreadman was a tech wiz and had encrypted his address. They offered to put a watch on her and her room, an offer she accepted. Teagan didn't dare tell her mother, because she would've freaked with a capital F. It was only two days until Thanksgiving when she could go home where she'd be safe. Hopefully, this maniac would be caught before school started up again after the holiday weekend.

The timer buzzed and Teagan stepped into the shower to wash out the dye. She wiped the fog off the mirror when she was done and breathed out a long breath of relief. She was no longer blond. Not only was she barely recognizable to herself, she no longer fit the description of the attacker's type.

Teagan dried her hair with the blow-dryer and studied her new look in the mirror. Hair color made a big difference in a person's looks, but she was still her. The way she stood, the way she walked, where she walked to. Eventually he would notice, especially if he were really looking for her.

The question was why? Why her specifically? The police confirmed that the other two victims hadn't received a similar message, which made them think this was probably a random prank. Did Teagan have any enemies? Any on-going disputes?

No, she told them. She kept to herself. Was generally well-liked.

It just didn't make sense.

Teagan startled when the message chime rang on her laptop. Was it *him?*

A quick look alleviated her fears. Sort of. It wasn't gingerbreadman, it was averagegeek99.

She wasn't entirely convinced they weren't the same person.

@averagegeek99: Are you there? Please. I don't know why you're mad at me. I just need to know you're okay.

Why wouldn't she be okay? Unless Marlow somehow knew about gingerbreadman? Maybe he wanted to warn her.

@art4ever: Yes. I'm here and okay.

@averagegeek99: This is going to sound weird, but I need you to confirm your identity. Quickly, so I know you're not scrolling through old texts, what is my biggest fear?

Teagan immediately began typing.

@art4ever: Snakes.

@averagegeek99: My roommate's name?

@art4ever: Zed.

@averagegeek99: First joke?

Marlow's urgency was scaring her. Her fingers shook, and she had to backspace to correct spelling while simultaneously chastising herself—who cared about spelling?

@art4ever: Knock, knock.

@art4ever: Marlow, what's up?

@averagegeek99: Sorry. Don't mean to freak you out.

@art4ever: Too late.

@averagegeek99: Something weird is going on. I can't explain it, just, I thought you were in trouble.

Teagan didn't know what had shaken him up so badly but she felt the need to comfort him.

@art4ever: I'm in my dorm. Door's locked. Just getting ready for bed.

@averagegeek99: Okay. Good. How are you? Is it okay for me to ask that?

@art4ever: I'm fine. Studying hard. I'm looking

forward to going home for Thanksgiving. Are you going home?

@averagegeek99: Nah. Holiday celebrations aren't really our thing. I've got a science paper to work on.

She really shouldn't have stayed online with him, but Sage was out again and talking to him made her feel like she wasn't so alone.

@art4ever: What's it about?

@averagegeek99: I haven't decided yet. It's for my quantum physics class. I thought I knew, but I think I'm changing my mind. The prof likes outside-of-the-box thinking so I have to pick something nerdy. Are you working on any cool art projects?

@art4ever: An abstract with mixed medium. Acrylics, fabric, bicycle parts.

@averagegeek99: Bicycle parts?

@art4ever: Gears and pieces of the chain. It's all about the texture.

@averagegeek99: I'd love to see it.

What was that? Was he suggesting they try meeting up again?

@averagegeek99: I mean someday.

@averagegeek99: Or just a picture of it.

@averagegeek99: Or never. Just forget it.

His obvious nervousness made her smile against her will. He was just so geeky! And adorable. He couldn't be gingerbreadman. It just seemed so ridiculous to her now.

@art4ever: I'd love to show it to you.

@art4ever: Someday.

Teagan smiled into her hand. It was true. She really did want to show it to him someday.

She heard another chime and her mother's name appeared. Her mom didn't usually write between their weekly sessions unless something came up.

@art4ever: My mom's online. I have to run.

@averagegeek99: Got it. It's been great chatting. Until next time?

@art4ever: Yeah. ☺

Talking to Marlow produced warm fuzzies in her belly, a happy sensation she hadn't experienced in a while. She had to change mental gears to deal with her mom.

@art4ever to @mylakeisthebestlake: Hey, Mom. What's up?

@mylakeisthebestlake: Good news! I'm at DU! There's a coffee shop by the park on the edge of campus. Believe in Beans. Do you know it? Can you meet me? I'd come to your room, but the campus is so large and confusing. I'm afraid I'd lose my way in the dark.

Teagan frowned at the screen.

@art4ever: What are you doing here? I'm going to be home in two days.

@mylakeisthebestlake: I don't want you to travel by yourself. It's not safe and I'm worried. And I thought it would be nice to spend some time together. I wanted to surprise you!

@art4ever: I'm surprised! Where did you plan on staying?

@mylakeisthebestlake: There's a hotel just off the highway. I booked a room. Do you want to stay with me? It'd be fun.

@art4ever: I would, but I really have to study.

@mylakeisthebestlake: I understand. How about a hot chocolate? I'd just feel better if I could see your face.

Teagan checked the time: 7:45. It would take her fifteen minutes by campus shuttle to get to the side of the campus her mom was at. She couldn't believe how directionally challenged her mother was. It was amazing she made it this far on her own.

@art4ever: Hot chocolate sounds good. But I can't stay long.

@mylakeisthebestlake: Great. I'll wait by the front door. See you soon!

Teagan pulled a pair of jeans over her pajama shorts and slipped into an extra sweater before putting on her jacket. The wind whistled through the window pane and she wrapped a red scarf around her neck for good measure.

She totally forgot to tell her mom about her new hair color. Her mother wasn't the only one with a surprise. Teagan ran to catch the bus.

Chapter 21

Marlow

IT WAS JUST another Tuesday. That was my first misassumption.

I stood in a long line at Java Junkie, catching a yawn with my free hand. Everyone looked puffy-eyed with bad hair and chins tucked into scarves or warm sweaters. Two girls stood in front of me, a brunette and a redhead. I recognized the brunette, Sage something. She was in one of my math classes. If she recognized me, she didn't show it.

By the time I got to the front of the line, ordered, paid for and got my coffee, I was running late for my calculus class. I pushed through the wind as droplets of rain dotted my glasses, causing the world to blur. I removed them and shoved them in my pocket, careful when I stepped up onto the sidewalk that I didn't misjudge the height. I didn't want to lose my caffeine fix. Fortunately, Professor Plats wasn't the type of prof to lock his doors. Once inside the building, I took a moment to retrieve my glasses and clean them with the edge of my shirt before sliding them over my nose.

The world came back into focus, and I grabbed an empty seat at the end of the room. Professor Plats was scribbling our assignment on the blackboard. It was strange to think of him as a professor. For one thing, he couldn't be that much older than I was—he must've been a quirky child prodigy. He had dirty-blond hair and squinty, brown eyes, like he needed glasses but didn't want to wear them. He wore sweater vests over white shirts with the tails hanging out over skinny jeans. He had a way of making nerdiness look cool. I should probably take notes.

He yawned and rubbed his eyes, and I wondered what could be keeping him up at night. Unsolved equations? Tests to mark?

A blond girl from the front row approached him. He snapped to attention like all guys did when they encountered a pretty face. His eyes widened and he nodded, then pointed to something in the textbook she held out. Even from my spot in the back row, I could see the girl blushing at the prof's attention. Maybe she was the reason he didn't get any sleep the night before.

Jake Wentworth sat two tables to the right of me beside his buddy Chet. Jake took a long pull from a tall paper cup of coffee. Chet gave in and lowered his buzz cut onto his arms on the table.

I stifled another yawn. It was the time of year. Midterms were a killer and everyone stayed up late, studying. My first exam was after lunch. No one was getting enough sleep.

I opened my textbook to the page Professor Plats marked on the board. It was a review of everything covered so far, prep for the next day's exam.

The class resumed in relative quiet, just the sound of pencils scratching and paper shuffling. The peace was shattered ten minutes before class ended when a girl who'd been playing with her phone instead of working out math problems started shrieking.

"Oh my God. It's happened again! Another girl has been raped and killed!"

Suddenly everyone was wide awake.

Who was it?

Do they know?

I've gotta call my roommate, make sure she's okay.

Who was it?

Oh, there's a name.

Another freshman.

The girl's name is Teagan Lake

Chapter 22

Teagan

TEAGAN SECOND-GUESSED the wisdom of taking transit alone after dark once she was on the bus. It was full of students she didn't know, mostly guys, and there were a handful that seemed to make a special note of her sitting by herself.

She wrapped her arms around her chest and stared at her reflection in the window. She was a brunette now. *He* wouldn't want her.

Besides, she couldn't leave her own mother hanging.

The bus came to a stop and her heart thudded when she recognized the couple that boarded. Nora and Jake. They walked right past her without even a nod of acknowledgment. That was when she knew her hair-color change had worked. Thank goodness.

Half a hockey team boarded at the next stop. Six guys oozing testosterone with bulky sports bags swung over broad shoulders pushed their way down the aisle, forcing other passengers to lean in toward the windows. They bellowed and guffawed, taking all the empty spots left, including the one next to Teagan. The guy shot her a quick glance as he sat down, then twisted so he could face his pals in the back.

"Hey Wentworth," he yelled. "You skippin'?"

"Nah," Jake shouted back. "I got my bag here."

Teagan slunk lower, hugging the window.

Two stops later, they all got off, allowing the remaining passengers to take a breath. Each stop after that had people getting off, but none getting on. Teagan had forgotten that the coffee shop her mom had mentioned was at the end of the line.

The campus populace had thinned out significantly. Maybe it was the time of night or maybe this just wasn't where the action was. Teagan shivered and wrapped her arms close to her chest.

A noisy freeway ran on the other side of a wide berm to the west. A forested park edged an empty parking lot to the north. A half-lit sign showed Believe in Beans and had an arrow pointing to the café. The windows were dark. It definitely looked closed, which would be odd for 8:00 p.m. at night.

Teagan wondered if her mom had gotten the name wrong.

Then she wondered if the message was actually from her mother. She froze. She wanted to turn around. Find another bus.

But if her mom were there somewhere, she couldn't just leave her.

Chapter 23

Marlow

BLOOD DRAINED from my face. It couldn't be. No. Please. Not her. I raced back to my dorm—rain pounding on my head, lightning flashing in bright, jagged streaks across the sky, thunder crashing in the distance. The universe was demonstrating the chaos going on in my heart.

I stood in my dorm, letting the water run from my body into a puddle on the floor, feeling numb.

I began to shake violently. Somehow, I managed to strip out of my wet clothes until I wore nothing but my boxers, and settled into my desk chair. I whipped open my laptop to double check the news. There must've been a mistake. Please, let it be a big mistake.

My fingers quivered along with my goose bump-covered body and I slumped as I read the newsfeed.

Third rape and second murder victim identified as Detroit University freshman, Teagan Lake. Her body was found in the park at the north end of the campus. Police are investigating and talking to persons of interest.

A picture of Teagan was posted alongside the story. It wasn't the same one she used on her chat profile. Her hair was longer, and the blue streak was missing.

My mind went crazy. Despite the newsflash in front of me, I couldn't accept it as truth. My fingers seemed to work autonomously from the logical part of my brain.

@averagegeek99 to @art4ever: Are you there? Please. I don't know why you're mad at me. I just need to know you're okay.

I pinched my eyes together. I was insane. Of course she wouldn't respond. Dead people didn't hang out in chat rooms.

Then I heard the ping.

@art4ever: Yes. I'm here and okay.

I knocked off my glasses in surprise. My heart took off like pebbles scattered across the pond. It couldn't be her. Could it? I scrambled to fit my glasses back on my face and began to type.

@averagegeek99: This is going to sound weird, but I need you to confirm your identity. Quickly, so I know you're not scrolling through old texts, what is my biggest fear?

A response came within seconds.

@art4ever: Snakes.

Good guess?

@averagegeek99: My roommate's name?

@art4ever: Zed.

Oh, God.

@averagegeek99: First joke?

@art4ever: Knock, knock.

@art4ever: Marlow, what's up?

It was *her*. It had to be. She knew my name!

@averagegeek99: Sorry. Don't mean to freak you out.

@art4ever: Too late.

@averagegeek99: Something weird is going on. I can't explain it, just, I thought you were in trouble.

@art4ever: I'm in my dorm. Door's locked. Just getting ready for bed.

I ran a hand through my hair and rubbed the back of my neck. I was so *confused*.

@averagegeek99: Okay. Good. How are you? Is it okay for me to ask that?

@art4ever: I'm fine. Studying hard. I'm looking forward to going home for Thanksgiving. Are you going home?

@averagegeek99: Nah. Holiday celebrations aren't really our thing. I've got a science paper to work on.

@art4ever: What's it about?

@averagegeek99: I haven't decided yet.

Maybe something to do with the last couple of lectures Prof Garvin gave on alternate realities.

Alternate realities.

No way. Was it possible? Was it possible that the

Teagan Lake I was chatting with now, wasn't the same Teagan Lake reported about in the news?

Could *my* Teagan Lake be in a parallel universe? I pushed away from the desk and paced around my wet pile of clothes. The idea was so crazy. But theoretically, it was possible.

And if my Teagan was still alive in another reality, a reality where the attacks were also happening, she could still be in danger.

How could I help her?

If I mentioned something crazy like this, she'd stop chatting with me again for sure and then it really would be impossible to help her.

If this *were* true, there must be a way to cross over. But how?

We continued to chat about lighter topics like her latest art project and she surprised me when she said she'd like me to see it. In the background my mind was racing, trying to unravel this mystery. Was this why none of our pictures or video efforts ever worked? She was over *there* somewhere and I was *here*? How did our chat sessions happen then? What was going on when I got her first message?

@art4ever: My mom's online. I have to run.

@averagegeek99: Got it. It's been great chatting. Until next time?

@art4ever: Yeah. ☺

I was still shivering from the cold induced by the storm and somehow made my shaky legs get me into a hot shower. My mind continued to spin as I soaped up.

The whole scenario was just so wild. Something nagged at the back of my mind, but I couldn't seem to grasp it in my exhausted and traumatized state.

I dressed in pajama pants and an old T-shirt, and brushed my teeth. I was spitting in the sink when it came to me.

The *storm*.

It was storming the day Teagan first contacted me. I remember getting shocked when I'd typed a reply.

Something happened that day to connect us. Maybe it originated from her side? I had to get over there somehow, had to do something to keep her safe.

I didn't know how to make a jump happen. Only one impulsive idea came to mind. I grabbed my laptop and ran outside into the rain.

Chapter 24

Teagan

TEAGAN WALKED up to the front door of Believe in Beans and peered inside. Only darkness. Chairs were stacked up in rows along a back wall. A sign hung on the window announcing it was closed for renovations and apologizing for any inconvenience.

Her mom must've gotten her cafés mixed up. She was probably waiting at one in an entirely different area of campus! She reached into her purse for her phone so she could text her.

"Teagan."

Her head jerked up at her name. It sounded like her mother's voice. "Mom?"

"Teagan!"

It *was* her voice. She sounded like she was in distress. Teagan searched the perimeter of the parking lot where her mother's calls seemed to come from. "Mom? Is that you?"

"Help!"

Teagan ran toward the sound of her mom's voice, into the darkness of the park. She didn't think twice that it could be a trap. The only thing on her mind was that her mother was hurt and that she needed to find her.

"Mom!"

"Teagan."

Ice cold prickles ran up Teagan's spine as she skittered to a stop. That was not her mother's voice. It was low and male.

"Thanks for coming," he said. "Of course, I knew you would. Mommy's girl."

Teagan spun slowly. He stood between her and the parking lot, his face in shadow so she couldn't identify him. She could scream, but she knew no one would hear her through the highway noise.

"Where's my mother?" she asked, hoping her voice didn't portray the fear she felt.

"She's fine. Probably happily banging my father again."

What?

He took a step closer. Teagan took a careful step backward. Her forehead broke out into a cold sweat. Her throat closed up. Her knees felt like jelly. She was in trouble. Deep, horrible trouble.

"You changed your hair. Tsk, tsk. You know I prefer blonds."

"Where's my mother?"

"She's not the one you should be worried about right now," he said.

"Where did her voice come from? I know I heard her."

He held up a small recording device. "As I have already indicated, your mother and my father are acquainted. All I had to do was to hack into one of their many communications."

Teagan's eyelids fluttered as she tried to process his implication. There was no way her mom would have anything to do with another man in that way.

Teagan took another step back, snapping a twig underfoot. The light of the half-moon filtered through the trees, which surrounded her on three sides. The dim parking lot lights pointed to the empty lot beyond, but *he* stood in her way. She wasn't an athlete. She was fairly certain she couldn't deke past him. The seconds boomed loudly between them as they remained frozen in their spot, waiting.

Then his voice broke into a soft, menacing song. "Run, run, run, as fast as you can. You can't catch me. I'm the *gingerbread man*."

Teagan spun toward the darkness of the park and ran.

PART TWO

Chapter 25

Marlow

"*AHHHHHHH.*" Tremors of electric shock shuddered through my body, a new pulse with every erratic beat of my heart igniting the system of nerves from the top of my head to my toes, each ending with sharp, fiery explosions. I couldn't stop yelling. "*Ahhhhhhhh!*"

"Are you okay, man?"

My eyes snapped open at the sound of a male voice. His face was a blur before me, the edges of my vision a creamy white.

"I think I'm going to be sick."

The guy pointed me toward a bright green bush, so green it looked emerald, like an over-exposed postcard.

I emptied the contents of my stomach.

"Pretty early in the day for drinking, huh?" I looked at the guy again and his face came into focus. Narrow jaw, long nose, squinty eyes.

I wiped my mouth with the back of my hand. "I'm not drunk. I might've been struck by lightning."

He chortled. "Dude, it's not even raining." His brow furrowed. "Maybe you should see a doctor."

"Yeah, maybe." I glanced to the ground, feeling embarrassed. "Thanks for your help."

He left me standing there soaked in my own sweat and I inhaled in short, dry breaths as I took in my surroundings. I stood in front of my dorm building, three floors of red brick with white window trimming. When I last saw it, cold rain drenched my skin and fogged up my glasses. Now there wasn't a drop in the sky. I squinted and cupped my eyes as I tilted my head back and looked up. The sky was a weird color, more green than blue, like I was viewing the world through tinted sunglasses. My hand went to my nose. I removed my glasses and examined them to confirm they were in fact my prescription lenses and not sunglasses.

Was this the place? A parallel universe where Teagan Lake was still alive?

Or was I having some kind of nervous breakdown? Maybe I was in a coma and this was a lucid dream. I could've caught a deadly bug like SARS or Ebola, or maybe I had been hit by a bus. I could be having an out-of-body experience.

If that were the case, shouldn't I being looking down at my body covered in a cotton sheet lying in a sterile room? Shouldn't there be a bright light beckoning me?

Or maybe this was real. Maybe I'd really made the jump from one reality to another. I had no idea how it happened, but if it did, there had to be a cosmic reason, and I believed that reason was to save Teagan.

But how?

In the last "normal" memory I had, I was standing in the rain with dark brooding clouds rolling overhead and the air charged with electricity. My laptop was open in my hands and I remember thinking I was an idiot for letting it get wet.

I stared at my bare hands. Where was my laptop? I scanned the area around where I had stood screaming like a wild man. The space was open with trimmed lawns and large coniferous trees. A neater, cleaner version of my own campus. Golden leaves floated down and scurried along the edge of the sidewalk stirred by a cool breeze.

I wrapped my bare arms across my chest, my sweaty, damp skin now cooled to goose bumps, and noted that I was wearing pajama pants and an old T-shirt. Great.

Unable to accept the loss of my main tool for doing *anything,* I scouted around the building and behind the bushes, hoping I'd just tossed my computer when I "landed" without damaging it too much. I was concealed behind a hedge when I heard Zed's voice. I felt like jumping out and hugging him, but then I heard another voice.

My voice.

I ducked lower, peeking through the bush. My jaw slacked as I watched Zed and a preppy version of me, without frameless specs perched on his nose, walk past and up the steps into my dorm.

My knees buckled, and I collapsed onto the damp ground not caring that my butt was getting wet. I cupped my hands over my mouth and breathed in and out—short, steady breaths.

I was definitely *here*. But what was I supposed to do now? I couldn't go into my dorm. I had to stay away from this Zed and anyone else who might know the other me. There was only one place I could think of to go. I wiped the cool earth off my rear end and jogged away.

Chapter 26

Sage

I DIDN'T NOTICE that Teagan was missing until eight o'clock in the morning. I'd gone out with Nora and the hockey players after their practice and had too much to drink. By the time I lumbered into our dorm room it was late, around three in the morning. I beelined to my bed and woke a couple hours later with major pressure on my bladder and a splitting headache.

Totally not worth it.

Teagan's blankets were all twisted and at first glance it looked like she was curled up in them. I crawled back into mine with a low groan.

Teagan's alarm went off at 8:00. I muttered loudly to her to shut it off and pushed my pillow to my ear. Normally, the high-pitched tone disappeared within seconds. This time it didn't.

"Teagan!"

When she didn't move, I threw a purple and green striped cushion at her. The morning light streamed through
the window in dusty beams. That was when I saw that her bed was empty. I assumed she was in the bathroom.

"Teagan! Your freakin' alarm is going off!"

When she didn't appear, I left my bed in a huff and swiped her phone, killing the alarm.

I crawled back into my bed with a heavy sigh of indignation. Teagan could be so self-absorbed sometimes, just lost in her own little world. I shut my eyes hoping for sleep to return, but in the back of my mind, in my subconscious, I knew something was wrong. For one thing, Teagan never came out of the bathroom. I didn't hear water running or any sound, and a second look revealed that the telltale strip of light that normally glowed from under the bathroom door was missing.

I sat up. "Teag?"

I'd removed my jeans at some point during the night but I still had my bra and blouse on. I tugged at them. So uncomfortable. My hair smelled of beer and cigarette smoke, making me gag. I ran to the bathroom, knowing I would find it empty, and dry-heaved in the toilet.

Teagan must've gotten up early and went out to scout for breakfast. I expected her to arrive any moment with her usual cheery smile and two cream and sugar laden coffees.

I showered and combed out my dark hair, letting it dry in natural straight sheets. Not one hint of a curl there. That was something I'd always envied Teagan for. My brown eyes had telltale bloodshot lines and grey half-moon circles underneath. This was one of the many reasons why I never went home with a guy—couldn't risk him seeing me looking like this in the morning.

Teagan hadn't shown up with my hoped-for coffee, so I dressed and went to the common lounge, hoping to find food in the fridge. Sometimes people put leftovers in there.

If it wasn't marked with a name, it was free for the taking. I didn't want to go to the café looking and feeling like a dishrag.

It was empty. Instead of eating I made a bad coffee in the machine, which did little to help my headache. I collapsed onto the couch, nodded to another weary-looking coffee-seeker, and closed my eyes.

Maybe Teagan had gone to one of her art classes.

But it was Saturday.

She might be working on a project.

I slipped my phone out of my pocket and messaged her. "Hey early bird, where'd you go?"

Nothing.

She could be really absorbed in her project.

Or?

I stiffened.

Did Teagan go out? She hadn't mentioned any plans. In fact, she quite clearly said she was staying in. But what if she changed her mind? What if she hadn't come home last night?

There'd been three attacks on freshmen girls since school started. All blonds like Teagan.

My heart tumbled about. I messaged again. "Teag? Just let me know you're okay. Okay?"

I waited. Her silence made my nerves flicker. A pit grew in my stomach and I suffered through another roll of nausea.

Teagan, come on. Text me back.

Then I remembered Teagan's phone was back in the room. Wherever she was she'd forgotten to take her phone. My veins iced over a bit more.

The entrance door swung open, and a wild-eyed guy with dark, messy hair, crooked glasses and dirty pajamas stumbled into the lounge.

"I'm looking for Teagan Lake? Do you know her?"

I stared hard at this strange guy. Both of us were looking for Teagan. A coincidence? I thought not. "Who are you?"

He puffed. "I just need to know if she's okay."

My heart fell two floors. "Why?"

"Is she? Please."

I felt sick again and my knees gave out. Thankfully, the couch was beneath me.

"I don't know where she is."

"Are you a friend?"

"Best friend. And roommate." I covered my face with my hands. So why didn't I know where she was? I glanced back at the guy. He grabbed at his messy hair and paced in small circles.

"You didn't answer my question," I said. "Who are you?"

He stopped and took me in like he was seeing me for the first time. "I'm Marlow Henry."

Good thing my coffee mug was empty. It fell from my fingers, breaking into several pieces on the tile floor. I knew that name. This was the guy Teagan had met online.

I shot daggers at him with my eyes. "If you've hurt her, I swear, I'll kill you."

Chapter 27

Marlow

"I DIDN'T *HURT* her. I'm trying to *save* her."

The pretty brunette eyed me suspiciously. "Save her from what?"

A girl with a short, leg-exposing housecoat tied around a narrow waist and a tall towel turban wrapped around her hair sauntered by in fluffy slippers.

I returned my attention to the dark-haired girl. "Is there somewhere we can talk? In private?"

She glared and I imagined cat claws springing from her fingertips. "How do I know I can trust you? That you won't, you know, try something?"

I threw my hands up in the air. "Look at me! I'm unarmed and wearing pajamas. I weigh a hundred and sixty pounds soaking wet. You could take me in an arm wrestling match."

That seemed to convince her. She was almost my height and she probably weighed around a hundred and thirty pounds. She had nice curves, and even without a stitch of make up, she was attractive.

Why couldn't Teagan's roomie be homely or at least ordinary? I seriously didn't need the distraction.

I caught the turban girl watching us. She raised an eyebrow in question, wondering probably, what on earth a girl like this nameless beauty was doing taking a wreck of a guy like me to her room. Teagan's dorm mate made a big show of leaving the door wide open.

Their room was a splash of color—reds, pinks, purples—from the bedding to the walls. One side was messier than the other, with clothes and art supplies scattered about. Several paintings hung on the wall. I felt drawn to them. I pushed my glasses up on my nose and stared.

"Teagan's?" I asked, even though I knew they must be.

"Yup."

I turned to the girl who was now sitting on the bed on the neat side with her back up against the wall and her arms wrapped around one knee. "What's your name?" I asked.

"Sage Farrell. Now tell me why you're here and what you know about Teagan."

I lowered myself to what I guessed was Teagan's desk chair, keeping as much distance from Sage as I could in the small room. "I'm assuming by your reaction to my name that she told you about me?"

"Yeah. You're the online creeper."

I winced at that. "We chatted on one of the forums and became friends."

"You stood her up."

"Well, not exactly."

"What do you mean? You either showed or you didn't."

"I showed, just not at the same… "

Her dark java eyes widened. "You went to the wrong café?"

"No, it was the right one."

"Okay, so the wrong time then?"

"I was there on time."

"Then what?" She flung a hand out impatiently. "You didn't recognize each other? Did you use a fake profile pic?"

"No." I motioned to the laptop on Teagan's desk. "You can check for yourself. I never once misrepresented myself."

"Then what happened?"

I ran a hand through my hair. "That's the part that's going to be really hard for you to believe."

"Try me."

"Okay, but don't freak out. And let me finish. And let me preface by saying that I believe Teagan is in grave danger, but that doesn't mean she's dead."

"Oh my God, Marlow! Spit it out!"

"All right." I rubbed damp palms on my thighs, knowing I was going to sound as crazy as I currently looked. "There was an electrical storm going on the night that Teagan contacted me online. I actually got zapped through my keyboard, seriously, like I stuck all five fingers into a socket. It lasted for only a moment and nothing else was affected—not the lights or other power sources. The storm never even made the news. I just shook it off as a weird random event."

Sage scratched at her arm and gave me a look that said, "Get on with it."

"Teagan and I connected. We shared interests and a sense of humor. We told each other about our secret fears."

Sage challenged me like it was a test. "Oh? What are hers?"

"She had nightmares about being chased and she didn't like storms."

Sage's eyes softened slightly. "What are yours?"

"I don't like snakes. So we dared each other to face our fears. I even went to the science lab and had my buddy take a picture of me feeding the boa there. The thing was, when I tried to send it to Teagan, she couldn't receive it."

"So?"

"Yeah, I thought it odd but no big deal. Then we tried to video chat online."

"I don't get what your computer glitches have to do with Teagan not being here right now."

"I'm getting to that. The next 'miss' was when we tried to meet in person. Everything we tried to do to connect outside of the chat forum never worked."

"Marlow, get to the point."

"The point is I'm from a parallel universe. That's why nothing worked. That's why when we both went to the same café on the same day at the same time, we didn't meet."

Sage met that statement with a stony stare. "If you're just going to mess with me, you can leave now. I'm going to call the police."

"I think you should call the police, but not about me. For Teagan. I believe the rapist has her."

Fear filled her eyes. "Why? Why do you believe that?"

"Because, in my time, she's the next victim." I left out the part where she's dead. I really didn't think that would help right now.

"Oh, God." Sage pressed up more tightly against the wall. "Are you the killer?"

"No! I told you. I want to save her."

"You actually expect me to believe you're from an alternate universe? Really?"

"I know it sounds crazy. I warned you it would. But look at me? If this was just a crazy plan to coerce an attractive girl to spend time with me, I would've at least gotten dressed first, right?"

Sage scanned me from head to toe with an unflinching expression. I tried not to squirm with embarrassment.

"Okay," she finally said. "Say I believe that *you* believe this story. You haven't convinced me it's true. Honestly, it's too ridiculous to believe."

My mind raced for a way to make her believe. I could think of only one thing. "Will you come with me? I want to show you something."

Chapter 28

Sage

CRAZY PERSON alert!

"I'm not going anywhere with you."

"We'll walk, okay? In public. It's still light." Marlow shifted uneasily. "I just want to take you to where the other me lives."

I scoffed incredulously. "The other me?"

"Yes. If you met a second Marlow Henry who looks like me living on this campus, wouldn't that be proof of my story?"

"You could have a twin."

"But why would I do that? Why would I spin such a crazy story?"

"Uh, because you're *crazy?*"

"Okay, then why would he? You can ask him yourself if he has a twin. Ask people who know him."

He shifted nervously in Teagan's chair and pushed his glasses up the bridge of his nose.

"Why don't you take those off?" I asked

His head bobbed up sharply. "Huh?"

"The glasses. I get how it feels like you can hide behind frames." I waved to my collection on my dresser. "But I'd just feel better if I could see your eyes."

Marlow slowly removed them. I examined his features. He had a nice enough face, nothing striking, but pleasant. His eyes were a clear pale green. He squinted like he actually couldn't see me.

"Stop that."

"Stop what?"

"Squinting like that. If you want me to go, just put them away and we'll go."

"But I need them to see."

"Please."

"Please what? These are prescription lenses. I can't see my hand in front of my face without them."

I scoffed. "You're kidding, right?"

"Why would I be kidding?"

I reached for his glasses and he let me have them. They were heavier than any of my frames. I tried them on. "Whoa. You *are* blind. Why don't you get your eyes lasered?"

"I don't have the cash."

"But it's covered by universal medical."

He burst out laughing. "Seriously? Ha. I'm definitely not in my universe."

I frowned at that. His story was bizarre, but since I couldn't report Teagan as missing until she'd been gone for twenty-four hours, I had time to humor this guy and maybe he'd give me a clue as to where Teagan went.

"I'll go with you, but you have to walk in front of me, more than an arm's length and I'll have my phone ready to dial the police."

"Deal." He stood and walked to the open door.

When he was six feet ahead of me, I got up and followed.

Marlow knew exactly where he was going, and with his long legs, I had to break into a near jog just to keep up to the six-foot mark behind him. The guy was on the tall side and lanky and with the way his hair swooped forward, he reminded me a bit of the character Shaggy from the cartoon *Scooby-Doo*.

The campus had a system of well-marked walking and biking paths that skirted around all the technical buildings and lecture halls and weaved through all the residential areas. Five minutes later, we arrived at a dorm that looked similar to the one I lived in with Teagan. Marlow ducked down behind a hedge, and when I didn't follow—because, hello, crazy!—he waved me over with frantic intensity.

I looked around and over my shoulder to make sure no one spotted my strange behavior and scooted in to duck down near him. The fall air was crisp and I noticed that he was starting to shiver. I wrapped my jacket tighter.

"They can't see me," he said in a near whisper.

"Why? Are you invisible now? Because I hate to break it to you."

"No, I mean, I can't let them see me. I don't know what will happen if the two *mes* meet."

I rubbed my temples. Marlow's stories were definitely making my headache worse. Teagan was probably back at our dorm right now, wondering where I was. She left early and simply forgot her phone. She was a bit of an airhead, her mind always on her artwork, and it wouldn't be the first time she'd left it somewhere. I'd gotten all worked up for nothing, and boy, wouldn't she laugh when I told her about this nut job.

Or maybe not. I was sure she actually had hopes for the Marlow guy she'd met online. I hated to be the one to have to break the bad news that he was *not the one*.

"Just go knock on the door," Marlow continued. "Ask to talk to Marlow Henry. Then ask him your questions. I'll wait here."

Couldn't he hear how psycho he sounded? But, since I was here anyway, no reason not to check it out. I made my way to the front door of the dorm, smoothed out my jacket, ran a hand through my hair and took a breath. Then I knocked.

A skinny guy with a beard answered the door. "Is Marlow Henry here?" I asked.

"Uh, yeah." He called over his shoulder. "Marlow, there's a girl here to see you."

There were a bunch of guys in a common room much like our lounge. This one had a large flat-screen TV in the corner and an old couch situated in front of it. My breath hitched a little when Marlow's doppelganger rose to his feet and came to the door. He looked exactly like the Marlow who was hiding behind the hedge, but without the glasses. I might not have noticed the mirror image if I hadn't asked Marlow to take off his glasses earlier. Each Marlow had a dark mole high on his left cheek.

"You're Marlow Henry?"

"Yeah."

"Do you have a twin brother?"

"No. What's this about?"

"You wouldn't happen to have ID on you?"

He folded his arms and leaned back defensively. "Is this about that Teagan girl?"

My heart jumped. "Why would you ask that?"

"I already told those detectives I've never met her. Never even heard her name before they interrogated me. I have no idea why she'd implicate me for such a horrible crime, but it was a cruel joke, and I'm not laughing."

I was there when Teagan told the police about her suspicions about Marlow after he'd warned her of a rape before it happened. She thought that since he'd warned her, he might've been the attacker, like he was telling her what he was going to do.

The Marlow standing before me claimed to never have messaged with Teagan and the police couldn't prove otherwise. Then another man was arrested.

"Look, unless you're here to clear my name or offer some other benefit to my wasting time talking to you," this Marlow said, "I've got work to do."

"Sorry to bother you."

My legs were shaking when I returned to the Marlow behind the hedge.

"Wow," he said. "I'm a jerk in this universe. I promise, *I'm* not like that."

I studied him, squatting like a toddler, his face full of concern and turmoil. He'd warned Teagan about a rape before it happened, *here*. Had it already happened *there?* Could this guy be for real?

"You said you had reason to believe Teagan was in trouble. Why?"

Marlow's gaze dropped to the ground. His shoulders sagged. "Because, in my world… she's dead."

Chapter 29

Marlow

SAGE BROKE INTO A SPRINT back to her dorm. I called after her, "Sage!"

"Stay away from me!"

"I can't. I need you to help me find her."

"She's probably back in the dorm right now, and if she is, I'm calling the cops on you!"

"And if she's not?"

Her pace slowed and she covered her face with one hand. Her voice was so quiet I barely heard her say, "She has to be."

Unfortunately, Teagan wasn't there when we arrived, just like I knew she wouldn't be. I wished Sage was right, that I was crazy. That I hadn't woken up this morning in another realm and gotten beamed out through a mysterious storm to this world where Teagan was missing.

Sage sat quietly at her desk and stared out the window. "Do you think she's dead?" she asked. "Here, I mean."

Her question gave me hope that she was starting to believe me. I needed her to believe me because I needed her help.

"I don't know. In my world they found her body right away. Since there's been no reports of another victim here so far, we can hope she's alive.

Sage grabbed her laptop and started typing. She scrolled through the news headlines. "No, there's no reports of a new attack." She spun to look at me. "She's probably fine and on her way home."

"Have you texted her?"

She flashed me an annoyed look and pointed to a phone on a small table beside Teagan's bed.

I sat in Teagan's chair and pulled her laptop close. "Do you mind if I check? Maybe there's a clue here to where she went?"

"Good idea." Sage pulled her chair up close to mine. She smelled good, fruity, and I tensed. I wasn't used to having girls sitting so close. And I probably smelled like a garbage dump. I shook my head and forced myself to focus.

Teagan hadn't shut down her computer or signed out, so all I had to do was click the return button to wake it up. I found the forum where we chatted still on the screen.

Sage shifted closer to read. It was strangely embarrassing, having one girl read the transcript of a conversation I had with another girl.

She glanced at me. "You're averagegeek99?"

"Yeah, well, I don't know how average."

She flicked her fingers at me and I stopped talking.

@averagegeek99: This is going to sound weird but I need you to confirm your identity. Quickly, so I know you're not scrolling through old texts, what is my biggest fear?

@art4ever: Snakes.

@averagegeek99: My roommate's name?

@art4ever: Zed.

@averagegeek99: First joke?

@art4ever: Knock, knock. Marlow, what's going on?

@averagegeek99: Sorry. Don't mean to freak you out.

@art4ever: Too late.

@averagegeek99: Something weird is happening. I can't explain it, just, I thought you were in trouble.

@art4ever: I'm fine. I'm in my dorm. Door's locked. Just getting ready for bed.

"That's creepy, Marlow." She glared at me. "Why would you try to scare her like that?"

"I wasn't trying to scare her. *I* was scared. I'd just heard that she'd been killed. All the news sources confirmed it."

I scrolled down to the bottom of the page, not wanting Sage to read any more between Teagan and me. I was looking for something else. Another conversation tucked out from underneath the forum window. I clicked on its edges.

"She went to meet her mother." I remembered now. "It was one of the last things she wrote to me."

Sage leaned in and I purposely took a deep breath of her scent. Somehow I managed to say, "Read this."

@art4ever to @mylakeisthebestlake: Hey, Mom. What's up?

@mylakeisthebestlake: Good news! I'm at DU! There's a coffee shop by the park on the edge of campus. Believe in Beans. Do you know it? Can you meet me? I'd come to your room but the campus is so large and confusing. I'm afraid I'd lose my way in the dark.

"That doesn't make sense," Sage said. "Teagan's mom is way overprotective. That's why I can't picture her asking Teagan to bus across campus to her. If she came this far, she'd come all the way to the dorm."

"Maybe she tried and got lost."

"It's not that complicated."

"Why wouldn't Teagan think it weird then?"

"I don't know. Her mother is very controlling. She says jump and Teagan jumps, no questions asked. It was one reason why Teagan wanted to go to an out-of-state college, to gain some distance from her and her mother. It was the only time I've seen her defy her mother's wishes."

145

"You've known Teagan a long time?"

"Since I moved in next door to her in sixth grade."

"Do you know how to get to this Believe in Beans place?

Sage nodded.

I stood, wishing I didn't look like such a dweeb, then reminded myself to stop being so shallow. How I looked in front of a pretty girl was of no consequence. What mattered was finding Teagan.

"Take me there," I said.

Sage nodded and threw an oversized hoodie at me. "I borrowed it from my brother. It should fit."

My mind went in a million directions as I took in the sight of this alternate world. It was a cleaner, wealthier version. The buildings all had new paint jobs and trimmed vines out front and the people wore high-end clothing. I felt like a complete bum and kept my arms wrapped tightly around my chest. I followed Sage onto the bus—she had a pass, and she threw some coins in for me—and took the aisle seat after Sage scooted next to the window. Her gaze remained outward. I didn't blame her for wanting to forget I was there.

We sat in silence as the bus went north, stopping every so often to let riders on and off.

Sage finally spoke. "Teagan is a really responsible girl. She doesn't even party. She's quiet, too. Likes to be alone. I've made a lot of new friends since September. She's met..." She glanced at me woefully. "...you."

I patted her arm. "We'll find her."

Her gaze cut to my hand still touching her and I sharply pulled it away.

"Mrs. Lake's message said it was dark out," I said, "which at this time of year means she left anytime after 5 pm."

"What time were you chatting?" Sage asked.

"Late afternoon. I'm not sure how synced up our times zones are."

"It's so weird when you talk like that."

"Like what?"

"Like you're from another plane."

I sighed. "You don't believe me?"

She snorted through her nose. "That's the problem. I do."

There were only a few passengers left when the bus came to the stop near Believe in Beans. I spotted the café sign through the window and stood. My face was slapped with a cold November wind as I hopped off the bus.

Sage stepped up beside me, her hands tucked deeply into her jacket pocket. "It doesn't even look open," she said.

My gut told me this was bad even before we got close enough to look inside. "If Teagan came here and saw this, what do you think she would do?" I asked.

"It depends on whether her mother was here waiting or not."

Or if *someone else* was waiting. I shivered and looked around. The parking lot edged along a forested park. I walked toward it.

"Maybe she went to the hotel across the highway," Sage said. "Maybe she's there right now, with Mrs. Lake."

"Yeah, maybe."

There was a noticeable path in the woods but it was impossible to tell if Teagan had been here. It would've been quite dark. There were no exterior lights.

We hoofed it over an overpass across the highway to where we could see a hotel down the road. A rush of dried leaves followed us inside the building when I opened the door to the lobby.

Sage went to the counter and spoke to the clerk. "I'm looking for a friend. She might be staying here with her mother."

"What's the last name?" the clerk asked.

"Lake. Her mother's name is Madison Lake."

The clerk typed into a computer then shook her head. "I don't have anyone here by that name."

I stepped forward. "What about last night?"

"No. No one by that name."

"Our friend has blond hair," I said

Sage added, "With a blue streak on the right side. Hard to miss."

The clerk shrugged sympathetically "I wasn't on duty last night. I can ask around."

Sage pointed to a hotel brochure. "Is this your email?"

The girl nodded. "I'm emailing you a picture of her. Would you mind printing it?"

Sage thumbed at her phone, sending a pic of Teagan and the clerk printed it. I couldn't help staring at the 8 x 11 image.

"Her name is Teagan," Sage said. "If you see her or if anyone here has seen her, please call me." Sage wrote her number on the bottom edge of the photo.

We stepped back outside into the blustery fall day.

"Now what?" Sage asked.

"Let's go back to your dorm," I said, sighing. "It's time to call the police."

Chapter 30

Sage

MY HEART PLUMMETED to the floor when I got back to our room and Teagan still hadn't shown up.

Part of me really hoped and imagined she would be there, flashing her welcoming smile and then freaking out when she saw who I was with. Part of me knew she'd still be gone.

I didn't want to believe Marlow's story. Even if he and the other Marlow were twins playing an elaborate joke to get back at Teagan for pointing a finger their way, it didn't explain why Teagan was still missing. And if it were a joke, this Marlow was an incredible actor. Tension and distress oozed off him. Plus, he wouldn't be calmly standing there watching me dial the police, would he?

"Hello? I need to report a missing person."

I glanced up at Marlow, and he rubbed his face before sitting in Teagan's chair.

"It's my roommate. Teagan Lake." I told the dispatcher that she left our dorm sometime last night and hadn't returned. She asked me if it had been twenty-four hours since I last saw her.

"Not yet. Almost."

"Kids take off all the time without telling dorm mates," she said. Had I called her parents? Kids, especially freshman, get homesick all the time.

"She wasn't homesick and she wouldn't have left without telling me."

The officer wouldn't budge. Told me to call in when Teagan had been missing for twenty-four hours.

"No go, huh?" Marlow said.

I shook my head.

"Do you mind if I use your shower?" Marlow asked. He ran a hand through rough-looking hair and inconspicuously sniffed an armpit. "It's, uh, been awhile."

"Yeah, sure," I said, pretending not to notice. "Knock yourself out."

If I was going to believe Marlow's story, and at the moment I couldn't think of an alternative, then that meant he "arrived" with just the clothes on his back. I made a decision to visit my brother, a senior who lived in a dorm not far from mine. He was here on a football scholarship and hopefully wasn't home. I needed to steal some of his clothes.

I got back to my dorm about twenty minutes later, with clothes and two sub sandwiches.

Marlow had showered up and sat on Teagan's chair. His wet hair was slicked back and his glasses were perched on his nose. The way he sat, all hunched over made him look like a scared little boy. He jumped a bit, looking startled when I breezed in.

"Sorry, didn't mean to scare you." I tossed him one of the sandwiches.

He smiled. "Oh, thanks! I'm starved."

"And here's some clothes," I added. "I thought you might like something clean."

Marlow picked through the jeans, long-sleeved T and fitted boxers with one hand, while stuffing his face with the other. "Whose are they?" he asked with a full mouth.

"Ben's."

"Boyfriend?"

I flashed him a look. Guys were guys were guys. "My brother."

He swallowed. "Right, you mentioned him."

"He's a senior. Football player."

"I'm glad you thought to bring me a belt."

I laughed. My brother was quite a bit beefier than Marlow. "Just get dressed before the cops get here."

He took another bite of his sub. "They can't see me, you know."

"Who?"

"The cops. No one can know who I am or that I'm here."

Right. Already a Marlow Henry on campus. I
saluted. "Okay, Mars."

"Mars?"

"That's what I'm going to call you. So I don't
have to say Marlow and the other Marlow."

"That's cool, I guess."

Marlow, or rather, Mars, disappeared into the
bathroom. I finished my sub by the time he emerged. I
held back a grin. "You look…"

"Like a geek?"

"No, I was going to say…clean."

I couldn't stifle the laugh this time. He looked
like a kid in his father's clothes.

"Shut up."

"You're welcome."

Mars returned to Teagan's laptop and started
typing.

"What are you doing?" I scooted my chair up to
him and noted that he definitely smelled better.

"Might as well use the time waiting to see if
Teagan left any other clues."

A wave of black washed over me. "Oh my God, I
can't believe I forgot."

He turned and raised an eyebrow. "Forgot what?"

"She got this creepy message last week. Someone
called the gingerbread man."

I felt him stiffen. "Show me."

I scrolled through looking for the message. "She
showed the police and they said they'd keep watch."

His eyes darkened. "What did the message say?"

"You're next."

He pushed away from the desk and into a standing position. "You're next? You're *next?*"

"The police just thought it was a prank because none of the other victims had gotten a warning message. They said they'd watch our dorm. And her."

Marlow waved an arm flippantly. "And yet, she's not here and neither are they. You need to call them again, Sage. Talk to someone else. We're wasting too much time."

His urgency amped up the level of fear I felt from concerned to desperate. My fingers shook as I dialed.

Chapter 31

HER VOMIT got in his mouth. He smacked her so hard she passed out. Just lay on the damp leaves like a rag doll. No fight. No fear.

No fun in that.

He lifted her over his shoulder like a sack of flour and carried her back to the parking lot. His was the only car left. He popped the trunk and threw her in.

He could've left her. He could've killed her. But he needed her. She was bait.

He cut onto the highway heading northeast toward the Canadian border. An hour out of Detroit, he turned onto a secondary road and then onto a gravel road almost hidden from view by all the wild brush. He winced as the branches of the overhanging trees rubbed against the roof of his car, but the grove made an excellent cover.

When he pulled up to the cabin, he heard banging and screaming coming from his trunk. He swore.

Should've tied her up and bound her mouth. Oh well, a little fight from the girl would add to his excitement.

He'd leave her there while he scoped out the joint. Hopefully tire her out. Break her will. He grabbed a flashlight from the glove box and flashed it along the exterior of the cabin. The windows were boarded up. The front steps were covered in leaves. The door was locked, but he had a key. He remembered swiping it from his father's dresser before leaving for college. He had no idea if the old place would even be livable but he knew his father never hunted anymore, not wildlife anyway.

He thought it might come in handy one day, and sure enough, he had been right.

The air was cool and crisp. Snow would be falling soon. Could be problematic. He didn't want the girl to freeze to death while he was gone.

Inside, things looked smaller than he remembered. His father had brought him here as a kid a few times, to hunt and fish and play "the game."

He flicked a switch. Damn. No lights or electricity. His flashlight skimmed over a kitchen table and chairs, a foldout couch and a chair with worn fabric on the seats, and an area rug. His nose twitched as his footsteps stirred up many years worth of dust.

There was a cast-iron wood stove in the corner. A pile of wood was stacked beside it. He didn't have much time. He bent down and got to work.

Chapter 32

Sage

THIS TIME I remembered the name of the lady detective, Kilroy, and asked to speak with her directly.

"I'm not exactly sure when she left," I said. I could hear the stringy tension in my voice. "But it was at least twenty hours ago if not more."

I'd been casting glances at Marlow throughout the call—he sat in Teagan's chair with wide eyes latched onto me—kind of made me nervous. I turned my back to him and faced the window.

"Please, she got that threatening text message, remember? I'm really worried."

I ended the call and turned back to Marlow.

"They're coming?" he said.

"Yeah. They'll be here in less than ten."

He nodded his head in approval while tapping nervously on his legs. He was a strange yet intriguing creature. If the circumstances had been lighter, I would've enjoyed his presence more. As it was, he was a distraction and a complication.

"So, Mars," I started. "What are we going to do about you?"

He stilled. "Huh?"

"You said you didn't want them to see you."

"Right." His eyes darted around the room. "The bathroom's not a good idea, in case they check it." He pointed to the wall behind me. "Is that your closet?"

"Yeah, why?"

"I'll hide in there. I can keep the door cracked a little so I can see and hear."

He took quick strides, easing behind me and grabbed the knob.

"Hey, wait!" I had personal stuff in there. Plus dirty laundry. It might smell. And I could see a black bra lying on the floor where it had missed the laundry basket. "Let me tidy it first."

He huffed. "I don't care about your mess."

Well, I did. I quickly picked up my bra and removed my dirty laundry basket, sticking it beside my bed. I pushed aside the clothes on the hangers, and tossed a couple pairs of shoes that were on the floor onto the shelf. "That'll give you more room."

Marlow stepped inside, but I was still self-conscious of the stale smell and quickly spritzed a shot of my body spray.

"Gah!" he blurted. "What was that?"

"Citrus Fresh."

"I can't smell that bad," he said indignantly. "I just had a shower."

"It's not you. It's the room." I placed a finger on my lips. "Shh, I hear something. I think they're here.

I shut the door on Marlow, leaving it open just a crack. I heard him stifle a cough and thought I might have overdone it with the spritz. I hoped he could hold it in when the detectives were here. Trying to explain why I had a guy hiding in my closet would be awkward.

I answered the knock feeling nervous. Like I was committing a crime by hiding Marlow. Maybe I was. I didn't know what to think anymore. Everything was so confusing.

"Hello, Miss Farrell," Detective Kilroy said. "You remember my partner, Detective Simpson."

"Yes, hello. Thanks for coming."

I opened the door wider and stepped aside. Our dorm room wasn't very big and it wasn't like I had a couch or anything other than the beds and desk chairs. I'd made my bed, but left Teagan's the way I'd found it that morning, in case it helped in some way. I didn't want to disturb evidence.

The detectives remained standing, each with a handheld device to take notes.

Detective Kilroy took the lead. "What makes you believe your roommate, Teagan Lake, is missing?"

"She didn't come home last night. And it's strange because she's the type of girl who doesn't go out much, and she specifically told me she wasn't going out last night."

"When did you first notice she was missing?"

"At eight this morning when her alarm sounded and she didn't turn it off."

"Was she home when you came in last night?"

"No. Well, I didn't notice. It was dark and as you can see by her covers..." I flung out my hand to direct their vision. "It looked like a body was in the bed." I didn't mention that I was somewhat intoxicated.

Detective Simpson cleared his throat. "Why did Miss Lake 'never go out' as you say?"

"It's not like she never went out. She just didn't like to. She has social anxiety issues."

"So she'd rather hang out with people she met online?"

"Sometimes."

"Is that how she met Mr. Henry?" he continued, "A.k.a @averagegeek 99?"

"Yes. But he's not the reason she's missing."

He cocked a dark brow. "You're sure of this?"

I nodded. "Yes."

"Why?"

"Because. Look, it's not averagegeek you should be looking into. It's the Gingerbread Man."

I went to Teagan's laptop, woke up the screen and pointed to the message. "Remember this? *You're next.*"

"I understand your concern," Detective Kilroy said with a smooth voice. "And we share it. We'll do everything we can to find out who is behind that message."

"Are you and Miss Lake close?" Detective Simpson asked.

"Yes. Best friends from grade school."

"But you don't hang out together much on campus?"

I hesitated. "No. She's in the arts program. I'm in math. Our paths don't cross that much."

He studied his tablet like he was trying to make sense of the notes he'd taken. "So, you're making new friends?"

"Yeah." I shrugged. "So?"

"Is it possible Miss Lake also made new friends, ones she didn't tell you about?"

"Yes, I suppose so."

He narrowed his dark eyes on me. "Why wouldn't she tell you?"

"How should I know? We don't tell each other everything." I tried and failed to hold in my frustration.

"What does this have to do with the fact that she's missing now?"

"We're just trying to gather information."

Detective Kilroy shot him a quick look then asked, "Do you have any idea where she might have gone last night?"

"To meet her mother at Believe in Beans."

"The cafe on the north end of campus?" she asked. "Isn't it closed down?"

"Yes, but I don't think she knew that."

"What makes you think she went there?"

I waved toward Teagan's laptop. "We scrolled

through her messages from last night."

"We?"

Oh man, I screwed up. I forced myself not to glance back at my closet. "No, I meant I. I scrolled through her messages. Here." I leaned over Teagen's laptop and scrolled down to the message she got from her mother.

"Except I don't think that was her mother."

"Why's that?" Simpson asked.

"I know Mrs. Lake. If she came here for her daughter, she'd have come directly to the dorm."

"Wouldn't have Teagan known her own mother, too?"

"Mrs. Lake is very controlling. Teagan doesn't always see clearly when it comes to her."

Kilroy smiled politely. "Do you mind if we take a look at her things?"

I swallowed, hoping they wouldn't ask to look at my things.

"Sure. This is her side of the room. That's her closet, her dresser."

It was disconcerting to watch two total strangers rifle through Teagan's mess. I felt violated for her, but if they found something that would help…

Simpson held up a blouse. "This is Teagan's?"

I nodded. "It's okay with you if we take it for the dogs to get her scent?"

I nodded again, the seriousness of this situation weighing heavier. After about ten minutes, the detectives shared a look, and then Kilroy said, "Thank you for your time. We will continue to investigate and let you know when we find out anything." She handed me her card. "If you think of anything else, please call."

They left, and I sat on the edge of my bed feeling worn out.

Marlow stuck his head out of the closet, and then stood in the middle of the room. I did a double take. It was weird seeing him in Ben's clothes.

"We can't wait for them," he said.

"What do you mean?"

"Someone has her. Someone with a violent streak. I don't think the police will move quickly enough."

A black knife of fear sliced my heart when he put it into words like that.

I locked eyes with him, imploring, "But what more can we do?"

Chapter 33

Marlow

"TELL ME ABOUT Jake Wentworth."

Sage sat on the edge of her bed and leaned back on two hands. "What about him?"

"In my world, Teagan and Jake walked around campus holding hands."

She cocked a brow. "In this world Jake is dating my friend Nora."

"Is Nora blond by chance?" I asked.

"No. Redhead. I really don't think it's Jake."

"Why?"

"I don't know. I have a feeling. He's a good guy."

I stifled a huff. "Guys like the one who took Teagan look normal. They *look* like good guys." I leaned forward, my elbows pressing on my knees, and stared at Sage with intensity, wanting her to get what I was about to say next. "That's how they get away with it. They hide in plain sight."

"Well, I was with Jake and Nora last night, so it couldn't be him."

"All night?"

"Late enough."

I eyed her. "You're a party chick?"

"No. Not really." She folded her arms across her chest defensively. "Sometimes I drink a little."

"Like last night?"

"Yeah, so?"

"Just, maybe you don't remember things the way you think you do."

She sprung to her feet in agitation. "We're not going to find Teagan by sitting around on our duffs." She searched for her jacket, finding it on the floor, having fallen off the back of her chair. She eyed me. "Let's go."

I stood to follow her. "Where are we going?"

"To ask a few of our own questions."

I liked how this girl thought. I was ready to get on with our own investigation. Teagan's life depended on it.

⁂

I still found it strange to view the world through this soft-green tinted lens. It made me wonder if Sage's skin was as porcelain as it looked. Flawless, even as her Romanesque nose grew pink in the cold.

I shook those thoughts off and huddled in under Ben Farrell's big hoodie. One girl on the brain was enough—especially for my nerdy brain. If I wasn't careful, I could blow a fuse.

"You and Teagan don't seem to be very much alike," I said. "For best friends."

"We used to be more alike. Something happened toward the end of senior year in high school. Teagan withdrew more than usual. I had developed a habit over the years to just do whatever she did. If she withdrew, then I did.

"But, by the time we graduated, I knew I had to branch out on my own or I could risk disappearing."

"Like Teagan?"

"Well, not literally. Just as a person, you know. I hate to say it, but if we hadn't already applied to be roommates, I would've picked someone else. It's not that I don't love her, it's just…"

"She was holding you back?"

"Kind of. Teagan's world is very small and she's happy with it like that. I wanted to expand my horizons. Not hugely, but some. You know?"

"Yeah. I get it. My world's pretty small, too. But not as small as how you describe Teagan's. I also have a best friend from high school who is my roommate."

"The guy with the beard?"

"Yeah, but not gay."

She shot me a questioning look. "You're gay?"

"No! The other Marlow and Zed. Maybe. Teagan thought so."

"I didn't pick that up when I talked to them this morning. But it's hard to tell sometimes."

I flipped the hoodie up over my head. To break the wind and to conceal my face. We had entered a populated corridor and I couldn't risk anyone recognizing me as the other Marlow.

"Where are we going?" I asked.

"Where a lot of students hangout this time of day. The dining hall."

My stomach grumbled at that. "I don't have a card."

"Don't worry, I'll take enough to share." She fluttered her eyelashes teasingly. It made my stomach flip. I tucked my chin in the hoodie and scolded myself. I was here for Teagan. Sage was out of my league, not to mention not even in my world. *Focus, man!*

The dining hall was in the same place as the one in my realm. It was a strange sensation because I knew my way around, and everything was where it was in my world, it just looked slightly different. Where the dining hall in my realm was a plain Jane brick building, this one had elaborate wood-crafted designs. Inside, the chatter of the students still ricocheted off the high ceilings, but this one had fancy light fixtures and dark wood decorative beams.

I took a seat at one of the round tables in the back while Sage stood in line. I watched as she heaped on a plate full of food, looked like roast, potatoes and gravy, and my stomach growled again. I normally ate something every couple hours. All I'd eaten all day was that sub Sage had picked up for me earlier.

She returned and handed me a fork and knife.

She moved a teacup off of a saucer and pushed a little of the food onto it before handing me the plate.

"Is that enough for you?" I asked.

"Yeah. I'm not really that hungry."

I was starved and gobbled up my pile in the same amount of time it took Sage to nibble her little portion.

"That's Jake over there," she said.

I recognized him from our short run-in in my realm. Cockiness oozed off both versions of him. "Who's the guy with him?"

"That's Chet. I don't know much about him, but Teagan didn't like him."

"Really? Teagan seems like the kind of girl who likes everyone."

"She is, but I dragged her out for drinks one night, and Chet threw a peanut at her, giving her a small welt on her forehead."

"Why would he do that?"

"I don't know. He probably likes her."

"Too far away to punch her in the arm?"

She grinned. "Juvenile, I know." Then she added, "Jake liked her at that time, too."

My head shot up in surprised. "He did?"

"Yeah, he asked her out the next day. For coffee."

The attraction leached over on both realms but for some reason, in this one, he chose Nora over Teagan.

Sage continued, "That was the night the first victim was raped. Teagan said the girl, Vanessa, had knocked over a display. Jake helped her clean it up. She left, and Jake left soon afterward."

"Coincidence?"

"I thought so, but Teagan wasn't so sure."

"What makes you say that?" I asked.

"The whole thing was really upsetting, and especially for someone like Teagan. She's very sensitive. She never watched the news and one of the reasons she wanted to come here was because of DU's reputation for safety."

Wow, this really was an alternate world.

Sage's gaze cast downward. "She suspected you as well."

"What?" I dropped my fork. "Why?"

"When you warned her about the rape in your realm, it hadn't happened in ours yet. So when it did, she thought maybe you were telling her in advance about something you were planning to do."

I sighed. "Ah, man."

Sage's gaze returned to Jake and Chet.

"Should we go talk to them?" I asked.

"They might recognize you," she said. "Not the Mars you, but, you know."

I pushed up on my specs, not sure what to say about that.

"The Marlow from here doesn't wear glasses," she continued. She tilted her head and examined my face, an innocent move that sent shivers down my spine. "He's clean-shaven; you're looking pretty scruffy."

"I haven't had a chance to shave." I pulled on my hood and rubbed my prickly face. "I'll hang back."

I didn't like Jake Wentworth when I met him in my realm, and I didn't like him in this one. He personified self-confidence and arrogance. Even though he did manage to look Sage in the eye once or twice, I was effectively invisible. Which I wanted to be, but man, he didn't need to make it so easy.

"Hey Jake," Sage said. "Have you seen Teagan?"

He shoved a fried potato slice into his mouth and answered mid-chew. "Nope. Why?"

"She didn't come home last night. I'm worried."

"Oh." Jake had the decency to look concerned. "I'm sure she's just out getting lucky."

Sage smirked. "You obviously don't know Teagan."

"Actually, I kind of do." He cocked a dark sleazy brow. "Which is why I'm with Nora now."

If he didn't outweigh me by at least fifty pounds, I would've socked him in the mouth.

Sage looked put off. "What about you, Chet?"

"Me?" Chet swept a swath of oily hair off his face. "I only met the chick once."

I took a step forward and asked, "Where were you guys last night?"

Jake shifted back in his chair, thick legs sprawled out, and scowled up at me. "Who are you?"

Damn. I should've kept my mouth shut and let Sage do the talking.

"This is Mars," Sage said. "We're just trying to

establish Teagan's whereabouts. Maybe you saw her last night and just don't remember. So, where were you?"

"We were at the same party as you, Sage."

"But after that," she pressed. "After I left."

Jake's eyes glazed over like he was bored, but I figured he was pissed off and trying not to show it. "I don't remember. You can ask Nora. I was with her. Now if you don't mind, we'd like to finish eating."

Sage pulled on my arm and led me out of earshot. "That didn't go so well."

"I guess you could call this Nora chick, see if his story holds."

Sage nodded and thumbed a message into her phone. "I told her I'm looking for Teagan and asked if she was with Jake after the party and if they saw her."

Moments later, Sage got a message back. "Nora says she didn't see Teagan and Jake was with her all night.

"That doesn't explain Chet, though," I said.

"Yeah, he's a bit of a black horse."

"Jake's henchman?"

Sage's gaze cut to mine. "What do you mean by that?"

"Maybe he does Jake's dirty work for pay. Or prestige. Or protection."

She lifted a shoulder. "I don't know. Maybe. I think we need to keep looking around."

"What classes does Teagan take?" I asked. "Maybe one of her profs knows something. Maybe she was working on a secret project?"

"Good idea. She had philosophy with Professor Madsen."

We headed outdoors and I followed Sage to the liberal arts wing of the campus. "What do you think the police are doing right now?" Sage asked.

"Probably scouring the Believe in Beans." I imagined them there with a dog, sniffing her scent from the shirt Detective Simpson took.

"I hope so. I really want this nightmare to be over."

"Me too."

I wondered if it would ever be over. Even if we found Teagan, I had no idea how I was going to get home, back to my realm. Was I stuck here? Would I forever be dodging the "legitimate" Marlow Henry? How would I live? I'd have to get a new ID.

Sage punched me in the arm. "Are you okay? You look kind of freaked out."

"I'm fine." *Get a hold of yourself, Henry!*

We trod through the thick fallen leaves that carpeted the walkway, leaving a yellow and purple wake behind us.

There were several cement steps to the impressive wooden doors of the ornate brick building. I tugged on the handle and waited until Sage passed through.

Students filed out of the lecture hall. I glanced at Sage in question. She frowned.

"Evening midterm," she said. "Teagan was supposed to be here for it."

The hall was on the large side and had theatre seating. The scent of nervous sweat lingered, and I was glad the fresh air followed us in.

Professor Madsen was packing up his satchel as we approached. He stifled a yawn with his forearm and then stood straight when he spotted us.

"Professor Madsen," Sage said as we neared. "I'm Sage Farrell a friend of Teagan Lake." Sage didn't bother to introduce me and I thought it for the best. I was there as an observer. Sage continued, "She seems to be missing, and I wondered if you've seen her recently?"

The professor was young, with dirty-blond hair and dark eyes. He looked like he could use more sleep. He folded into his chair at the news. "Missing? I wondered why she didn't show for the exam."

"When was the last time you saw her?" Sage asked. "We're just trying to create a timeline."

"I don't know. Must've been the last class of mine that's she's in. Honestly, so many students come through those doors, I don't always notice who's here and who's not."

I wanted to believe him, but it all seemed too convenient. And why wasn't he sleeping at night? Violent kidnappings had a way of interrupting your rest.

I spouted off. "Where were you last night?"

Sage flashed me a look.

"I was here until late, marking papers. And then I went home." He eyed me like he knew he didn't have to answer to me. "Who are you, anyway?"

"A friend."

Professor Madsen got to his feet. "I'm sorry to hear about Teagan. I'm assuming you've called the police?"

"Yes," Sage answered.

"Then I suggest you leave the investigation to them." He left the hall without saying good-bye.

"Interesting character," I said.

Sage nodded then asked, "Now what?"

"We keep digging."

A lone student with dark hair and an open laptop remained in the room. He was in a short desk tucked in the shadows behind Professor Madsen's, which was why we didn't notice him at first.

We were about to leave when he called out, "I saw Teagan Lake last night."

Chapter 34

THE ROOMATE and her skinny, hooded accomplice were asking questions. He had to admire their audacity. As if they could track him down. Here he was, sitting one table over, listening in as they badgered a jock. He'd be insulted if it weren't so amusing.

He stuffed a bun and an apple in his coat pockets to feed the Lake girl something when he got back to the cabin. He'd bring soap too. Her vomit had gotten in her hair and the smell was a real turnoff.

He found he didn't mind waiting for her. Instant gratification wasn't everything. The anticipation and buildup to the event aroused him as well. And it gave him time to be creative. Maybe he'd produce a video and send it to his old man. He could just picture the bastard coming to the rescue of his whore's daughter.

Then he'd kill them both. First the girl with his dad watching, then him. He'd have to think of a way to make his father suffer, make the pain and suffering drag on. Pay back for the years of bruising and innumerable broken ribs he'd endured.

He smiled with contained amusement as the jock blew the roommate off. He waited thirty seconds after the girl and her thin companion left, then followed them. He was curious as to where their little "investigation" would take them. He laughed into his hand when he watched the two of them head to Madsen's lecture hall.

Amateur imbeciles. He checked the time. It was dark. He felt a buzz in his nerves, worried suddenly that he'd been gone too long. The girl might die if he didn't get back to the cabin soon and then all his plans would be ruined.

Chapter 35

Sage

I TOOK MARLOW to the pub for a drink. If ever there was a time when a person could use a drink it was when their best friend went missing and a killer was on the loose.

"Can I buy you a beer?" I asked Marlow, knowing that he didn't have any money.

"Won't they card you?"

"I'm nineteen."

"Don't you have to be twenty-one?"

I shook my head.

He shrugged. "Okay, then. Sure."

I ordered at the bar and we took two seats by the window. The room was much warmer than outside and I shook off my jacket and hung it on the back of my chair. I scratched at my arms and jiggled my knees. I couldn't stop thinking about Teagan and how she was out there somewhere, scared to death.

Oh, God. Bad choice of words. Teagan couldn't be dead. She just couldn't be.

The server brought us two foamy glasses, and I took a swig, wiping the foam mustache off my face with my sleeve.

Marlow eyed me with concern. "Are you okay?"

"No. Do you expect me to be okay?"

"I didn't mean that. I just meant, well, you look a little pale."

"I'm not going to faint or anything if that's what you're worried about."

"I'm not worried."

I closed my eyes and took a long breath through my nose. Then I looked at Marlow, still hidden away in the hood of the hoodie. "I'm sorry. I don't mean to take it out on you. I'm just scared. And I hate not knowing what's going on."

"I understand. I'm freaked out too."

"I imagine you are. Tell me about your home." If it weren't for Teagan I'd have been all over Marlow about this apparent parallel universe thing. "I mean, I still can't comprehend it. My brain is going off in all directions right now." I emphasize this by pointing all ten of my fingers at my head. "Is it much different?"

"It's bluer."

"Bluer?"

"Yeah." Marlow wiped condensation off the side of his glass. "The sky is bluer. The general hue is lighter. It's kind of green here."

"That's weird. Why is that I wonder?"

"Your sun must be cooler than ours. Oranger. The colors refract differently, making the sky look green rather than blue like ours."

"Our sun *is* orange," I said. "Yours isn't?"

"Nope. It's yellow." He flashed me a charming crooked smile. "That's what we're taught in school, anyway. It's actually a prism of colors, which I expect is similar to yours, only somewhat hotter."

I hummed. "Interesting."

"The economy here seems to be a lot better," Marlow added. "We're in a recession in my world. Detroit was hit hard, especially the auto industry. Most of the factories are shut down."

I wrinkled my nose at him. "Sounds like a dystopian novel."

He laughed. "Yeah, it is."

"And no universal health care?"

Marlow shook his head and adjusted his glasses to reiterate. "Nope."

"If I were you," I said, "I'd be tempted to stay here."

We locked gazes and his eyes softened, like he was looking deep into my soul. I swallowed nervously. I hoped he wasn't developing a crush or something. I wasn't interested in him that way. I averted my eyes, casting my gaze to my hands.

"There's already a Marlow Henry here," he finally said. "One is enough, I should think. Though, to be honest, I'm not sure how to get back. I don't know if I'm missing in my realm or if I'll return to the same moment as when I left. That's assuming I get back somehow. I don't really know anything."

We drank in silence for the next few moments, each of us trying to process everything. I know I certainly was having a hard time of it.

A TV screen hung in the corner and a new report came on. A ticker ran along the bottom. SEARCH FOR MISSING GIRL IS ON. ANOTHER DETROIT UNIVERSITY VICTIM?

I pointed, "Mars, look!"

On the screen we could see the police with dogs scouring the wooded area by Believe in Beans. Detectives Kilroy and Simpson stood solemnly by police cars that had their blue and red lights flashing.

A reporter thrust a microphone in Detective Kilroy's face. "Is this the DU rapist's third victim?"

"At the moment Miss Lake is considered a missing person," Detective Kilroy replied. "We've yet to find evidence that foul play was involved or that her disappearance is linked to the other crimes."

"Is that why you have the search dogs out in the park? You have reason to believe she was here?"

"We have reason to believe she was in this vicinity. We have yet to conclude where exactly. But be assured, we are doing everything in our power to bring Miss Lake home safely."

The story cut back to the basketball game that had been playing.

I cupped my face with my hands. "This can't be happening."

I heard a chair scoot over and felt Marlow's arm drape awkwardly over my shoulders. He didn't say anything but just his presence brought me some peace. The warmth of another human touch. I leaned into him and buried my face into his chest. I stifled a major sob that threatened to erupt. Marlow stroked my hair.

A part of my brain detached itself from my current situation, the horror and the mystery, and only acknowledged Marlow. His comfort. His inner strength. I found myself reconsidering my earlier judgment. Maybe Marlow Henry *was* my type after all and I just didn't know it.

Marlow tensed suddenly and pulled away, tugging on his hood.

"What's the matter?"

"I know those guys."

I twisted around and spotted the two guys who'd sauntered in with all the coolness and confidence money and good genes could buy.

"Paul Meadows and Steve Dubeki?" I asked. Paul was shorter and stockier and was a hockey star whereas Steve's taller athletic build made him all-star basketball material. They both had pretty eyes and dark curly hair. Neither had ever given me the time of day. They pulled up chairs and sat on them backward, leaning casually over the back wooden frames. The girls they had joined giggled flirtatiously.

"They're dorm mates of mine," Marlow said. "And definitely not as cool in my world."

"So, there are doubles of everyone?"

"Seems like it."

I tilted my head. "Even me?"

"I haven't met the other you, but I imagine so."

"The same but different?"

Marlow shrugged. "That's what I don't get. Some people seem to be the same, like those Jake and Chet guys. They're douches in both realms. The other me is more metrosexual than I am, but Zed looked and acted exactly the way he does in my realm."

"Interesting."

"Yeah. I've spotted a lot of familiar faces. Some dress the same way and emit the same confidence or lack of confidence. Others are so different I have to look twice."

Marlow drank the last of his beer, and I finished mine soon afterward. "What should we do next?" I asked.

"We could go to where the investigation is taking place? See if the detectives found anything."

"I wonder if they'd tell us if they did," I said. "But, I doubt if they're still there. It was light out when that footage was taken." I waved to the window beside us. "It's dark now."

Marlow pushed back his hoodie, ran fingers through his hair and pulled it back over his brows. "I wish there was a way we could find out who the Gingerbread Man is."

Maybe there was. I cocked a brow, leaned over the table and whispered, "How are your hacking skills?"

Chapter 36

Marlow

WE WENT BACK to Sage's dorm expecting quiet and privacy so we could put our combined hacking skills to use, but instead we were accosted in the common room by an emotionally distraught couple that I quickly concluded were Teagan's parents.

"Sage!" Mrs. Lake threw long thin arms around Sage and squeezed. Pulling back, she grabbed Sage by the shoulders and implored her. "Please, tell us everything you know."

"Of course," Sage said, leading us down the hall and into her room. She offered a chair to Mrs. Lake, and then pointed to Teagan's as she spoke to Mr. Lake. "There's a chair for you if you'd like."

Mr. Lake studied the chair, and the knowledge that it belonged to Teagan flashed across his eyes before he crumbled into it. He was the same height as his wife, but rounder in the belly. His facial features were unremarkable and the hair on his head was thin and streaked with grey—not exactly a handsome man, which was why I couldn't stop staring at Mrs. Lake.

She was mesmerizing. Though she had to be in her mid-forties, she could easily pass for much younger. She had glossy blond hair that hung in waves over narrow shoulders, bright blue eyes and delicate facial features. She dressed like an upscale business person in slacks and a shimmering blouse.

I was amused and strangely comforted to see this odd coupling. It gave me audacious hope that someone like Teagan, or Sage, could actually be interested in a skinny geek like me someday.

"We've talked to the police," Mr. Lake said. "Frankly, they weren't a lot of help."

"What happened?" Mrs. Lake asked. Gold bangles clinked together at her wrists as she motioned to Sage. "Do you know where Teagan is?"

Sage sat on her bed and scratched at her arms, a nervous habit I'd noticed before. I stood by the door like some kind of guard.

"I'm afraid I don't know where she is, Mrs. Lake. I was out late with some friends."

Mrs. Lake cut her off. "Teagan wasn't with you?"

Sage shook her head.

"But you two went everywhere together. You were inseparable."

"I know, but since we've been at DU, we've made new friends. We're on different study tracks, so our paths don't cross as much as you would expect."

Mrs. Lake let out a small "oh," then motioned for Sage to continue.

"It was late when I got in and I didn't want to wake Teagan so I didn't turn on the lights. That's why I didn't notice she wasn't in her bed."

All eyes darted to Teagan's bed, which was still a mess of tossed and twisted sheets. "I didn't even know she was gone until the alarm on her phone went off."

"Where is her phone now?" Mr. Lake asked.

"The police took it along with her laptop."

"Mr. and Mrs. Lake," I said, breaking in. "Do you have any enemies?"

Their heads both shot up to look at me. Mr. Lake shook his head, like the question was preposterous. Mrs. Lake's eyes fluttered, and her neck flushed red. She narrowed her eyes as she scanned my sloppy, baggy look. "Who are you?"

I cleared my voice. "A friend."

"Of Teagan's? Do you have a name?"

Sage jumped in. "He's actually a friend of Ben's. Just offered to walk me home tonight. She stood and ushered me through the door. "Wait for me in the lounge," she whispered sternly.

I nodded and left, agreeing that my being there wasn't a good idea. It was never a good thing when someone took notice of me and started asking questions. How could I explain that I'd met Teagan online. That we'd become friends but that we hadn't actually met. And that I wasn't from this realm so they shouldn't bother asking the other Marlow Henry about Teagan because he didn't know her.

I collapsed in a heap on the couch. What a mess.

The lounge was a weigh station where the girls from this building met up. A lot of coming and going this time of night. Some getting coffee in preparation for a long night of cramming for exams.

I should be doing that myself. I already missed a major physics exam.

Unless I didn't.

I decided to help myself to a coffee. Something about me caused the girls in the room to give me a wide berth. Maybe this hoodie and baggy pants gave off a badass vibe. Had to file that info for later. I poured the strong-smelling dark liquid into a mug that looked relatively clean. I heard whispering.

"Sage Farrell brought him home."

"Is she slumming it?"

"Maybe he's helping her study."

"Or she's scoring drugs."

"No, he's got something to do with Teagan Lake. Did you see her parents blow through here?"

"So sad. I hope they find her."

I scooped an extra sugar into the coffee. It looked like mud, but it was better than nothing. I went back to the empty couch pretending I hadn't heard a thing the girls said.

I decided to take stock.

Three weeks ago, a freak storm shocked me through my laptop just before I met Teagan online. We had no idea we were chatting through two realms.

There were two of everyone, well, except now, there was only one Teagan. A wave of sadness consumed me and I let myself soak in it as I finished my coffee.

Teagan from this world chatted with me after the Teagan from my world was dead. This was what convinced me that all the crock Garvin had fed us in physics class could be true. Another freak storm appeared. I ran outside with my laptop. I jumped, my laptop didn't.

At least I hadn't arrived naked.

So what was causing the storms? My gut told me the answer to this question was key.

In my realm Teagan's body was found in a park the next day. Was it the same park that was behind Believe in Beans in this realm? I'd never had reason to visit that end of the campus before. I didn't even know if there was a Believe in Beans in my realm.

So why wasn't Teagan's body found in this realm? Not that I wanted her dead. It was why I was eager to jump, so I could do something to save her.

But the question remained. What made the villain change his MO? Teagan's body hadn't been found, so I hoped that meant she was still alive. But why was the villain keeping her alive when he obviously didn't care about the other victims?

The detectives told Teagan when she reported the warning she'd gotten from @gingerbreadman that none of the others had gotten a message.

What made Teagan different?

My head jerked up to a slight commotion in the lounge. Girls voices twittered, "Hi Ben!"

Ben? Sage's brother? The one whose clothes I was wearing? I folded myself into the couch and kept my head down. Ben was tall with broad football player shoulders. Like Sage, he had dark hair and eyes. He walked with quick strides, on a mission to get to Sage's room, and he didn't give me a second look. I heard him rap on Sage's door. It opened and he disappeared inside.

I wondered how long I'd have to wait for Sage. And where exactly was I going to sleep tonight? In this lounge on this lumpy couch?

A bigger question niggled at the back of my mind as I yawned into my sleeve.

Why was Mrs. Lake lying?

Chapter 37

Sage

"I DON'T LIKE that boy," Mrs. Lake said after Marlow left the room. She played with her gold bangles, then looked up at me from under damp lashes. "It's always the bad ones we're attracted to."

I noted her slip up, using the word "we" as if she were part of the equation. Mr. Lake was a good guy. I didn't think he had a bad bone in his body. The way he sat slumped over with his face in his hands, so helpless and weak-looking. I pitied him.

Mrs. Lake wasn't the easiest person to live with. She was an enigma, a dichotomy. She was cold and distant while being outgoing and friendly. Flamboyant and something else… frightened?

Teagan couldn't resist her charms, doing everything Mrs. Lake asked, never once disobeying her, at least not aggressively. Teagan had developed a large passive aggressive toolset to cope.

Teagan was cute and adorable, but not nearly the beauty queen her mother had been at the same age. Mrs. Lake was a hard role model to live up to. Her moods were as unpredictable as the weather, high or low.

"Mars?" I asked to clarify. Was he the "bad boy" she was referring to?

"That's his name?" she said with a huff. "His mother named him after a planet?"

"I'm pretty sure it's a nickname."

"That's what they always do," Mrs. Lake said softly, "the ones that are hiding something. The deceit begins small, then grows with time."

I cut a look to Mr. Lake wondering what he was making of his wife's comments, but he kept his head down.

Talking about Marlow with Mrs. Lake wasn't a good idea. I searched for something else to say, some words of comfort, but I was at a loss. I scratched at my arms and looked anywhere but at Mrs. Lake's face.

My dorm room was small and with the three of us, it was like we were meeting in Mrs. Lake's walk-in closet. The longer Teagan's parents stayed, the more it shrank.

We jumped at a hard knock on the door. I thought it was Marlow checking in, but was surprised to see my brother's face.

"Ben?"

"Hey, I heard." He nodded at me then quickly said, "Hi Mr. Lake, Mrs. Lake."

Mr. Lake reached out to shake Ben's hand. "Good to see you," he said.

"I wish it were under better circumstances."

Mrs. Lake's eyes washed over Ben from head to toe. Her appraisal of my brother had always been favorable. It kind of creeped me out, especially once Ben grew taller and

filled out. Even though he was my brother, I knew he was good-looking. All the girls liked him.

I was sure that Mrs. Lake liked him. She was beautiful and alluring. A perfect cougar.

"Hello, Ben," she said smoothly.

"Mrs. Lake. Is there anything I can do?"

She pressed a fist to her mouth. "I don't know. We're waiting on news from the police."

"Teagan's picture is looping on the news," Ben said. "An alert has been broadcast."

"There must be more," Mrs. Lake insisted.

"We can put out flyers," I said. "I'll make them tonight and if Teagan hasn't been found by morning, we can canvas the area."

Mrs. Lake smiled weakly. "That would be wonderful." She stood. "We should go. We're at the Riverside Hotel if you need to reach us."

She gave me a quick hug and then moved on to Ben, holding him a little longer than necessary. I closed the door behind them and let out a long breath.

"For a slim woman," I said, "she sure takes up a lot of space."

Ben smirked. "She sure does. I'd hate it if our

mother looked like that."

I wasn't sure what to do about my brother being here, knowing that Marlow was sitting in the lounge wearing Ben's clothes. I was surprised Ben hadn't noticed him coming in. Chances weren't good that he'd miss him on the way out too.

"You don't look great, Sage."

"Thank you?"

"I mean, this is just such a shock. You and Teagan are so close."

The sob I'd been pushing back all day finally surfaced.

I ran to the bathroom to grab toilet paper for my tears and blew my nose like a foghorn. "I didn't even notice she was missing until this morning." My voice was muffled by the tissue paper. "She'd been gone all night. If I'd noticed earlier…"

"Sage." Ben reached for me. "It's not your fault. No one expects you to be at Teagan's side twenty-four seven."

I let my brother hold me. We weren't the huggy-kissy type, but tonight I needed him.

When it started to feel weird, I pulled away and finished wiping my tears and blowing my nose. I winced at my reflection in the mirror. My eyes were bloodshot and my skin was blotchy and all I could think of was how I didn't want Marlow to see me like this. I washed my face with cold water hoping I could also wash away my vanity.

Ben sat on my bed while he waited and stood

when I walked out.

"Are you going to be all right? I'm supposed to meet friends but I can stay with you if you want."

"No, I'm fine." I was still wondering how I was going to get him past Marlow. "You can go."

"I'll help hand out flyers tomorrow. I can round up a bunch of help."

"That would be great, Ben. Hopefully, we won't need to. I'll text you in the morning."

He reached for the door handle. "Well, get some rest, okay?"

I couldn't chance that he'd notice Marlow. "I'll walk you to the door." I'd distract him with conversation or something if I had to.

Turned out it wasn't necessary. The lounge was empty, and Marlow was gone.

Chapter 38

Marlow

I DIDN'T WANT TO CHAT with Mrs. Lake again or chance running into Ben Farrell so when I heard voices coming from down the hall, I took it as my cue to head outside. Turning left outside the door, I swung around to the side of the building and rested against the brick wall. I kept my eye on the entrance so I'd know when it would be safe to go back inside.

Mrs. Lake walked ahead of Mr. Lake by a measure of one stride. Mr. Lake slumped with heavy shoulders and reached for his wife, touching her elbow. She paused and stiffened. He let his arm drop to his side with a weariness I could sense from my hiding spot. I didn't need a degree in counseling to see that all was not well in their relationship and that it was something that went beyond the disappearance of their daughter.

Mrs. Lake slipped into the passenger seat, and I had to admit that she had nice legs. Ben didn't appear for another fifteen minutes, and by that time I was chilled to the bone. Iwas grateful for Ben's hoodie, but the temperatures had dipped, and I needed something closer to a winter jacket to keep warm in this weather.

I waited until Ben finally drove away and then hurried back inside. My lips tugged up into a soft smile when I saw Sage waiting in the lounge for me.

"Where were you?" she asked, her face filled with real concern.

"I stepped outside when Teagan's parents left. And I didn't want to risk having your brother notice my clothes."

"Yeah," she agreed. "That would be hard to explain." She turned and started down the hall. "Come on. We have work to do."

Sage pulled both chairs up to her desk, sat in one and began typing away on her laptop.

I rubbed my arms to stimulate my body heat. "What are you doing?"

"Hacking into Teagan's laptop."

I stared at her in surprise. "You're a hacker?"

"Sort of."

This girl never failed to surprise me. I thought she wanted me to do the hacking. "How can you be a sort-of hacker?"

"I sort of do it as a hobby, and I sort of don't tell people and I sort of practiced on Teagan."

Wow. "Did she know?"

"No. Our friendship was already becoming strained and I didn't think she'd be cool with it. I mean, who would? I wouldn't if she were doing it to me. I didn't invade her privacy, much. It was a while ago. I only did it a few times to exercise my chops." Her eyes cut to mine. "I didn't know about you and your chat forum, if that's what you're worried about."

I was kind of. "I'm not worried."

I watched as Sage worked her magic. I had a kindergarten level of skills when it came to hacking. She easily showed me up in the computer tech department.

"I'm taking math and computer sciences," she said, as if that explained things. "There, we're in."

"We're in?"

"Yeah. Teag's laptop is sitting open in an office at the police station."

I looked at the window on Sage's laptop and gaped. What I saw was someone's desktop. There was a pile of paper to one side and a dirty coffee cup next to that.

"You linked into her webcam?" I asked

She nodded, and I sensed a spot of pride under the surface.

"Can't they tell you're spying?"

"They could if they were looking for me," she said. "But it looks like whoever was examining her laptop has left his or her desk at the moment. Perfect timing."

She typed some more.

"What are you doing now?"

"Bringing up the last message Teagan got, the one from @gingerbreadman. I'm looking for an IP address. I'm sure the police have done the same thing, but no reason why we can't both look."

A bunch of code came up on the screen. Sage sighed. "No IP address. The guy knows computers."

Most people our age did. Even I knew how to cover my tracks if I wanted to. What I didn't know is if computer technology worked the same in this realm as it did in my own.

"Did you check his echo?"

"Echo?"

"Sometimes there is a residual echo, a cyber shadow. We think we've covered our tracks but there's always a little something left."

"Like digital DNA."

"Like that."

"I think I know what to do." Sage kept typing code over code. I couldn't help fidgeting while I waited. Sage cut a look to my bouncing knees and I forced myself to go still.

"Here," she said. "This thread embedded here. I think that's him."

I smiled. "Gotcha."

"What should we do?" she asked.

"Message him back. Tell him that we know who he is."

She glanced at me with alarm. "But we don't."

"He doesn't know that. Maybe it'll flush him out. Just make sure you cover your trail. Piggy back your message to IP addresses all over the globe."

Sage nodded like she knew what I meant. It took her awhile, but she finally sat back with a satisfied sigh. "It's sent."

Chapter 39

Sage

NOW THAT WE HAD DONE what we set out to do, sitting so close to each other felt uncomfortable. I excused myself and used the bathroom. When I returned I stretched out on my bed. Marlow never moved from his spot on the chair. He was spaced out again. He did that a lot. I guess that was to be expected in someone who suddenly found himself in another universe.

I still couldn't believe his story, but I couldn't *not* believe it either. I scratched at my arms. My nerves were shattered with Teagan's disappearance. My mind seemed determined to go to the darkest place. Some evil guy had her and was doing something awful to her. Or worse, she was dead in a ditch somewhere.

I was aware of the statistics. The more time that elapsed after she went missing the more likely the outcome would be terrible. I pressed my palms into my eyes. I felt like a horrible friend. I had virtually ignored her these last few weeks, running off with Nora, partying, and all the while Teagan was being stalked.

"Should I leave?"

Marlow's voice brought me back. I'd almost forgotten he was there.

"Where would you go?"

"I don't know. Is there a shelter somewhere?"

"A shelter? Like for dogs?"

"No, for homeless people."

"We don't have a lot of homeless." I checked the time. It was past midnight. "It's probably too late to start looking anyway."

"Can I sleep in the lounge?"

"No. That's strictly forbidden. Security will kick you out." I stared at Teagan's empty bed. "You could stay here."

Marlow's head jerked my way and his eyes popped open. "With you?"

It came out in kind of a squeak. I bit my lip to keep from laughing. "I promise I don't bite. Besides, I'd rather not be alone."

Marlow's gaze moved from my face to Teagan's bed and back again. "Are you sure?"

"Absolutely. It's settled." I scampered out of my bed to my dresser and removed a pair of pajamas. "I'm going to use the shower."

The shower felt luxurious and a wave of guilt washed over me with the warm water as I thought about Teagan. Did she have a place to sleep? To shower? How badly was the Gingerbread Man treating her?

Because as much as I hated the guy for taking her, the idea that he had her somewhere, out of the elements and alive, was a better option than the alternative.

I dried off and dressed and brushed my teeth. I combed out my hair and blow-dried it until it was almost dry.

I stepped out of the bathroom and motioned to the door. "It's all yours."

Marlow's jaw dropped and his cheeks flushed red. That was when I remembered I was wearing nothing but a pair of pajama shorts and a skimpy camisole with no bra. I wrapped my arms across my chest and skipped to my bed, slipping under the covers. I could feel Marlow's eyes follow me.

"What?" I snapped.

He pulled his gaze away sharply and ran for the bathroom. I heard the shower go, his second one of the day, but I expected this one was cold.

I felt bad. Ben had told me how easy it was for a guy to get turned on, but I just forgot. It's not that way for girls. I mean I get turned on, but it doesn't happen with one look. Rooming with Marlow could be more complicated than I first thought.

I turned the light off on my side of the room and pretended to be asleep when Marlow finally emerged. He wore only boxers since his pajama pants remained in my hamper. Note to self, do laundry tomorrow.

Marlow removed his glasses and placed them on Teagan's night table. He leaned against two pillows propped against the wall and clasped his hands together on his chest. He was skinny but not without muscle. I was actually surprised by how toned he was.

"You could get your eyes fixed while you're here," I said.

His eyes darted my way. "I thought you were sleeping."

"Not quite. What about it?"

"About what?" he asked.

"Get your eyes fixed."

"Just walk into a clinic, no ID?"

I leaned up on my elbow. "You have ID, just not on you."

He glanced at me again, then shook his head in frustration.

"You can't see me, can you?" I asked.

"I don't need to see you. I'm going to sleep."

"Mars, when else will you get the chance to get it done at no cost to you?"

He frowned, and I couldn't help but think he was kind of cute.

"What are you thinking?" he asked.

"We borrow the ID of Marlow Henry who lives here, who's in the system. You go in as him." I relaxed onto my back. "No harm, no foul."

"And how do we get our hands on his ID?"

I wiggled my fingers at him and waved to my laptop. "Just leave it to me."

When he didn't respond, I pressed my point. "I had the procedure done when I was twelve. It's not a big deal, I mean, if you're afraid of pain or something."

"I'm not afraid of pain." He sighed, tiredly. "I'll consider it."

I left him alone after that and promptly fell asleep. When I awoke in the morning Marlow was already awake and dressed and sitting at Teagan's desk with my laptop.

"I hope you don't mind my borrowing it," he said.

"Sure. Any news?" I asked hopefully.

My heart dropped when Marlow shook his head. "No. I'm afraid not."

"I guess I better get up and get those posters made." I whipped my covers off and Marlow held out a flat palm. He stared off to the side, refusing to look at me. "If you don't mind lending me the money, I'll go make a coffee run. No offense, but the coffee in the lounge sucks."

I pulled my covers back over my body and reached for my purse. There was something refreshing about seeing a guy being so modest. I pulled out a couple bills.

"I'm covered up, Mars. You can look at me."

He glanced down with an embarrassed blush and took the money. "I hope I can pay you back somehow," he said.

"Just helping me to find Teagan is help enough."

"Okay, good." He pulled up his hood and tucked it down over his brow before leaving. The guy was a geek, but a cute geek.

No time to entertain such frivolous thoughts. Teagan was still out there. I hurried to the bathroom. I wanted to make sure I was fully dressed and ready before Marlow returned.

Chapter 40

Marlow

I WELCOMED THE COLD SNAP of wind to my face when I headed outdoors. Java Junkie was nearby and I moved in that direction. I fingered the money in my pocket, glad to get out of that dorm. It smelled too much like girl.

What was the matter with me? The whole reason I was here was because I'd grown attached to Teagan. She was the girl I wanted to see, not her roommate. It frustrated me that Sage's mere presence affected me the way it did. I wished there was a switch I could turn off. Sage was attractive and sexy in a way I didn't think she realized.

I slapped my face and picked up my pace. I needed a coffee, bad. I had to clear my head and stay focused. First priority: find Teagan. Second priority: find a way home.

I kept my head down. The cool fall weather was a

helpful ruse. Everyone wore thick coats or sweaters with chins buried into scarves. Except for my oversized jeans, I sort of fit in.

I spotted a small convenience store and ducked in to buy a toothbrush. I didn't want to kill Sage with my breath, and I almost knocked myself out when I woke up this morning.

The line at Java Junkie was long, so I didn't notice who was at the front of it until it was almost too late. My roommate and best bud, Zed Zabinski, turned from the counter with a green breakfast smoothie in hand. I fought back a chuckle. So he liked those disgusting drinks in both realms?

I swiveled my back toward him as he passed by and watched as he pushed through the glass door. It felt weird to not call out to him. He looked just like *my* Zed. It made me wonder for the millionth time how I was going to get back to my world.

I was beginning to think that running outside into the storm was a mistake. What was I thinking? That I'd be some kind of big hero, swoop in, rescue Teagan and save the day? So far I'd done nothing much to help. Sage's hacking skills were beyond mine, so she didn't need me for that. I had no clue how to go about finding a lost girl and every time I opened my mouth, I just got stern looks from Sage.

Why was I here?

I pushed back at the heaviness that settled on my chest and focused on the menu. When I reached the front of the line I ordered two coffees and two breakfast sandwiches.

Carrying the small bag and Sage's coffee in one hand, I sipped at mine as I made the trek back. Sage was heading up a flyer blitz across the campus and into neighboring communities.

I wasn't going to go. It could get ugly if someone recognized me. Plus, I had something else I wanted to do.

Thankfully, Sage was fully dressed when I got back. She had black-framed glasses on and I did a double take when I saw her.

"Those make you look different," I said as I handed over her coffee.

"I know," she said. "That's why I like them. People take me more seriously when I wear them."

"Really?"

"Yeah, especially guys. For some reason, glasses work as a barrier. I get far fewer unwanted advances with them on."

I pushed my glasses up. "So that explains things." I grinned. "Maybe I'll take you up on that offer for eye surgery after all."

"Ha, ha." She unwrapped her sandwich. I was already halfway through mine.

"That's not why I suggested it," she said after chewing. "It's for your convenience. And ultimately it'll save you money since you don't have to keep buying eyewear."

"You keep buying them."

"Just frames with clear lenses. They're cheap."

I finished my breakfast and produced the toothbrush I'd purchased. "I hope you don't mind that I bought one of these?"

Sage feigned relief. "Thank God!"

"Do you mind if I use your toothpaste?" I was just being polite. I'd borrowed some the night before and finger brushed.

"Go ahead."

Sage's small printer was going strong when I returned. Page after page of Teagan's face spit out. Sage carefully placed them into a tall pile.

"Ben organized a team. We're meeting her parents at the dining hall in twenty minutes."

"I'm going to hang back, if you don't mind. It's best if I don't show my face to too many people around here."

Her dark eyes cut to mine. "What are you going to do?"

"Visit the physics lab."

"Oh? What do you hope to find there?"

"I don't know." I shrugged, knowing it was a long shot. "Help getting home?"

She nodded like she understood. Sadness shrouded her, and I wished there was something I could do to lift it. I knew the only thing that would really help was finding Teagan alive.

"Any word from the Gingerbread Man?" I asked.

"I was so busy making flyers, I completely forgot."

Sage typed into her laptop and brought up her

encrypted message board.

I sucked in a breath. I honestly didn't think that Sage could do it, but the evidence was there in black and white on her screen.

@gingerbreadman to **@Ifoundyou:** Nice handle if a little misguided. You see, I know you didn't find me. But I've found you.

Chapter 41

Teagan

TEAGAN'S BREATH came out in short puffs, producing small smoke-like ghosts in the cold room. Her body shivered violently. Sweat dried to her temples. She itched with no way to scratch it out. She'd wrestled against her bonds, but no amount of fighting would set her free. Teagan's wrists burned behind her back, and her shoulders ached. Her feet had gone to sleep. Every part of her body hurt.

She peed her pants.

What did he think she was, a machine? Just leave her tied up for hours on end, alone in a dark room, tied to a chair, with nothing to do but watch the fire go out?

Teagan gagged at her own smell. Urine, nervous sweat, dry breath. Good. She hoped she stank to high heaven. She hoped she was a real turn off.

She screamed until her voice was gone, but no one came to her rescue. She had no idea where she was, but wherever it was, she was alone.

She was going to freeze to death.

Which was preferable to what she knew was coming. Either way, she was going to die.

She'd seen his face. She knew who he was.

Chapter 42

Sage

MARLOW SPOKE with an edge of deep dread to his voice. "Don't write him back."

"But…"

"Don't! It's bad enough he has Teagan. This guy is a psychopath. And now he wants you."

I gave into a voluntary tremble at his words.

Marlow straightened and pushed his glasses up on his nose. I was beginning to see this was a nervous habit rather than a case of slippery specs.

"You should call the cops," he said.

"I can't. I hacked him. It's illegal. Besides, he's bluffing."

"How can you be sure?"

"Because I know how this works. I've covered my tracks. There's no way he knows who I am, or where this message came from. Just like we don't know who or where he is."

I typed quickly before I lost courage.

@Ifoundyou: Who are you?

He must have been sitting at his computer waiting for me to respond because his response was lightning quick.

@gingerbreadman: ha ha. I thought you knew.

@Ifoundyou: Where is Teagan?

@gingerbreadman: She's safe and sound. Well safe anyway.

@Ifoundyou: Why did you take her?

@gingerbreadman: You ask a lot of questions. She's a means to an end.

@Ifoundyou: What end is that?

@gingerbreadman: REVENGE

I gasped and glanced up at Marlow who stood close behind me, reading over my shoulder.

"I'm hoping to get him to reveal a clue." My voice came out in a dry whisper.

Marlow nodded. "Keep him talking."

@Ifoundyou: What does Teagan have to do with it?

@gingerbreadman: Ask her mother.

I sucked in a breath.

@Ifoundyou: What does Mrs. Lake have to do with anything?

I tapped my desk with my fingertips, waiting nervously for his reply. Marlow rubbed the stubble on his face.

Nothing. I cracked my knuckles. Marlow removed his glasses and cleaned them with the edge of his shirt.

I felt deflated. "He's not answering back."

"He gave us the clue we wanted."

"Mrs. Lake?"

Marlow nodded. "I'm not surprised, somehow. When I asked her if she had any enemies, she looked…"

"Scared?"

He nodded. "Scared."

I checked the time and jumped to my feet. "I gotta go."

"Right," Marlow said. "So, we should talk to Mrs. Lake again soon."

"I'll talk to her at the blitz. I'll find a way to get her alone."

Marlow stared down at me with a softness that made me feel warm inside. "Sage?"

"Yes?"

"Be careful."

Chapter 43

Marlow

A LARGE CROWD gathered outside the dining hall. Good. I'd admonished Sage to stay with a group of people at all times, preferably her hulky, football-playing brother. I hiked up my pants and walked on by.

I'd made the trek to the physics lab so many times I could do it in my sleep, but once I got to the front door, I paused. I had no idea what I thought I would find there. Professor Garvin, likely. Would he be able to tell I'm not the Marlow Henry from this world?

I hiked up my jeans again.

Probably. The Marlow Henry from this realm wouldn't be caught dead wearing these clothes.

I slipped inside the building and padded quietly down the hall until I got to the lab. I tested the door. It was unlocked, and I peeked inside. There was one person, a guy, wearing a lab coat. His back was turned to me.

Emboldened, I stepped inside.

"Hey," I said.

The guy turned around and I blinked. Blaine Tucker?

He looked at me incredulously. "Marlow?"

I lifted my chin. "Blaine."

"What are you doing here?"

"Just, I don't know, checking things out."

He smirked. "Regret dropping the class?"

I dropped out of physics?

"Um, yeah, you could say that."

"There's always next semester," he said.

He turned back to his project and I decided to probe a little. "What are you working on?"

He jerked his head like he didn't have time for me and my questions, but then answered anyway.

"I'm convinced that Everett's Many Worlds theory is correct, and I believe I have a way to prove it."

I knew the theory: a measurement taken of a quantum object causes an actual split in the universe. The universe is literally duplicated, splitting into one universe for each possible outcome from the measurement.

A dry lump filled my throat. I swallowed hard. Was Blaine responsible for my being here?

"Not only that." He flashed a smug look and continued, "I'm working on a mathematical formula that I believe will open up a gateway of sorts between universes."

"You think realm-jumping is really a possibility?" I asked.

"In theory."

"So you've never tried it?"

He cut me an impatient look. "It's still in experimental stages."

"Do you notice anything unusual about the weather, you know, when you experiment?"

Blaine froze. "Well, actually, now that you mention it." He tilted his head and eyed me. His gaze took in my clothes, and I could see his wheels turning.

"Why are you here?"

"Here in this room?" Or here in this realm?

"Yeah, sure? Why are you here in this room?"

"I was late for the Teagan Lake search blitz. So, I just ended up here."

He blinked hard. "I heard about the missing girl. Too bad."

"Yeah."

"Well, if you don't mind," Blaine said. "I'd like to get back to work."

"Sure. See you around."

He gave me a strange look as if to say, why would that happen? He didn't know what I knew, that I'd need his help to get home.

Now wasn't the right time. After Teagan was found, but not now. I was here for a reason. I had to be.

I left the physics lab and squinted at the late morning emerald hue. I shoved my hands into my pockets and the fingers of my right hand touched paper. I pulled it out and smirked. Sage had tucked a ten in my pocket when I wasn't looking. I examined the bill. It was shiny and made of plastic, similar to the money in countries like Canada and Australia in my world. I didn't recognize the face on it. I realized I didn't even know who the president was here. I just assumed it would be the same guy, but maybe not. My curiosity was piqued. I should go back and do some digging on Sage's computer.

I decided on a long route back. I needed time to think. I used Sage's ten at a campus sandwich shop and washed down a ham and cheese with a glass of Coke.

Though populated for the most part, a lot of the paths that went through the area were isolated and off the beaten track. I don't know what possessed me to take one of these paths. Maybe it was the need to process all the information and all my new feelings where it was quiet.

I thought about Blaine Tucker and his experiment. Blaine was a pompous ass in both realms, but his experiment was intriguing. He thought it was still a theory, but he must've triggered something on the quantum level that caused me to jump. I don't know why it was me and not him, though. That was another mystery. I needed to pick this Blaine's brain before I went back to my world, so I could rub my newfound knowledge in Professor Garvin's face. For sure I would ace my next paper.

The afternoon sky grew darker, and it smelled like

a storm coming. I tensed. Did I have to be wary of all storms or were there special ones for jumping? What was Blaine doing back at the lab? Something that would shoot me off into another realm? There were infinite possibilities. Including the one where I never made it back to my home world.

I didn't get a chance to ponder further because the next moment there was a thick arm squeezing tight around my neck. A voice I didn't recognize said, "Mind your own business."

I gasped for breath as the edges of my eyesight grew black.

Chapter 44

Sage

BEN HELPED to organize everyone into groups of four and we spread out into the different areas that bordered the campus grounds. Ben and I were in the group with Mr. and Mrs. Lake. Ben was going to go with his buddies, but I remembered the look on Marlow's face when he made me promise I'd stick with Ben. I tugged Ben's sleeve and pleaded.

"Please, I need your support if I'm going to spend the next several hours with the Lakes."

He had pity on me and I think deep down he wanted to support me or at least protect me. He squeezed my shoulders. "Anything for you, Sis."

Mrs. Lake looked terrible, and that said a lot since I'd never seen her look anything but fabulous in the twelve years I'd known her. Her hair was pulled back in a tight ponytail, her eyes were dull and circled with gray. Her clothes looked like she'd just pulled them out of her suitcase without the benefit of ironing them first. I felt sorry for her.

Mr. Lake didn't fare much better, but he hadn't looked that great for years.

The idea was to knock on doors, show Teagan's picture and ask if the occupants had seen her. The point person in each group was to make note of any possible tips. Other groups went around to businesses and hung the posters up on boards and posts. We wanted to get everyone thinking about Teagan and looking out for a sighting or for strange behavior from anyone they knew.

After two hours I was exhausted. My feet hurt, my lower back ached and I had a raging headache.

Ben handed me a bottle of water.

"Thanks."

"We're out of posters," Mr. Lake said. "I think we should head back."

Mrs. Lake almost protested but then just covered her eyes and sighed. Ben drove us back to the campus and said good-bye. He'd made plans to meet his girlfriend, who had a class and was already late.

"Thanks for all your help," I called out as he strolled off.

"Glad to be of help," he shouted back.

That left me standing awkwardly with Mr. and Mrs. Lake. Mrs. Lake took my hands. "I can't thank you enough, Sage."

"I wish I could do more."

Mrs. Lake hugged me, and I hugged her back. Mr.

Lake looked uncomfortable. "I'm going to go use the restroom," he said.

That left me alone with Mrs. Lake, the perfect opportunity to ask hard questions. The wind had picked up and I pulled my jacket tighter. "Can I ask you something?" I said.

"Anything."

I stared at the ground feeling like the little girl I used to be and not wanting to talk to the intimidating mother of my friend. But Teagan's life might depend on this question. "When we asked you the other night, if you had any enemies, you didn't answer." I looked up and held her gaze. "Do you?"

"Sage, what kind of question is that?"

"It's a valid question. Someone took your daughter. Maybe someone who has something against you. Or your husband."

"That's ludicrous." Her hand went to her purse and she pulled out a pack of cigarettes. "I don't normally smoke, well, not that much, but this…" She stuck the cigarette in her mouth, lit it and breathed in deeply. She let out a plume of smoke and sighed with relief.

"There is something Teagan doesn't know, or her father." She took another drag. "I'm involved with someone."

"Another man?" My voice squeaked as I said the words.

"For God's sake, keep your voice down. Yes, another man. I'm having an affair, and it's news that wouldn't benefit anyone should it get out. I'm trusting you will keep what I say confidential."

"Okay."

"He's a little… controlling. He doesn't like that I'm here with Bill. He hates that we're sharing a hotel." She took another drag, dropped the butt and crushed it with her shoe. "I need to get back to Illinois."

"Are you afraid of him?"

Her eyes cut to mine. "He doesn't have anything to do with Teagan, if that's what you mean. He's not a pedophile."

Teagan wasn't a child anymore, but I didn't say that aloud.

"What's his name?"

"That's none of your business. I already told you more than I should. Now, thanks again for your help."

Mr. Lake appeared then, and Mrs. Lake slid into the passenger seat of their car. She didn't wave when they drove away.

Marlow was probably back at my dorm by now, but I wanted to make a quick stop at Ben's before heading back. Ben's dorm mate, Ryan, had a build closer to Marlow's. I snuck in quietly, because where I had been borrowing from my brother, I was stealing from Ryan. I had no way of knowing if I could return what I was about to take, and it wasn't like I could ask. Eventually, I'd have to take Marlow into the city and shop for clothes. It made me wonder how long I'd have to take care of him. What happens after the Teagan crisis is resolved?

A bridge to cross later.

I'd been to Ben's dorm a few times so I knew my way around. Ryan's room was cleaner than Ben's, so I didn't have to trip over piles of junk on the ground. I moved quickly, taking a shirt from his closet, and a pair of jeans and a pair of boxers from his drawers.

I was just about to sneak back out when I heard the front door open. Footsteps moved quickly toward me. I could tell by his gait that it was Ryan. I dropped to the floor and rolled under the bed.

Chapter 45

Marlow

MY HEART skipped as I choked for breath. My assailant flipped me onto the ground. I landed on my stomach with an "oof" as the wind was knocked out of me. For good measure, he kicked me in the stomach. I curled up like a baby, covering my head with my hands, anticipating more, but that was the end.

I looked up in time to see a blurry vision of my attacker's back as he disappeared around the corner.

I raked the rough walkway with my fingers in search of my glasses. Pain ripped through my body as I reached. Finally my fingers brushed over them and I curled a fist around the frames. I groaned. They were busted.

Good thing I knew my away around, even in the dark, though I did stub my toe a couple times just to add to my already considerable pile of pain. I held my ribs tight. It hurt to breathe.

I made it to Sage's dorm, but was disappointed that she wasn't there. Were they really still out canvassing?

I washed up in the bathroom, and stared at my blurry image in the mirror. *What the hell is going on, Marlow?* I thought. Or should I say *Mars?*

I played around on Sage's laptop. In order to see anything I had to wear my busted glasses. The left lens was completely shattered, but the other was merely cracked. I could make out the text if I covered my left eye.

I typed in "president of the United States." The current president was none other than Mrs. Hillary Clinton. I laughed at that. In this realm, she beat out Senator Obama with a wide margin.

I couldn't find Facebook, but a search took me to a site called Facefacts. Basically the same thing and also founded by a group of Harvard students. I looked up Blaine Tucker. He had a lot of friends. Boasted of many science accomplishments. Had a girlfriend. Not Gina, a different one.

I searched for Marlow Henry and frowned. His friend list wasn't nearly as boisterous, and he rarely posted. He liked TV shows I hadn't heard of, and said he was in a relationship. I saw a picture of him with his arm wrapped around a blond chick. I took a closer look and sucked in a hard breath. The girl's name was Vanessa Roth. The first victim.

I did a web search on Vanessa Roth. She'd been raped on campus, but her boyfriend, whose name hadn't been released, had alibied out.

Was this Marlow Henry Vanessa Roth's boyfriend? First of all, kudos to my alter-ego for snagging a girlfriend—Vanessa Roth was cute. But what happened to them? I rechecked Marlow's Facefacts timeline. No new posts or pictures since the day of Vanessa's rape.

Did he break up with her because of the assault? He was an ass if he did. Maybe she broke up with him. That could explain why he was in a foul mood the day Sage went to their dorm.

My eye ached from squinting so hard. I had to take a break. I checked the time. Almost four o'clock. Where was Sage?

Tendrils of slippery concern vined through me. I was about to struggle back into Ben's hoodie, something my ribs did not want to do, and go on my own search for Sage when she finally returned.

"Where were you?" I asked.

"Sorry. I know I'm late. I got held up at my brother's. But here…." She held out an armful of clothes. "These should fit you better."

"Not Ben's?"

One side of her mouth tugged up in a grin. "No. And don't ask."

I forgot about my ribs when I reached for the clothes and let out a small yelp.

"What's wrong?"

"Someone jumped me."

Sage's eyes widened. What?"

I lifted my shirt to show her the bruising. "I don't think anything's broken but my ribs hurt like a bugger."

"You need to put ice on that and get it wrapped up."

"I can't go to the doctor."

She agreed. "I'll be right back."

Sage returned moments later with a handful of ice cubes wrapped in a tea-towel.

"Take off your shirt."

I blinked at her. What?

"Mars? I can't tend to this through your shirt. Do you need help removing it?"

I nodded numbly. I raised my arms. It hurt like hell. Sage nimbly pulled my shirt over my head and tossed it on the bed. I sucked in a breath as the ice pack hit the heat of my skin.

"Tell me what happened," she said.

"I went to my physics lab, or rather, your version of my physics lab." It hurt to breathe. It hurt to talk. I had to pace myself out. Sage waited with questioning eyes.

"There was a guy there working on experiments to do with jumping universes. He talked like it was all just theory and not something he'd tried himself."

"He didn't know you were a jumper?"

"I don't think so. He spoke to me like I was the Marlow from this realm. In my realm we're in the same class. Apparently, in this one, I dropped out."

"Weird. What's the guy's name?"

"Blaine Tucker. Do you know him?"

She nodded her head. "I've only really had a chance to meet people in my own study track."

"So Teagan wouldn't have known him either?" I was trying to make the connection between me, Blaine's experiment, Teagan and the killer.

"I doubt it," Sage said. "Teagan's in the arts program. And she hardly ever went out."

"Did you get a chance to talk to Teagan's mom?"

Sage shook her head and grimaced. "She's having an affair. That's why she didn't want to talk about it. Teagan doesn't know, and neither does her husband."

"Oh." I guess I shouldn't have felt so shocked. Mrs. Lake was hot, and Mr. Lake had let himself go.

"If this was a random attack, Teagan would be dead, and we'd be at her funeral already."

Sage's shoulders sagged when I said this and I felt bad. I paused for another breath.

"Going with the assumption that she was targeted," I continued, "and the Gingerbread Man's messages support this, who around here *did* Teagan know?"

The ice had melted and Sage took the soaked cloth from me. She opened up a mid-sized first-aid kit and removed a roll of gauze.

"A gift from Mrs. Lake," she said at my look. "She always wants Teagan to be prepared for any disaster. Teagan has cases of bottled water in her closet, just in case there's an emergency."

I leaned forward in the chair as she began to wrap my chest. I tried to ignore how wonderful it felt to have her fingers trace along my skin. I closed my eyes to her nearness.

"Well, we talked to Jake and Chet," she said, answering my first question. I'd almost blanked on what she was referring to. Right. Who did Teagan know? I focused on her words. Her words, words, her words. Not her body, not her fingers. Her words.

"And Professor Madsen, her philosophy teacher."

"The TA," I added. "He said he saw her on the bus, but what if he had been following her. His admission sounded like an alibi, but maybe it was a tease?"

Sage taped the gauze so it wouldn't fall and then sat in the chair beside me. "There must be other people we can talk to."

"She didn't mention meeting anyone new?" I asked

She eyed me. "Other than you?"

It made me think about the Marlow Henry from this realm. He liked blonds. Was it possible he raped his own girlfriend? Maybe Teagan had been in touch with both of us? Maybe *this* Marlow had arranged to meet her and succeeded?

"What's wrong?" Sage asked.

"I think we need to ask the resident Marlow Henry a few more questions."

Chapter 46

Teagan

TEAGAN HAD NODDED OFF. A door slammed followed by a round of swearing.

"You filthy pig."

She didn't bother to look at him. Blood prickled up her arms and legs as he cut through the tape that bound her to the wooden chair. He grabbed her roughly and dragged her down the hall. It felt like a million little sharp knives cutting into her legs, and she cried out.

He pushed her into the bathroom. "I brought you some food. You don't get it until you've cleaned up." He placed a bag on the bathroom counter and closed the door. Teagan rubbed her arms and legs vigorously, wincing as her circulation returned to normal. Her wrists and ankles had ugly red marks.

There were clothes in the bag. Brand new with tags still on. Yoga pants, a sweatshirt. Underwear. She ran the shower and scrubbed herself with soap. Scrubbed, scrubbed, scrubbed. Tears mixed with the hot water. She'd never be clean enough after today.

Teagan thought about Sage and what she was doing without her there. She thought about her mom and how worried she must be right now. Teagan knew they'd be crazy and doing everything they could to find her.

She had to find a way to stay alive. For them.

Teagan dried off and dressed in her new clothes. She turned the knob and had a fleeting thought that maybe she could escape, but the door was locked from the outside

She sat on the toilet seat and waited.

Chapter 47

Sage

WRAPPING MARLOW'S RIBS was strangely erotic. I felt my face flush and I had to look away. I pushed my chair farther from his to get some distance. "You want to investigate the other you?" I asked, working to keep my voice steady.

"I know it's weird, right?" he said, "but he did date the first victim and he kind of dropped off the social scene since her rape happened."

"That doesn't say guilt to me. More like remorse. He couldn't protect his girlfriend. And he's also probably heartbroken because Vanessa dropped out of university. I heard she broke up with him."

"Well, put like that, I suppose it makes sense," he said. "And I'm relieved, obviously. I'd hate to think any form of me could be capable of something as evil as that."

Marlow's eyes darted around the room, at everything but me, and I wondered if my nursing efforts rattled him a little as well. He even forgot he wasn't wearing glasses and jabbed the middle of his forehead with his index finger.

"Ow," he said.

I laughed. "Do you make a habit of stabbing yourself in the head?"

He stared at me with eyes that appeared slightly crossed. "I broke my glasses in the fight."

"You really can't see, can you?"

He bit his lip and shook his head.

"Do you think you can get a shirt on?" I asked. I knew he was in a lot of pain.

"You didn't happen to bring me a button-down, did you?"

"In fact, I did." I pulled the flannel shirt from the pile on the bed. "Here."

He stood, and I helped him get it on. He pulled back when I tried to do the buttons up for him. "My fingers aren't broken."

"Fine."

He took the other clothes into the bathroom and came out ten minutes later looking quite fab. Ryan's clothes were a much better fit. I muttered, "You look... good."

His chin dropped like he was embarrassed. His bashfulness was really quite adorable.

"While I was waiting, I put my hacking skills to work," I said. I handed Marlow a piece of paper. "Your health insurance number. We're going to get your eyes fixed."

"I guess I have no choice now, unless I concede to walking with a stick." He hugged his wounded chest. "I hope it's not far."

"A ten-minute bus ride just outside of campus. I know a walk-in place that's open after hours."

I helped Marlow ease into the hoodie but left the zipper up to him.

"Is it going to hurt?" he asked. "Because I've had enough pain for one day."

"Only a little." I tapped him lightly on the arm.

"Ow!"

"Baby."

Chapter 48

Marlow

SAGE GAVE ME a couple of painkillers and they'd kicked in nicely while we were on the bus. The odd bump only made me yell out a little. I couldn't believe I was preparing to go under the knife. Yeah, I was feeling melodramatic, but who wouldn't in my shoes. These were my eyes we were talking about.

"Maybe I should just see an optometrist and get new prescription lenses?"

"Don't tell me you're chickening out already?"

"I'm just being pragmatic."

"Well, I hate to break it to you," Sage began. "Since most people get their eyes fixed, there's not a lot of business for prescription lenses. You can get them, of course, but it takes a couple weeks. We could get you that stick and I'll lead you around. Maybe a pair of dark sunglasses to complete the look?"

"Ha, ha. You're funny."

The bus took us out of the DU grounds and it was my first look at a Detroit not affected by a recession. Except I couldn't really see it. The outlines of the skyscrapers in the distance poked the sky, but the edges were blurry. I couldn't make out anything up close. I sighed and faced the facts. I needed this surgery.

After several stops, Sage nudged me to get off. I was careful to hold onto the seat backs and the rail as I exited. Last thing my ribs needed was for me to fall on my face.

The medical clinic looked like many others I'd been to, at least as far as the smell went. A tinge of cleaner mixed with the musk of air ventilation.

Sage spoke to the receptionist on my behalf. "My friend is nervous, but he just broke his glasses, so now's the time!"

The receptionist smiled. "You're a hold out, huh? Don't worry, honey. It won't hurt a bit, and you'll be so glad you did it."

Since I couldn't read the form, Sage filled it out for me with the other Marlow's info.

"Won't he already be in the system?" I asked. "Since he's already had this procedure?"

Sage the hacker gave me a sly look. "He was." She passed the forms over to me and I signed my consent. Next, I was led into a small examination room where one of the doctors ran me through an eye exam to establish my current prescription. She gave me a Valium to help me relax and drops to numb my eyes, then she sent me back to the waiting room to sit with Sage.

"How are you doing?" she asked.

"Okay. I'm on Valium so I'm no longer responsible for anything that comes out of my mouth."

She snorted before turning her attention back to her phone.

"Any news?" I asked.

She shook her head. "Nothing new on the newsfeed, just that an investigation is ongoing. Nothing from Mrs. Lake. Not even anything from the Gingerbread Man."

I patted her arm, but didn't say anything. I couldn't tell her that everything would be all right, because I didn't know. And with each passing day, a happy ending became less likely.

"I just wish I could turn back the clock," she said softly. "I wish I would've stayed home with her. I didn't even have a good time. Had too much to drink and got sick."

"It's not your fault," I said.

"You keep saying that, Mars, but I can't help thinking I should've been there for her. She's my best friend and I blew her off."

"You're her friend, not her mother. You're not her husband. You're not her babysitter. There was no way for you to know, and I doubt there was a way you could've stopped this. If he hadn't taken her that night, he would've done it another. No one could've known that Teagan was being hunted, not even you."

She leaned into me and rested her head on my

arm. My heart rate rose a little as I breathed in the fresh scent of her shampoo. I liked the feeling of her body pressed up against mine. I loved that she felt comfortable enough with me to do it.

I almost reached over and stroked her hair when my name was called.

Sage straightened up, then asked, "Do you want me to come in and hold your hand?"

"Yes," I said without hesitation.

"Seriously?"

"Damn right." She might've been joking, but I was dead serious. I hated needles, doctors and anything to do with poking out my eyes. Plus, I really wanted to hold her hand.

The doctor directed me to a chair that looked very much like what you'd find at the dentist. I almost opened my mouth and said "ah."

She let me hold Sage's hand but gave me a squeeze ball for the other so I wouldn't reach for my eyes. She promised to tell me everything each step of the way but my stomach turned at "corneal flap," and I asked her to stop. I focused all my attention on the red light I was meant to stare at. I tensed when my vision went totally black and fought the panic that I might now be completely blind. Sage stroked my arm and I was overwhelmed by all the sensory input. I could swear I smelled flesh burning.

"Right side is done, Mr. Henry," the doctor announced.

"Already?" I let out a breath in relief. That only

took a few minutes.

I braced for the sensation of pressure on my left eye and breathed through all the digging around. The Valium had kicked in nicely and if it weren't for all the activity happening around my face, I might've broken into a show tune.

"All done," the doctor said.

I looked at Sage and frowned. "It's still a blur."

The doctor gave me a pair of sunglasses. "Your vision will clear up gradually overnight. Wear these for the next three days, even to bed." She handed me a bottle of drops. "Put a drop in each eye twice a day for the next week. No screen work or any kind of reading for twenty-four hours. Take a day to rest."

I put the sunglasses on my face and the bottle of drops into my pocket. We thanked her, and Sage helped me to my feet. My legs felt a little too relaxed and I buckled slightly against her.

"I'm fine," I said, straightening. I gathered all my dignity and pushed my sunglasses up tight to my face.

We headed back toward the bus stop. The wind had picked up and suddenly we were in the center of a leaf-ridden vortex. The air was dry, but lightning flashed in the swirl around us.

Everything happened so fast. I pushed Sage with as much strength as I could muster with my wounded ribs, thrusting her outside of the vortex, just as I felt the shock of jumping riddle through my body.

I screamed as the leaves settled around my feet.

"Sage!"

I pressed the sunglasses against my face and searched for her. She wasn't with me. I had jumped again. My heart sunk three floors when I took in the landscape around me. I had jumped, but I wasn't home.

Detroit City lay in complete ruins around me, all dust and decay, like an atomic bomb had gone off.

PART THREE

Chapter 49

Marlow

I HAD TO BE hallucinating. My knees gave out and I crumbled to the broken earth, bits of rock and debris poking through the denim into my skin. What I stared at through my darkened lenses completely distracted me from those minor points of pain. Detroit City, *my* city, was in *ruins*.

Ahead of me, in the near distance, were the tall office buildings of the city center—windows shattered, paint erased, the top floors missing. The whistling wind was the only sound. Gone was the constant rumbling of motor vehicles and the beehive of pedestrian activity. The clinic I'd just left moments before with Sage by my side, the euphoria I felt over facing a lifelong fear of getting my eyes lasered—all gone. I was surrounded by dusty rubble.

"What the hell happened here?"

The words escaped my mouth as my brain refused to conclude the obvious. A bomb had gone off. A major one. Probably more than one.

I swallowed dryly with a thick throat and choked on the dusty air.

I grabbed my head and panted. I wasn't home. I wasn't with Sage. I was in another, hellish universe. It took every ounce of my will, to rise to my feet. As far as the eye could see was lifeless destruction. I blinked, hoping I was hallucinating, dreaming. That maybe I was about to wake up in a hospital bed with Sage at my side, holding my hand, imploring me to hold on. Had I been struck by a car?

I crumbled to the ground. It felt real enough. Ash and dust sifted through my trembling fingers. If this were a dream, it was nothing like any dream I'd ever had before.

I must've jumped. Into the freaking end of the world. How long until the mysterious storm would come to sweep me up and take me away again? Would I ever find my way home?

If I wanted to live, I had to move. Find shelter. Water and food.

I headed in the direction of the campus, though I had no reason to believe I'd find anything intact there. The only other place I was tempted to go was my house, to check on my mother. My old neighborhood was on the other side of the city, a much farther walk, and any woman I might find there wouldn't be my real mother anyway. I was thankful she was safely at home in my own world, probably chewing sunflower seeds and drinking diet Pepsi while watching *Wheel of Fortune.*

The atmosphere in this world was orange. Smoke particles filled the sky blocking the rays of the descending
sun, effectively removing natural shadows. I glanced around for my shadow, and not seeing it, I felt a bit like Peter Pan. The effect was unnerving.

All the landmarks were gone or destroyed. Fires dotted the darkening horizon. Plumes of smoke washed the tangerine sky. I covered my mouth with the cuff of my shirt and tried to swallow my spit. The street lamps lay in rows of twisted metal. Burned out cars, buses and a variety of SUVs were scattered in the ditches and crumpled into buildings. I skirted around fallen golden arches and broken Texaco signs.

Approaching a Dodge minivan that looked not too worse for wear from my vantage point, I wondered if there was any way to jump-start it. I should've paid more attention to those cop shows. Driving would beat walking. I peered inside when I got close to it, but hopped back with a screech when I saw a body in the driver's seat. Dark singed hair concealed the face of a woman. Her skin was puckered, red and gray. Two smaller bodies were strapped into car seats in the back.

The smell of decay hit me like a wall, and I bent over toward the ditch and hurled.

From my position with my head between my knees, I could see the half-circle sun blushing along the horizon. I had to find shelter for the night. It would be cold and who knew what kind of wild, hungry post-apocalyptic creatures were on the hunt for their next meal.

I forced myself to keep walking. It was like I'd landed in the middle of a massive graveyard, one that hadn't been tended to in a couple hundred years. Green regrowth had poked through the cracks and concrete, vines crawling up the blown-out structures.

There were several abandoned cars parked in lots and on the side of the road, empty. I tugged on a few handles, but the doors were locked. I came to an old Ford Escort, tugged on the handle and it clicked open. The interior was lined with a film of dust and ash. I scooted into the driver's seat and searched for a key. In movies, there was always a spare under the floor mat or in the visor, but this was real life and I had nothing. The dash was blank. I reached underneath, looking for wires, but whatever was there was encased in hard plastic. Even if I could get inside, I had no idea what to do. I had no choice but to keep walking.

I finally reached the campus grounds and my first stop was Sage and Teagan's dorm. It was damaged and empty, but the stairwell and all the rooms up to the third floor were intact. Despite the odds against finding anyone, I climbed through the debris and called Sage's name.

Next, I went to my own dorm. I actually found myself hoping I'd see a third Marlow Henry and a third Zed. Our building was even worse off. There were no staircases intact at all. It smelled like an old, sooty fireplace. No one could've survived if they were here when the bombs fell. My third self and best friend were likely dead. I felt a strange detached form of grief, like holding onto a helium balloon. I had to keep my emotions at a safe distance in order to keep moving on, but they were still there, tied to my wrist with a long string.

Sage's dorm, at least, would provide some shelter from the elements, but wouldn't keep wild dogs out. I had a little time before nightfall to find something better. It was spectacularly creepy to be the only person on the whole campus in the aftermath of an incredibly terrifying event.

All the trees were burned black and leafless. Some lay prostrate on the earth with exposed broken trunks. I broke a branch off one of them and swung it through the air like a sword, a weapon of minimal efficiency, in hopes of fighting off potential night creatures.

My sunglasses made everything appear dark and eerie. I removed them and slipped them into my pocket. I took a moment to put the drops in my eyes and blinked back at the dusty atmosphere. My vision had cleared, and I could see better than I ever could before. I wanted to keep it that way.

I headed for the science labs. If I was going to find anything of value to me, it would be there. I breathed out in relief when I saw the building was still standing. The upper windows were all blown out, and the brick exterior was darkened by soot, but the three-story building was in one piece.

I sniffed the air. Smoke? Dusk had descended in a murky gray glow. The smoke smelled fresh, like a fireplace, but I couldn't see it. I didn't see flames either. The world here had a stench of death and soot. It was entirely possible that my mind was playing tricks on me. After everything that happened in the last couple days, I wouldn't be surprised if this was all part of a mental breakdown, a trauma induced psychosis.

I bit my lip until I tasted blood. Real blood. I wasn't imagining things. Squinting, I continued on. Was that light coming through one of the basement windows?

A click. The unmistakable sound of the cocking of a gun. My nerves flushed with cold fear. I wasn't alone.

"Stay where you are."

My head jerked to the side. I knew that voice.

A girl with wild, dark hair came into view. A gas mask covered her nose and mouth. She wore what looked like hospital scrubs over thicker winter clothes. She narrowed her dusky eyes and lowered her weapon. "Henry?"

"Sage?"

Her arm snapped back up and she held her pistol

firmly with both hands.

"Get down on the ground!"

"Sage? It's me."

"I don't know who you are but I know who you're not. Now get down or I'll shoot you. Don't think I won't!"

I believed her. I got down.

Chapter 50

Marlow

SAGE STOMPED on my back with an army boot and I cried out. This Sage didn't know about my damaged ribs.

"Who are you?" she demanded.

I snorted dust. "Marlow!"

The weight on her heel lessened. She bent over and stared at my face. "Except for the hair and clothes, you kind of look like him." She laughed. "A wimpy, hipster version of Henry."

I took offense. I wasn't a hipster.

She roughly forced my arms behind my back and bound them with plastic tie-ups. Then she poked the back of my neck with her gun. "Get up, soldier."

I grunted and groaned as I twisted from my stomach to my back. I bellowed as I did the sit-up necessary to pull myself to my knees and then to my feet.

"What is wrong with you?" Sage asked. I eyed her as I got my breath. She looked like a wild-child version of Laura Croft: boots, weapons, tough-guy stance. No braid, but something close to dreadlocks.

"I hurt my ribs." My shirt had popped open in the effort, and I caught Sage staring at the bandage wrapping my torso. I almost told her she had been my nurse but thought it wise to keep certain things to myself.

She raised her chin in acknowledgement. "Walk."

"I don't know where I'm going."

"Where were you headed?"

No reason not to tell her the truth. "The science lab."

"Perfect. Keep going." She opened the door for me when we reached the scorched building and prodded me to go down the steps.

"It's dark," I said, pausing at the top. "I don't want to fall." I sounded juvenile, but my hands were tied behind my back. No way I could break a fall, and it was nearly pitch black.

I felt her hand on my elbow and the nose of her gun in my side. "Don't do anything stupid."

"I just want to make it to the bottom of the stairs alive."

"Good goal."

I followed her lead, stepping down when I sensed she did. She had obviously made this journey in the dark many times. I felt as blind as I was when the ophthalmologist lifted my cornea.

I nearly lost my footing on the last step, and Sage tugged up on my arm, saving me from a face plant. My ribs screamed out but I bit my lips to keep from joining in.

"You don't happen to have any painkillers here, do you?" I asked.

"Sorry, those are rationed."

She pushed me into a room, and I pinched my eyes shut to the light. "Ouch! I just had my eyes done!"

"Shut up!" She pushed me hard from behind, and I stumbled forward. "You are such a baby!"

"Sage…"

"Stop calling me that!"

Her volatile response surprised me. I guess I'd be a little high strung if I'd survived a holocaust. "What should I call you?"

"Farrell."

"OK, *Farrell.*" My eyes automatically squeezed shut against the light. "There's a pair of sunglasses in my pocket. Would you mind putting them on my face?"

She grunted, but I soon felt her hand sift through my pocket. She pushed the glasses onto my face. I glanced at her in relief and was about to thank her, but she wasn't looking at me. She had my eye drops in her hand.

"Don't take those, okay? I don't want to go blind."

"Oh, stop whining already. I'm not going to take your stuff." She shoved the drops back into my pocket.

We entered a hallway and walked past many labs to a door halfway down. I recognized the room. It was where Blaine Tucker from the green world had been testing his theories on multi-universes. This third version of him turned as he heard us enter. His hair was greased back behind his ears. He wore a soiled lab jacket.

"Is there something you need to tell me, Tucker?" Sage asked.

Blaine Tucker's jaw dropped, and then his face broke into a satisfied dimple-bearing grin. The coyote who caught the bunny. "Where'd you find him?"

"Snooping around the science buildings. Does Henry have a twin he never mentioned, or a cousin?"

"I don't believe this is Henry's twin," Blaine said with an amused twinkle in his eye. "More like Henry's double."

"What are you talking about?" Sage demanded.

"Henry and I, our experiments. We were supposed to go *there*, but it looks like he came to us instead."

Sage slapped her hands down on the table and glared at Blaine. "What the hell are you *talking* about?"

"When we tease photons and stir up the light particles, we can redirect the quantum energy to create a gateway to a parallel universe."

"You're telling me that your experiments actually… worked? That this guy—" She waved a hand in my direction."—is a second Henry from another realm?"

Blaine laughed and two big dimples popped up on his face. "Yes! This is great!"

I decided to jump into the conversation. "I'm glad you're having such a good time. I'm actually not." I turned to Sage and hoped she could see my imploring look through my glasses. "By now you must know that I'm no physical threat. And I'm unarmed. Could you please cut these binds?"

"Tucker, what are we going to do with him?" she asked, ignoring me. "What's going to happen when Henry returns? Will there be a split in the universe or something? Because, a bombed-out city with millions of dead people is enough for us to deal with right now."

Blaine hesitated. "I'm not sure. I doubt it, but for insurance, we should keep them apart. Fortunately, Henry's not due back for some time."

"Sage?"

Her attention finally returned to me. "Farrell."

"Farrell, please." I turned and attempted to wiggle my fingers. My shoulders burned from the tension, and my hands had fallen asleep. I was ready to beg and plead, but I hoped that she'd spare me the humiliation. She branded a knife, and I held my breath. With the hard look in her eyes, she could just as easily slit my throat.

She reached behind me, and in seconds my arms slumped to my sides. Razor blades ran up and down my arms, and I rubbed them frantically to encourage the blood flow. I felt sick.

"Is there a chair?" I asked. "And water?"

Sage pushed a wooden chair my way, and I collapsed into it, lowering my head to my knees. *Breathe.* In and out. Sage left the room—hopefully to get me something to drink. My throat felt like rope.

Sage returned with a glass of tepid water, and I almost drowned myself gulping it back. Blaine watched me with continued amusement. Sage didn't share his good humor. She had produced a device the size of a cell phone, and she waved it over my body. I knew what the instrument was: a dosimeter. She was measuring my radiation levels.

"He's hot," she said, shaking her head. She nodded at Blaine, and he strode toward me quickly, each of them taking one of my arms.

"Hey!" I shouted.

"I'm afraid you need a decon shower."

"What?" I knew what that was, naturally. I watched TV. They were going to high-pressure wash me. It was going to hurt. Worse, it was going to humiliate me because Sage demanded I strip down to my birthday suit.

I sputtered, "With you in here?"

She shot me a look. "This is no time for modesty."

They ushered me into the staff room. It existed in my realm too, but I'd never entered it before. It had been carefully closed to students, so I hadn't known that there were shower stalls inside. One of them had two decontamination sprayers set up on either side.

Blaine opened up a garbage bag. "All your clothes in here."

Sage pulled off my glasses and tossed them into the bag. She ripped off my shirt while Blaine unzipped my pants.

"Hey! I can undress myself."

"It's imperative that we accomplish this as soon as possible," Blaine said. I was stumbling on one leg as my socks were pulled off. Sage removed the gauze around my ribs and I laughed out loud at the irony."

"Please stay calm," she said.

Seriously? How could I be calm, standing completely naked in front of her and Blaine while they power-hosed me? The soapy solution stung like a million bee stings. The spray against my ribs dug deep like a gunshot blast. I pinched my eyes shut and covered my nose, and hoped like hell I still had skin left when it was all over.

Finally, the water turned off. Sage handed me a towel, and I quickly covered up my man parts. Her expression when she looked at me was of complete indifference.

I didn't like this version of Sage Farrell.

Blaine returned with what amounted to hospital scrubs. "Sorry, dude, that's all we have for clothing in a pinch."

Blaine escorted me back to the lab. My eyes had adjusted to the light, and another poke to my forehead reminded me that I no longer needed glasses. Thank God for small mercies.

"So, Tucker," I began. I wasn't so daft to see that last names were "in" around here. "How about you bring me up to speed? Looks like your weenie roast got away on you."

Blaine settled into a chair behind Professor Garvin's desk. He leaned forward and threaded his fingers together. "Your world is different?"

"If you mean, have we blown ours to smithereens like you have yours, then yes, it's different. So far we've managed to avoid World War Three."

"Good! That's great!"

"Yeah, for them. Why does it make you so excited?"

"Desolation is a great motivator for science," he said. "Wouldn't you want to escape this place if you could?"

Actually, I did want to escape this place, but I knew what he meant. "Most people would look at ways to colonize other planets."

"That involves technology and finances beyond the scope of this civilization," Blaine said. "But what if there's another universe out there, parallel to ours but not destroyed—why not go there if you can?"

"Well, because of the whole parallel thing. There's already one of you in each of them."

Blaine studied me with a confused look. "You mean both of them."

"No. I mean each of them."

"No way! There's more than one?"

"I can safely say there's at least three."

Blaine clapped his hands. "This is great!"

"If you say so. Except, why am *I* here?"

Blaine leaned back and clasped his hands behind his head. "Well, I'm actually not sure. Henry and I have been experimenting on ways to manipulate quantum matter for some time, since long before the bombs fell. It was my hope
that we'd be the ones going to you. Not the other way around. Obviously, we haven't mastered directional activity."

"Obviously."

Despite their lack of control I had to give Blaine Tucker credit for trying. And the other Marlow Henry. I had a hard time wrapping my mind around the fact that this was a world where I was a friend and partner of Blaine Tucker. That we'd developed an experiment that was responsible for my jumping universes. I didn't even take my own physics course that seriously. I just wanted a passing grade.

I snorted.

"What?" Blaine asked.

"I just think this is all so crazy."

Sage returned and another heat wave of mortification rushed over me as I recalled the decon shower. I tried to act nonchalant, leaning back in my chair and stretching out, but it was hard to pull off cool wearing baggy, mint-green pajamas.

"Who's crazy?" she asked.

"Not who," I returned, though I suspected maybe this version of Sage Farrell *was* crazy. "Just everything.

This. Me here."

I cut a quick look to Sage and then to Blaine. "Where is everyone, anyway? Can't be only the two of you here?"

"No, there's more," Sage said. "But not many."

Sage and Blaine shared a look.

I leaned forward, feeling awash with new anxiety. "Can you tell me what happened?"

Sage's eyes actually welled up with tears. She looked away, her expression hard, as if crying was a sign of weakness or something.

Blaine started and what he said sent shivers down my spine. "We lost the war on terror."

I nodded wanting him to go on, but dreading what he'd say.

"Just like with the towers and the Pentagon, they had a one, two, three plan. First DC, then New York, then Chicago. Each city obliterated by a single 'small' nuclear bomb. The initial attacks were by citizens of Arab countries, but they didn't act alone. Russia and China attacked from the north with incendiary missiles hitting Seattle and Detroit, and from the west, hitting Los Angeles and Houston. Their collaborative goal was to incapacitate America's democracy. It looks like they succeeded."

I assumed the cell towers were out. "How do you know all of this?"

"The lab is equipped with a ham radio," Blaine said. "We get the emergency broadcasts. A contingency government is trying to rule, but no one has even heard of the acting president, he's so far down the chain of command."

Sage added solemnly, "The whole cabinet was wiped out in the DC attack." She crossed her arms. "We weren't prepared. We lived life like everyday would be the same as the previous one: went to class, studied, partied."

"It wasn't like we didn't have a clue. The news about the unrest on the other side of the world went on ad nauseam," Blaine said. "We just didn't think it was something we'd have to deal with now. Professor Garvin knew we were in trouble, though. He was the brains behind this makeshift bunker. He was the one who'd acquired the decontamination showers, the gas masks, dried food rations, guns."

"Is he here?" I asked. I was curious to see this Rambo version of Professor Garvin.

Blaine's eyes washed with sadness. "That's the irony. He was in Chicago for his sister's wedding when it happened."

"No one in Chicago survived," Sage added, "and very few in Detroit. Not just from the fire bombs, but also from the fall out cloud from Chicago that blew over the city.

"You and Teagan are from Chicago," I said.

Her eyes welled up again. "Her parents and mine are gone."

"Teagan's okay, though?"

Sage nodded. "She'll arrive with the others."

"What about Ben?" I asked.

Sage blinked. "How do you know about my brother?"

"You have one in the realm I came from. I just met him yesterday."

Her jaw dropped. "He's alive?"

"Yeah," I said, stretching the word out.

She choked out a small laugh. "He died when I was ten. He had a peanut allergy and went into anaphylactic shock."

"I'm sorry. He's a nice guy. And a good brother to you."

Sage couldn't stop the tears this time. She wiped her face on her sleeve with a loud sniff. My heart went out to this softer version of Sage. I could see why she had to go all tough-guy just to survive emotionally.

"So how did you guys survive the attack?" I asked.

"Luck?" Sage said. "Providence?"

"Henry and I were working late in the lab," Blaine said. "Professor Garvin was our biggest fan and he gave us permission to work whenever we wanted."
Sage sighed. "Teagan and I were out with Jake and Nora. We'd been up all night partying and we were looking for coffee, but it was too early for the coffee shops to open. Then we saw Zabinski walking out of this lab with a coffee in his hand. We charged the door thinking we'd get one here."

My heart leaped at the mention of Zed's name.

"Zed's alive?"

Sage nodded and continued. "That's when we felt the earth shake. At first we thought it was an earthquake, but Zabinski suspected it was something more. Detroit's not exactly on a fault line. He rushed back into the lab and we followed him in.

"By this time the cell towers along the East Coast were down, and Tucker had set up the ham radio. That's when we heard about the three explosions that had taken place at dawn, each ten minutes apart."

"Then the bombs dropped on Detroit. It all happened so fast. Henry—" Her eyes caught mine. "Uh, our Henry, ushered us into the shower room where we huddled together until the noise stopped."

"That was three weeks ago," Blaine said. "Welcome to our nightmare."

Before I could ask any more questions, we were interrupted by the return of the others. Several gas masks were dropped on the stainless-steel table closest to the entrance, along with numerous other items— canned food, flashlights and batteries, black garbage bags filled with soft items. A couple gasoline containers sat by the door.

Jake Wentworth, a redhead I assumed was the Nora chick Sage mentioned, Zed and Teagan, all stripped off the scrubs they'd been wearing over their clothes. Blaine walked around with a garbage bag as they tossed their discarded items in. Sage followed with the dosimeters. "Clear," she said, after scanning each one. Obvious relief settled on their faces once it was confirmed they didn't need to get their skin scrubbed to a thin layer.

I couldn't take my eyes off Teagan. This was the girl with whom this whole adventure started: art4ever.

Her blond hair was back in a long ponytail, mussed from removing the gas mask. She didn't have a blue streak. Her face was drawn and tired, nothing like the happy profile picture I'd stared at for weeks.

"Syphoned eight gallons of gasoline," Jake said, breaking my reverie. "Should keep the generator going for a while." He removed the winter coat he'd been wearing under the scrubs, revealing a tight long-sleeved T and fitted designer jeans.

"Blankets and more clothing that should fit," Nora said. "It's creepy looting empty homes." She flung red hair over her shoulder. "I keep thinking I'm going to stumble over a dead body or worse, a half-dead one."

"Zombies, baby," Jake teased. "The zombie apocalypse is next."

She pointed a finger. "Don't even joke!"

Zed and Teagan stared at me. Jake and Nora finally noticed my presence and the room got quiet.

"You cut your hair?" Teagan asked. She continued to scrutinize me. "Why are you dressed like that?"

Zed stroked his beard. "He's not Henry."

Teagan's eyes flashed with confusion. "What?"

"This *is* Marlow Henry," Blaine started, "just not ours. He's from another realm."

The wind sucked out of the room as everyone

took a disbelieving breath.

"Are you saying," Zed began, "that your experiment worked?"

"What experiment?" Jake asked.

Blaine ignored him and responded to Zed. "Kind of. Except our Henry was supposed to go there."

The lines in Jake's thick forehead buckled deeper. "I thought he went to check on his mother?"

"He did," Blaine said. He looked put out having to answer Jake the jock's questions. By the measurable increase of tension, I gathered there was some bad blood between them. "At least, I think he did, right after our last effort."

"I watched him leave this morning with a bicycle and a gas mask," Zed said.

Jake stared hard at me, his mouth morphing into a smirk. "Sorry, dude. Bad deal for you."

I ignored Jake the jock, like I did in every realm. "Where is his mother?" I asked. My mother, sort of.

"She's in Indiana visiting her sister," Blaine answered. "She should be fine."

I nodded, relieved, picturing her playing Scrabble with my Aunt May. I hated to think of her suffering anywhere.

Teagan stepped closer, pulled up a chair and sat. "What's it like over there?" She smiled softly. "Must be better than here."

I sucked in a breath. For most people it was a hundred percent better, but not for her. "Yeah," I said simply.

Chapter 51

Marlow

THE SCIENCE WING had laundry facilities to wash lab coats and lab rags. The staff room had a small kitchen where I assumed Zed and Teagan went with the canned goods they'd brought back.

Sage had disappeared, leaving me with Blaine.

I was suddenly overcome by a wave of fatigue. "I don't suppose there's a place I could lie down?"

"Sure. There's a cot in the staff room, beyond the kitchen."

"Where do you guys sleep?"

"We've pulled mattresses from nearby dorms into one of the labs. We needed to clean off the soot, but fortunately they weren't poisoned. We'll drag the cot in later tonight for you. It's warmer if we all sleep in one room together."

The eyes of the others watched me as I shuffled by in my scrubs, and I let out a long, hard sigh when I was finally alone. My mind went crazy processing everything that had happened, jumping from my life experiences in all three realms. The first one, mine, I didn't even know Sage. Teagan was a chatroom fling. Zed and I played video games in our free time. I was basically a slacker in all areas of my life, including my studies. Then Teagan was killed.

In the next realm, the green one, I met Sage. We had one goal and that was to save Teagan who had gone missing. I started to fall for that version of Sage. Despite the dark circumstances, she was strong and at times funny. There were moments when I thought she saw me as something more than a friend, but then she'd turn it off, and I'd feel stupid for even thinking I had a chance with someone like her.

Besides, she wasn't from my world, so it was just stupid overall.

Now in this world, Teagan was safe but millions of people were dead and the United States was on the brink of losing its democratic government, if it hadn't actually happened already. Blaine and my counterpart were driven to build a contraption that would transport them out of this world and into another. I didn't blame them.

It was a wonder I fell asleep.

What felt like seconds later, I awoke to a soft knock. Sage peeked in. "Supper's ready if you're hungry."

My stomach growled. I was starved.

Supper was a humble affair of warmed-up canned spaghetti, canned creamed corn and stale crackers. We sat on tall stools around one of the stainless-steel lab tables: Blaine at one end, Sage, Teagan and Zed along one side with me, and Nora sitting across from them. Jake took the other end of the table opposite Blaine.

Everyone was looking at me.

After several bites of spaghetti and corn, I finally said, "Are we exactly alike?"

"Well, your hair is shorter," Teagan said. She'd mentioned the hair difference before. "Our Henry wears a long ponytail."

I offered a half-grin. So this version of me was a hippie. I guessed that was cool.

"He doesn't wear hipster clothes," Sage added wryly.

"For the record, those clothes weren't mine. They belonged to a guy named Ryan."

"Why were you wearing some other guy's clothes?" Sage asked.

"My own were in the wash. You stole them for me, actually."

Sage's mouth dropped open. "I did?"

"It's a long story."

She smirked. "I can't wait to hear it."

"What did you do in the other world?" Nora asked.

"In my world I'm a science student at Detroit University. Zed, uh, Zabinski, is my roommate."

"Is your world under threat?" Zabinski asked.

"Yeah. There's always some war going on, often more than one. Jerusalem and Palestine, Russia and Ukraine, extreme Islam in the Arab states."

"Much like here," Sage said. "Are your towers down in New York?"

I nodded. "Yes, but not in the world I was at before this one."

"Wild," Jake said as he scraped the last of his spaghetti from his bowl and spooned it into his mouth.

The conversation turned to the last looting raid. "We need to keep going out," Sage said. "Before things deteriorate further. We need to go wider, away from the fallout path."

"What's your plan?" I asked.

Jake threw me look of superiority. "To survive."

"I gathered that. I mean, in the long run?"

"We're hoping to get rescued," Sage said. "If we can survive long enough, the army will arrive. The emergency broadcasts say they're out looking for survivors. It's still too soon after the bombs. Their resources are stretched."

"We'd hoped for some help from Canada," Teagan said, "but the border cities are dealing with fallout from Chicago as well."

"Why don't you just drive out?" I asked. "There are plenty of abandoned cars. There must be a way to hot-wire them."

Blaine shook his head. "The bombs emitted damaging electromagnetic pulses that screwed with the digital systems."

"So, older cars then? Before digital?"

Jake scoffed. "There aren't any older cars. The federal government recalled all old vehicles in 2000, offered a rebate as an incentive, though no one really had a choice. Within five years everyone had a new or relatively new car and the American auto industry was rebooted."

"Ah," I said. Germany in my world had a similar program and a thriving auto industry to go with it, though I didn't think they forced anyone to do it.

It didn't take long before we'd eaten to the bottom of the pot, and since I considered myself a guest, I took a spot on the couch in the staff room while the others cleaned up.

After about twenty minutes, Teagan wandered in. She sat in a chair across from me. "This must be so weird for you."

Understatement. "It is."

"I'm sorry."

"For what?" I asked.

"That Tucker and Henry did this to you. I'm sure you'd rather be back in your world."

Back in my world I'd been chatting online with this girl. Back in my world, she had died.

"I'm trying to look at it like an adventure. An education if you will."

Her rosebud lips pulled up into a smile. "Great attitude."

"It does in a pinch."

Her gaze dropped to her folded hands. I couldn't stop staring at her. If things were different, if a homicidal maniac hadn't been let loose on campus, she and I could've been friends. Could've been more than friends, even. Her lashes flickered and she looked like her mind was racing for the next thing to say. I understood her social discomfort and wanted to relieve her of it.

"Knock, knock."

Her head snapped up, and by her confused expression it occurred to me belatedly that Knock-knock jokes may not have been my best option. Why didn't I ask her what music she liked? Something normal?

She drew out her answer. "Who's there?"

"Iva."

"Iva who?"

"I've a sore hand from knocking."

She laughed. "You're a geek."

"I know."

She placed her fingers over her mouth. "It almost seems sacrilegious to laugh. Things are just so unimaginatively terrible."

"It's even more important to have a sense of humor then," I said. "Sometimes it's the only way to get through a day."

Sage walked in and I was sure I saw a hint of disapproval cross her face. "Ten minutes until lights out. We go to bed early around here to preserve energy. Marlow, since you're new, you can use the lavatory first."

"Sage, you called me Marlow."

"That's just to keep from confusing you with Henry. And the name's still Farrell." She motioned to Teagan. "Hey, Lake, let's give the guy some space."

Teagan released a small sigh, like she was used to taking orders from Sage, and left me alone.

Chapter 52

Marlow

IT WAS BACK to finger-brushing my teeth. Someone had filled a petri dish with baking soda and I shook a little on my index finger. I grimaced at the sharp taste, rinsed my mouth and ran my tongue over my teeth. Better. My face was still tender from my involuntary power wash, so I decided to leave it alone for a day. My flesh had a rosy hue to it from the ordeal, like I'd spent one too many hours in the sun without sunscreen.

True to his word, Blaine pulled the cot from the small nursing station into the lab room next door to the one we ate in. This one was freezing cold, since it hadn't any heat or lights. An emergency candle burned on a counter that ran against the wall, shedding enough light for everyone to find their own beds, but not so much that you felt completely exposed to your neighbor.

The mattresses were tucked pretty close together, to make the most of body heat, I assumed, and I felt like the odd man out with my elevated cot. Let me be truthful. I was even *more* of the odd man out. How much odder could you be than the guy who arrived from not one but two other universes?

Sage and Teagan's mattresses were pressed together, as were Jake's and Nora's. I was shoved against Zed and Blaine. It wasn't a big lab room.

When we were all tucked in like schoolchildren, Sage blew out the light. No one said anything. Not good night, no prayers, no nothing. Soon the room filled with light snoring and heavy breathing. Before long, I joined in.

The early light of dawn streamed through the high windows, and I was pulled out of sleep. It took me a few seconds to remember where I was. This was the second time in three days I'd awoken in a bed that wasn't my own, and the second time I awoke in a new realm. The mattresses on the floor around me were already empty, blankets straightened and pillows arranged like we were in an army camp rather than on college grounds.

This world had raised military-minded students, more so than the others. They might not realize it, may think they were oblivious to the dangers that had loomed outside their walls, but on a subconscious level, they were more disciplined, more capable than their counterparts. I suspected their childhood may have been similar to those who'd grown up in the fifties in my world, subjected to the ever-present fear of a nuclear Soviet attack. All those drills in school and at home, all those backyard bunkers. It had to have an effect on a kid.

Teagan gave me a sympathetic glance when I shuffled into the staff room kitchen. "We only have toast, but at least there's lots of peanut butter." She motioned to the jar next to the open bag of bread next to the toaster.

I made my toast and carried it to the other room, not wanting to miss the plans for the day. Everyone was already dressed and putting on scrubs over their winter coats. They each chose a gun, checked the magazine and made sure they were loaded up before strapping the weapons on.

"Who are you afraid of?" I asked. "I thought you expected the Army to arrive?"

"That's who were hoping will arrive," Jake said. "But the terrorists have infiltrated. There are a lot of desperate people out there. We don't know who will show up. Could be friend, could be foe."

"What are you going to do?" My question was directed at everyone, but Sage answered. "Tucker will stay with you. Maybe figure out a way to send home. We take turns guarding the lab." She nodded at

Zed. "Zabinski's up for that. The rest of us scout. Food, supplies, whatever."

I liked the idea of getting sent home. But really, I wanted to go back to the green realm. Teagan's life was still in danger there. It was easy to forget that when another Teagan stood only feet away from me, safe and sound.

They blew out of the lab leaving Blaine and me standing there in awkward silence. The way he watched me—I'd noticed his eyes on me often though I tried to ignore him—made me nervous. I felt like I was nothing more to him than an oversized lab rat, or a hairless chimpanzee.

"Even though I'd like to go home," I said, "I need to go back to the world I came from for a little while first."

"Oh?" Blaine said. "Why?"

"Got unfinished business. Can you program your experiment to do that?"

"I can try. No promises. Remember, I didn't even know we'd brought you here in the first place."

I had to be content with the effort. "Okay, but I don't suppose you have something else I can wear? I tugged on my loose pants. "I'd rather not arrive to wherever I end up in this."

"Sure, follow me." Blaine led me to the room where all the lab coats and rags were washed. I knew my way there, since I'd had reason to wash a lab coat or two in my own world. I was happy to see a stack of clean, folded clothes sitting on a counter.

"Pick out whatever you like," Blaine said. "Let me know when you're ready."

I found a pair of jeans whose previous owner shared my long legs and slender torso. Knowing I was likely slipping into the clothes of a dead man, probably a former student, someone I might even know in my world, was slightly macabre. There was a T-shirt that had "resident insomniac" printed on the front, and a dark green zip-up hoodie. I put on both of them.

Blaine had donned lab glasses and a long lab coat. I didn't know how necessary either item was, but some things were just habit, especially when it came to the lab.

"I've had the privilege of meeting two other Blaine Tuckers," I said. "Both are in the science track, but neither of them are as driven as you."

Blaine shot me a look. "I guess you could say the same thing about you and our Henry."

"True. What's different here?"

"Besides World War Three?"

"You didn't know this was going to happen. Or maybe you did, but you didn't know it would happen now. Is that why? Were you just trying to find a way to escape?"

"At first? No. At first it was just the rush of breaking through. And I thought it might be cool to see if my dad were alive another world. He died when I was three."

"I'm sorry to hear that."

"I barely remember him. And I'd tossed out that

possibility because I'd wrongly concluded that if he were dead here, he must be dead everywhere. But your story about Farrell's brother proves I was wrong. It excites me that Dad could be alive somewhere."

"But then the bombs?"

"That changed everything as you can imagine. Henry and I were really stoked about the possibility of escaping this world. That's why he left to see his mother. He decided he needed to say good-bye. When he gets back, we're going to work on our experiment until we're both the hell out of here."

"What about the other *yous*? The ones in those other worlds? No worries about splitting the universe and all that?"

"We'd have to leave Detroit. Start over. Get new names. Just make sure we never meet. I mean, I don't really know what would happen if we met. But as a precaution, I'd make every effort not to."

The addition of Blaine Tucker and Marlow Henry into another world had to effect the cosmos somehow, even if they didn't meet their counterparts, and probably not in a good way, especially if it was permanent. But for right now, I couldn't worry about that. I just had to work with Blaine to get out of here myself.

The experiment took place in a converted storage room. Blaine instructed me to stand on a circular pad. An identical pad hung overhead. Blaine fiddled with knobs and numbers. "We're creating an energy field. You'll feel electricity, like a shock, as the photons and electrons are scrambled."

"Dude," I said, "just fyi. When I jump, it feels like I'm being struck by lightning."

Blaine flashed a crooked grin. "Good to know."

Time ticked by. My legs and back grew sore from standing. My nerves were taut with the anticipation of bone-rattling shock waves. I threw Blaine a look of frustration.

He scratched his head. "I don't know why it's not working."

"Let's take a break," I said. "My legs are tired and I'm getting a tension headache."

Blaine checked the time. "The others will be back soon anyway. They never stay out for more than two hours."

"Because of the radiation?"

"It's dying down, thankfully, but it's still better to be safe than sorry. What we need is a good rain."

Or a good storm. "The weather was always wonky, each time I jumped," I said. "Well, the first time I made contact through another realm was through the Internet."

Blaine stilled. "What do you mean?"

"I'd made contact with Teagan, actually. My realm to hers, but only through a chat room online. It wasn't until the second freak storm that I physically jumped to Teagan's world. And it hurt like hell. Like I said, I thought I'd been struck by lightning.

"Interesting. We've had unsettled weather the last couple days. Sheet lightning. Maybe something is

happening on a molecular level in the atmosphere. Maybe the effect of our experimentation isn't limited to what we're doing in the storage room. Maybe the recent injection of radiation has something to do with it." He scratched his head again. "Let
me think about this."

I decided to make myself useful and went to the kitchen to start lunch for everyone. Truth was, I was getting hungry. I rummaged through the canned goods finding several cans of soup. I opened up four of them, added water and began to heat them on the stove. Good on Professor Garvin for securing that generator.

I made toast and used the last of the margarine, hoping they'd somehow managed to find more of it on their raids. I had the lab table set with bowls when the crew returned. They didn't show up with smiles this time. There was something close to panic etched on their faces. I counted heads and a cool liquid dripped down my spine.

"Where's Teagan?"

Chapter 53

Marlow

"ONE MINUTE she was with me," Nora said in a thick voice. "And the next, she was no where to be found. I called for her, even lifted this stupid mask off my face." She grabbed it off the top of her head, her hair catching its static and springing out in a red halo. "Risking my own life! But she never responded."

"Calm down, babe," Jake said. He stood in front of her with his palms up. "Where were you?"

"We took the neighborhood in the northwest end, by Paddy's creek. I know we aren't supposed to split up, but we both thought we could cover more ground." She bit her lip as she stared at the bag of goods she'd retrieved at her feet.

"We have to go back and find her," Sage said.

Blaine had the dosimeter out and he scanned each one. "You guys are hot. You must've walked through a radioactive pocket." He shook his head. "You all need a decon showers ASAP." He pulled a black bag out of the cupboard and opened it. Jake and Nora were already stripping down.

"I'm going back out," Sage said. "I can't leave Lake out there to die."

"We won't leave her," Blaine said with a slow, steady voice. "As soon as the numbers are down, you can redress and go out again."

Zed pulled off his scrubs. "He's right Sage. Use your head."

"I'm not waiting," Sage said through tight lips. She stared at Nora. "Where exactly were you, O'Shea, when you last saw her?"

Nora rattled off the address. Sage reached for the door.

"Wait," I said. "I'll go with you."

She considered me. "You risk contamination."

"I don't care."

I quickly shucked on a winter jacket and clean scrubs and grabbed another gas mask. Zed handed me a backpack with two water bottles, a couple energy bars and a flashlight inside. Sage handed me a gun.

"You know how to use one of these?"

I grimaced. "Not really."

"Well, you probably won't need to use it, but if so, slip the safety off, aim with two hands and pull the trigger."

She put hers into her pocket. I did the same with mine. It was heavy. I had to lean left a little to compensate.

The mask fit tight against my face and my breath made Darth Vader-like noises. I felt slightly claustrophobic. Sage was obviously unaffected by her mask or the weight of her gun. She strode in a near jog and I scrambled up the steps to keep up with her.

It was midday with a clear fall sky. The air was cool despite the sun. The atmosphere remained smoky and particle-filled. My shadow was still missing.

You don't realize how much you depend on shadows to give perspective and direction. North, south, east, west. Near or far. I knew the campus and Detroit City, but this catastrophic mess was enough to throw my inner compass off.

Sage consulted a handheld GPS.

"That still works?" I asked.

"The terrorists have yet to find a way to bomb space stations." Her voice through the mask made her sound far away, which messed with my senses. At least I could hear her and we could talk.

Sage wasn't in a chatty mood. It gave me time to think about Teagan. Was she destined to die in every realm? Was it impossible to save her? It made me wonder if the bombs in this world had prevented a rapist from taking her here, and so the universe had found another way.

"Sage…uh, Farrell?"

"Yeah."

"Before the bombs, what was going on at campus?"

"What do you mean?"

"Were there any crimes?"

"Other than cheating and plagiarism?"

"Yeah, like serious crimes. Like rapes and killings?"

That slowed Sage down. She flashed me a murderous look and pulled out her gun. "If you even think ..."

"Not me! God, Sage! Farrell, whatever, what the hell."

She lowered her weapon. "Are you talking about your world?"

"Mine and the next one."

"Doesn't sound like paradise there either. Don't tell Tucker. He'd be so disappointed."

"Okay, I won't. Thing is, Teagan ..."

I paused, second-guessing if I should tell. What was the point anyway.

"Teagan what?" she prodded.

"Nothing."

Sage stopped and looked me in the eye. We breathed Darth Vader noises at each other. "Tell me."

This version of Sage intimidated me. I squared my shoulders. "In my world, Teagan Lake is raped and murdered."

I could see the color drain from Sage's face through her mask. "In the green world, she's missing, but her body hasn't been found. You and I believe she's still alive. We're trying to find her."

"You and me?" she said. "We're friends?"

"In the green world we are."

She resumed walking. "Why do you call it the green world?"

"The sky there is greener than it is in my world. It gives everything an emerald shimmer."

"What color is your world?"

"Well, the sky is blue, but there's no shimmer. We do have shadows, though."

"We had shadows before the atmosphere filled with a smoky, radioactive haze." Sage inspected her GPS. "This way," she said, and we turned a corner.

"Are we good friends?" she asked without looking at me. "Because here, we're not. I mean the other version of you. I only met Henry the day of the bombs."

"We've only known each other for a couple days. I feel like we became friends quickly, though. Maybe because we both really want to save Teagan."

"I can see why I would want to save Teagan. She's my best friend. But what drove you? Were you friends?" Her eyebrow arched to the top of her mask. "More than friends?"

"We met online. I felt like I knew her. I cared for her enough that I didn't want to see her die twice."

A silence fell between us. I didn't understand this Sage. At all.

"I'm sorry," she finally said. "Life in this world didn't just start getting hard for me three weeks ago. I know I'm bristly."

"You do remind me a little of a porcupine."

That actually mad e her eyes smile. For about a

tenth of a second.

We turned another corner and Sage stopped. "This is the area."

The suburb reminded me of wartime pictures I'd seen on the Internet. Rows of empty homes with walls and windows blown out, glass shards and broken red bricks scattered about, chimneys knocked over and shutters askew. I followed Sage into the first house on the right. A small twisted bicycle lay in the ditch. Sage turned on her flashlight, and the beam coasted across a dust-laden living room, everything just as it was before the occupants fled.

"Teagan!" Sage called out.

We searched the second floor and the basement. Except for a family of mice, the place was empty. The next three houses were variations of the same.

"This is taking too long," Sage said. "Let's split up. Go door to door, call her name." She reached into her backpack and produced a whistle. "Lake has one, so listen for this. If you find her, blow as hard as you can. I'll do the same. Meet me at this address in one hour if you don't find her. We'll have to regroup."

I took the whistle wondering how I'd manage to use it with my mask on. Not possible. I'd have to risk radiation to use it. Fine.

Sage was already at the front door of the next house. When it wouldn't open, she disappeared around the back.

I took a deep breath and started in the opposite direction. To say the place was eerie was an understatement. A bombed-out ghost town. Just me and my noisy breath.

Some houses were burned-out shells, while others remained surprisingly intact. People who fled at the news of the Chicago bombing fared better than those who waited until after the Detroit fires.

The front doors were usually locked, and in those cases I searched for an open or broken window that Teagan may have gained entrance by.

I searched the next house as quickly as possible, calling Teagan's name as I went. I thought I heard something in one of the bedrooms. Heavy breathing? Was Teagan here? Hurt?

"Teagan?"

I heard the breathy sound again, but it wasn't the sound of someone breathing. It was hissing. I jumped back and screamed. A snake slithered across the floor. I fell against the dresser, knocking a lamp onto the floor. It landed with a crash. The reptile disappeared under the bed.

Sweat broke out on my brow under the mask, and my own short breaths roared like crashing waves in my ears. I scrambled out of the room, down the dark hall and out the open front door.

Bent over at the waist, I rested my hands on my knees. It was just a snake. Probably a harmless pet or just a creature looking for its next house mouse meal.

Shake it off, man.

I admired Sage's courage. I agreed that we would cover more ground if we separated, but I missed her company. Safety in numbers, and all that. Good thing I couldn't see my own shadow or I'd likely jump at that too.

A howl in the distance. I stopped short. Great. Mutant wildlife. What else could go wrong?

Even though we were on a mission to find Teagan, Sage had grabbed two empty canvas bags before we left in case we stumbled across something valuable. Mine hung over my shoulder with six boxes of mac and cheese and a tub of unopened margarine that I'd found in the last house. Unlike butter, margarine was an edible oil product and I wouldn't be surprised if its properties were sufficient to stand up against radiation fallout.

I turned onto Riddle Street. Another row of brick and wood single story homes with in-ground cement basements. Trees leaned like naked fairies, their leaves on the ground and escaping in the nearly freezing breeze.

I reached for the next handle, turned it and blinked when it eased open. Teagan could be inside. "Teagan?"

The floorboards beneath me creaked. My ears perked up at the sound of high-pitched squeaking and what sounded like sand being thrown on the linoleum. The mask on my face made for unclear peripheral vision. Something brushed against my leg.

I yelled and did a jig. A row of rats scurried around me, disappearing behind the worn couch in the living room. I grabbed at my heart. I hated rodents.

Almost as much as I hated snakes. Apparently, underground creatures had the best chance of surviving apocalyptic events.

Nervous sweat broke out on my brow. I breathed deeply, urging myself to carry on. The air smelled off. More off than usual. The mask filtered poisonous fumes, but it couldn't block the rancid stench that grew in intensity as I walked down the hall.

Bad smell. Bad body smell. Bad dead body smell.

Oh, God, please let it not be Teagan.

The bedroom door was open a crack. I pushed on it. My heart thundered in my ears. Sweat dripped off my eyelashes and I blinked to clear my vision. The door creaked as it swung wider. A body lay on the bed.

Chapter 54

Marlow

WIRY WHITE HAIR spread over the pillow and along the temples of a wrinkly old man. His nose and cheeks were missing. Damn rats! I backed up and bent over my knees. I couldn't vomit. I didn't want to remove my mask. *Breathe, Marlow!* In. Out.

I raced outside. The only thing I wanted to do was rip off my mask. I felt claustrophobic, like I'd been stuffed into a man-sized test tube. I tugged on my hair until it hurt, bringing myself to my senses.

It was just a dead body. That was all. The poor guy probably had a heart attack in bed. He'd lived a long life and left the stage before he had to deal with the horrors that now lay outside his door. He was luckier than most.

I had to stay focused on Teagan. She was out here somewhere. Alone. I had to get my shite together and find her. I inhaled deeply and shouted, "Teagan!"

A noise came from the house next door. Knocking? I cocked my head and strained to hear. Yes, knocking. The house looked stable, with no missing windows or loose bricks. I ran to the front door. Locked. Circling around back I could see that the front of the house concealed the damage at the back. A covered porch had collapsed and debris was strewn across the yard. I approached carefully, noting that the wooden steps were brittle with age and weather.

"Teagan!"

Again the knocking, but it sounded like it came from behind me. A soft tap, tap, tap.

"Teagan!"

"Help." The call was faint but distinct. I spun around and saw a broken wooden crate on the ground. I hurried toward it. It looked like a cover to a cellar or a bunker. I grabbed the broken pieces and pulled, ignoring the sharp slivers that stabbed through my gloves and bit my fingers.

The area below was dark. I reached for my flashlight and worked a grid with the beam of light. Teagan lay at the bottom of the stairs. Blood dripped on one side of her face and her arm was bent in an unnatural angle.

She stared up at me through her mask, eyes wide with fear. "Who are you?"

"It's Marlow. I'm with Sage. I'm here to help."

Teagan winced. "I fell down the stairs and hit my head. I must've passed out. I twisted my ankle, and God, does my arm hurt."

The cement staircase lacked a railing. I eased down not wanting to be a second casualty.

"You're okay," I said when I reached her. "I'll get you out."

"My bag," she said, pointing. It had landed out of reach of her outstretched arm. "I need water."

I pulled her bag closer, dug inside and handed her the water.

"Can you help lift my mask?"

I nodded and held it up while she drank. I placed it back when she was finished. Capped her bottle and returned it to her bag. I then removed a bottle from my bag and followed suit. I eyed the steep stairwell, imagining myself carrying Teagan out. I should've spent more time at the gym. Correction: I should've gone to the gym.

"I thought the cover was just a scrap piece of wood. I should've known better than to walk across it," Teagan said.

I flashed my light to better take in our surroundings. Looked like an old bunker. A radio sat on a dusty desk. Canned food stuffs lined a shelf. An old dog-eared pin-up calendar featuring a voluptuous blond wearing a pointy brassiere, hung from a nail in the wall. February 1952.

I scoured the place looking for something I could use as a brace for Teagan's arm. A broom leaned up against the wall. I lifted a knee to break the handle over my leg. I underestimated the strength of it. Pain exploded in my thigh and I jumped around as curse words flew from my lips. Teagan watched me with great apprehension. I came to my senses and looked for tools. Surely a bunker would be equipped with a toolbox. I found one under the desk. The snap flicked open easily and I found a hammer. I thought maybe I could pound the middle of the handle until it weakened, but then I spotted the handsaw underneath.

I lay the broomstick on the desk and sawed until I was halfway through. I used my other leg this time to complete the break. There was a length of rope I cut into two pieces with a less-than-sharp hunting knife. I was a sweaty mess after the exertion.

"Okay," I said with my Darth Vader voice. "I'll be as gentle as I can, but it's probably going to hurt."

Teagan nodded with eyes glazed over by fear and pain. She gripped my scrubs as she screamed bloody murder, then collapsed in a heap. I thought she might've passed out with the pain.

"Teagan?"

Her eye's flickered open. "I'm all right."

I worked as quickly as possible, tightening the piece of broom stick to her forearm with the rope, and fashioned a piece to loop around her neck as a sling. It occurred to me that I should take a moment to blow the whistle, to alert Sage, but I didn't think she would be able to hear us from down here.

Besides, we had bigger problems. Dusk came early to Michigan this time of year. The hungry nocturnal beasts were awakening. I heard a low growl from the top of the stairs. Two red eyes peered down at us, a feral face marked with patches of missing fur. It growled again, baring two rows of sharp, pointy teeth.

It looked hungry. It looked diseased. It looked desperate.

We were in trouble.

Chapter 55

Marlow

"MARLOW! My gun!"

Teagan's yell snapped me out of my frozen stance and I remembered the weight in my right pocket. I reached for the gun and aimed it at the creature—a dog or coyote, a wolf—it was hard to tell in the near darkness. It crouched down and I could see the silhouette of its neck, its stiff fur standing on end. It was going to pounce.

I gripped the gun with both hands, which were shaking so much it would be a miracle if I shot anything at all. I pulled the trigger, but it didn't budge. I'd forgotten the safety.

The creature growled again.

"Marlow!"

Safety off. Aim with two hands. Pull the trigger. I wasn't prepared for the kickback, and I stepped backward, tripping on what was left of the broom, and landed hard on my ass. I heard a yelp and then a howl.

I'd nicked the animal, but not enough to deter it. Hunger and rabid craziness overruled any natural fear of man it might've had. It crouched back on its hind legs and leaped toward me.

I aimed and shot, and this time I didn't miss. The body of the beast fell in a heap half way down the steps and tumbled to the bottom. I pushed back on my butt, not wanting to touch the thing. Unfortunately, it lay directly in our escape path. I had to touch it.

I tentatively reached for one of its back legs. In my mind, I saw it spring back to life and clutch my throat, its whole playing-dead thing a ruse to trap me. Its fur was coarse and dry, the skin beneath it warm. It didn't attack. I dragged the body to the back of the bunker.

"Let's get out of here," I said, returning to Teagan. I helped her onto her good foot and slipped my arm around her back. "Lean on me." She hopped one step at a time, and I tried to bear as much weight as possible. We made it to the front of the house where I took out the whistle that Sage had given me. I blew on it until she appeared. Even through her mask I could see the look of relief on her face. She rushed to Teagan, leaned away from her injured arm and gave her a hug, which also, because Teagan was leaning on me, meant Sage was pressing up against me too.

I didn't mind at all.

"You scared me," Sage said.

"Thanks for coming back for me."

"Of course, Lake. I know you'd do the same for me."

"Yes, I would."

Between the two of us, Sage and I got Teagan back to the lab where we all endured decon showers—girls first, then me. Blaine rigged up a cast for Teagan's broken arm and produced a crutch. Then it was time for dinner.

The good thing about living in a science lab is that if you don't have the drugs you need, you can usually make them. Teagan was particularly grateful for my talents when I produced fairly strong painkilling drugs. I was sure Blaine did his best to set her ulna but he wasn't a doctor. I feared Teagan may have to live the rest of her life with a crooked arm, but at least she was alive.

It gave me hope that the other version of her might have a chance as well, that maybe Teagan's death wasn't inevitable.

"Marlow was *ammmazzing*!" Teagan was high.

We gathered for a dinner of mac and cheese, lounging on the couches and chairs in the staff room instead of around a lab table, since Teagan couldn't sit up by herself yet. Her foot was propped up on an ottoman.

"That coyote was going to *kill* us and Marlow just

shot it." She made me out to be some kind of Indiana Jones. "He broke a *broomstick* and *tied* it to my arm."

My face flushed with embarrassment. Sage's lips tugged up with amusement. "How's it feel to be a hero?"

"All in a day's work," I said lightly. "Nice work on the cast, Blaine." I hoped to remove the attention off me.

"We should call you Dr. Tucker," Jake said. Then with a mocking glance my way, "Or should I say, Dr. Blaine."

"You're welcome to step in," Blaine said. "With no actual doctor on the premises, you can be my guest."

Nora poked a finger in the air. "He's just giving you a hard time, Tucker."

"My dad's a doctor," Zed said. He placed an empty bowl on a small table beside him. "He wanted me to follow in his footsteps."

"Why didn't you?" I asked. I knew Zed, and he was smart enough.

He rubbed his beard. "I hadn't decided not to. I might've yet, if this hadn't happened."

"My dad's an accountant in New York," Jake said. "Or was."

The room grew quiet. It was easy to forget that whole cities and millions of people had disappeared from the face of the earth.

"My dad died when I was three," Blaine said. "I'm glad he didn't live to see this."

"Do you remember him?" Sage asked.

"Not a lot. I have this memory of him at a cabin in the woods. I think my parents went there to escape the city on weekends. We'd play this chase and tickle game. He'd sing a nursery rhyme." He quoted the next part with a singsong voice. "*Run, run, run, as fast as you can. You can't catch me, I'm the gingerbread man.*"

I dropped my fork. The staffroom elongated like a long dark tunnel. My mind spun. *The gingerbread man.* Could it be? Could Blaine Tucker be the assailant in the other worlds?

I stared hard at the Blaine Tucker who sat languidly on a couch across from me.

"Dude," he finally said. "Are you all right?" He sat up under my piercing gaze and choked out a chuckle. "Do I need to get the medical kit?"

I averted my gaze and covered my eyes. This line of thought was crazy. "No, sorry. Just zoned out there for a moment. Rough day."

"Yeah, well, time to kill the lights soon." Blaine yawned. "I'm hitting the hay.

Chapter 56

Marlow

I DIDN'T SLEEP much that night. My thoughts went to the missing Teagan in the other world, captive to some monster and wondering if it were really possible that the monster was Blaine Tucker. Though Zed, Teagan, Jake and Nora seemed much the same in this world as they were in the other worlds I knew them in, Sage was different. This Sage was tougher, harder. But they were both fighters.

The Blaine Tucker from my world, the one I sat beside in physics on occasion, was cockier and sleazier than this one. He was a player. Even though he had a girlfriend, Gina, rumor had it he didn't mind fooling around on the side.

This Blaine seemed more levelheaded. I hadn't seen him hit on any of the girls once. Maybe the seriousness of their day-to-day reality, the looming presence of real-time danger, gave him focus.

Maybe it was because his dad had died when he was three.

I didn't know. I just knew that no matter what world I was in, I didn't trust Blaine Tucker. If I'd learned anything since I began jumping it was this: nothing was as it seemed.

The consensus the next day, since everyone had been exposed to higher levels of radiation than was recommended the day previous, was that it was time to take a day off from exploring and exploiting. Zed hung out with the ham radio in case there was any new news: continued reports of rampant looting in all major cities, riots in the Midwest, and all the problems and issues that came with a mass population relocation. Refugee-style camps dotted the Mississippi River.

Nothing about rescue teams sousing out the cities that had been attacked. The assumption was that everyone in them was dead, and if they weren't dead, they would be before help could arrive. The resources were diverted to pockets where survival was most likely.

Which meant this little group was on its own.

"Maybe we should head south like Henry did," Jake said. "We could round up enough bicycles."

Blaine shrugged. "It sounds worse out there than it does here. At least we have shelter and food enough for the winter."

"I agree with Tucker," Sage said. "They can't handle the numbers they have. Best to wait until the weather warms up. By then things will have settled down."

"Are you sure we have enough fuel for the winter months?" Jake asked.

Blaine nodded. "Garvin was ready for a hit. We're good until March at least."

"Can you get me out?" I asked. "I need to get back to where I was before I jumped here."

"I don't know," Blaine said with a shrug. "We can try."

"Now?"

Blaine eyed me with suspicion. "What's the rush?"

"One less mouth to feed?"

"I don't know. It takes a lot of energy. I don't think we can spare it."

"You spared it to get me here."

"That was an accident."

"You were willing to try earlier," I said. "What's changed?"

Blaine shrugged. Maybe he'd been in a more generous mood earlier.

Teagan was in the room, and even though she seemed kind of out of it, I still didn't want to talk about her death and abduction in the other realms in front of her. I doubted it would be enough to change Blaine's mind anyway. He didn't seem all that attached to the people here, except for the fact that they were willing to do the raids and risk radiation exposure. He hadn't gone outside once since I'd been here, and no mention had ever been made to suggest that he'd gone out before.

I didn't think he would care about a Teagan Lake

in another world.

Blaine left the room, and I felt a strange sense of relief. Sage took a seat beside me. She shifted to face me, pulled her knees up and wrapped her arms around them. "What's wrong with you?"

"What?" I asked.

"You're really uptight. More than usual, I mean."

"I need to get back. It's urgent."

She tilted her head. "Why? What's going on?"

I lowered my voice and leaned in. Sage met me halfway, her ear turned to my face. "Remember how I told you that Teagan was killed in my world and abducted in the next?"

She nodded. "Uh, huh."

"I think Tucker might be the assailant."

Sage pulled back and shot me a look that said I was crazy. "Why would you think that?"

I hushed her and beckoned her with my fingers to come close again. "His story about the gingerbread man. Gingerbreadman is the assailant's online handle. You, the other you, hacked his computer but you couldn't track him. He tracked you though. *You* are also in danger."

"That could just be a coincidence."

"Maybe. But I know the Blaine Tucker from my world. There's something off about him."

Sage sagged back and closed her eyes. "I still have a hard time accepting the whole concept of alternate universes. If you weren't right here where I can touch you, I'd say it's all nuts."

She laid a hand on my knee. Hot nerves shot up my leg. Her hand was rough, yet dainty. I wanted to hold it. I didn't want her to move it.

She cleared her throat and pulled her hand away. "I don't know how to help you. It's not like I know how to operate the experiment."

"I know, but you can help me convince Tucker he needs to try."

Chapter 57

Marlow

THERE WEREN'T A LOT of places to be alone—not if you also wanted to be warm. With six of us in one functioning lab, the staff room and the sleeping lab, we were bound to be in any room with someone. Zed kept Teagan company in the staff room while Jake and Nora were "napping"—read, making out—in the bedroom. Blaine had set up his "personal" lab space in the back corner of the lab next to the small adjoining room where he and the other Marlow Henry conducted their experiments. At this moment he sat on a stool at the table with his nose in an old textbook.

Sage and I approached him. "Tucker," she said. "We need to talk."

Blaine groaned. "Let me guess, little Marlow Henry is homesick."

We pulled up stools across from him. I clasped my hands and rested them on the cool surface of the table.

"This is serious," Sage said.

"We tried earlier and it didn't work," Blaine said stubbornly. "I don't see the point."

"The point is you're messing with alternate worlds. You need to take some responsibility."

"Responsibility for what?"

"What goes on there. And right now, Teagan is in trouble."

"I gather you're not talking about her twisted ankle?"

"No. Tell him, Marlow."

"In my world, Teagan Lake is the victim of a serial rapist and is killed." I took some satisfaction that Blaine blanched at that. "In the next world, the one I was at before I jumped here, she's abducted. Sage and I," I glanced at Sage. "Another Sage and I believe she's still alive."

Blaine raised a brow. "Why?"

"For some reason, in that realm, the assailant didn't follow his MO. Normally, he attacks and leaves the victim behind. In this case, no body has been discovered. Plus, he left a threatening note before Teagan disappeared. And then, afterwards, another taunting message."

"What's his email address? Maybe I can track him from here?"

"It was a chatroom handle." I paused and watched his expression. "It's @gingerbreadman."

His eyes flickered but not in a way that indicated guilt or a guilty conscience. "Okay, that's weird. I don't know if I can track it, but I'll try."

"I doubt it. He's a high-level hacker."

"It sucks that other Teagan Lakes aren't faring well in their worlds," Blaine said, "but I don't see what I can do about it, or why, really, I should intervene."

"Because it's you," I said.

His eyes flickered wildly this time. He shook his head sharply. "It's me? What?"

"You are the assailant. In those worlds, you're messed up, man."

Blaine snapped his textbook shut. "If this is a joke, you're not funny. Now if you don't mind…" He nodded to the door as if that would make me excuse myself and leave.

"It's you, Blaine. And now you have a chance to make things right. Help me stop you before you hurt anyone else."

"Do you hear yourself? You're accusing me of being a rapist and a murderer!"

"Not this you," I said as kindly as I could. "Another you."

"But why would I?" He looked truly stricken and for the first time, I felt sorry for him.

"I don't know."

He shifted off his stool and grabbed his head. "This is too much."

"Tucker," I said. "You mentioned a cabin yesterday. Where is it located?"

He cut a sharp look my way. "Why?"

"Because, maybe that's where you've taken her. If you send me back, I can check."

"It can't be me. You have to be mistaken."

"Maybe I am. There's only one way for me to find out. Either way, you'll be helping Teagan. Maybe you'll save her life."

I hoped that he'd take that rope. A hero in this world, even if he's a villain in another.

His eyes darted to Sage as if he were pleading with her. *Take my side.* Instead she said, "You have to try. Besides, Marlow doesn't belong here. And Henry might come back. We can't risk having them both present at the same time."

Tucker let out a heavy breath and then with shoulders back, nodded toward the storage room. "Okay. Let's do it."

⁂

Blaine motioned for me to step on the circular metal pad. I was tempted to say, "Beam me up," but thought that might undermine the seriousness of the situation.

"I didn't have to stand in a special chamber to get here," I said as I took position. "Can't you just summon up a freaky storm?"

"In essence, that's what I'm going to do. Except it's indoors in a controlled environment. Or as controlled as a quantum tornado can be."

"Do you want to say good-bye first?" Sage asked.

I'd been here only a day and a half. I hardly needed to make a scene surrounding my departure. Besides, this might not work, and then it would be all "forget about the good-byes, I'm still here."

"You say it for me," I said.

Sage nodded like she understood. "I hope it works. I hope you save her."

The friendship between Sage and Teagan transcended worlds. It warmed me and made me believe in humanity. It made my quest all the more urgent.

Blaine flicked switches and turned knobs. He put on a pair of tinted glasses and instructed Sage to wait outside the room. "You ready?" he said to me. I nodded. He pulled on a lever and my eyes blurred. I felt like I'd been stung by a dozen stingrays. My body trembled. Every bone shuddered.

Then it stopped.

I opened my eyes. It was dark. The room smelled dusty and stale, like the door hadn't been open in weeks. It worked! I was in a storage room that functioned as a storage room. I worried that I might be locked in. A line of light leaked in under the door. My eyes grew accustomed to the darkness, and I fumbled my way around bookracks and shelving. I held my breath as I tried the knob. It clicked open.

I was in the science lab. Sage and Blaine were gone. Professor Garvin sat at the desk at the back of the room, squinting in front of a computer screen. I still couldn't tell if I was in my own realm, the green one, or yet another new one. I moved as quietly as I could toward the door but my sneakers squeaked on the linoleum. Professor Garvin's head popped up.

"Mr. Henry?"

"Oh, hi, Professor Garvin. I thought I forgot my book bag here, but I guess I must've left it in my calculus class."

He frowned at me like he suspected I was up to something but couldn't think of what. I skipped out of the lab as fast as I could before he could question me further, and up the stairs to the outdoors. I had to see what color it was. *Where* was I?

I exhaled. Green. Now I just had to find Sage.

Chapter 58

Marlow

I WASN'T SURE where to find Sage so I figured I'd go to her dorm. If she wasn't there, I'd wait for her. The walkway was covered in dry leaves and lined with wrought-iron lampposts. My mind did a double take at all the signs of life: undamaged brick buildings covered with autumn-colored vines; a couple walking hand in hand; a girl wearing a wool cap, her head bent as she thumbed a message on her phone: a gang of hockey jocks, punching each other in the shoulders and cracking crude jokes.

All of them dead in the smoky realm. All this beauty destroyed.

I cupped my mouth with my hands, in part to keep them warm with my breath and in part to keep from hyperventilating. I moved forward with my head down, my mind a swirl. I shoulder-butted a body trying to pass me.

"Pardon me," I said. When I looked up, my breath caught in my throat. Blaine Tucker stared back at me. This version of him had pasty drawn skin with gray circles under
his eyes like he hadn't been sleeping. He almost looked frail, but then I considered how hard it felt to ram into him. He was strong underneath his winter coat.

"Watch where you're going, Henry," he said as he kept walking.

"How's Gina?" I called after him. He twisted and gave me a sour look. "She's fine."

How could a guy who had a girlfriend like Gina Upton and a full course load have time to kidnap a girl? Sure, he was an ass, but that didn't make him a killer. I slowed as I pondered it all. Maybe I'd jumped to conclusions. Maybe I'd accused the wrong guy. Maybe I was about to lead Sage on a wild goose hunt.

Sage didn't answer her dorm door when I rapped on it. I tested the knob. It was locked. With no other options that I could think of, I settled down on the couch in the lounge to wait. The seconds ticked by slow and painfully. I stuffed my hands into my pockets and jiggled my legs, releasing nervous tension. The room smelled of old coffee, but at that point I'd settle for old over none. I helped myself to a mug, loading it with two sugar cubes and a couple creamers, then returned to my spot on the couch. The caffeine didn't help with my nervous tension, and my anxiety felt like an itchy wool blanket under my skin.

My eyes trained on the door and when I saw her, I jumped to my feet, almost spilling the dregs at the bottom of my near-empty mug.

Sage stilled when she saw me. "Marlow?" Then she ran to me and bear-hugged me. I wrapped my arms around her with uncertainty. So many moments in my life over the last couple days have registered high on the surreal scale, and this embrace was among them. I couldn't stop myself from taking a whiff of her shampoo.

Sage grabbed my arm and pulled me down the hall to her dorm. "You just disappeared!" she said with a failed effort at keeping her voice down. She unlocked her door and practically pushed me in. "Into thin air! I almost had a heart attack. Can you imagine?"

"I…"

"What the hell happened to you?" She narrowed her dark eyes at me in further scrutiny. "You look like crap and…" She wrinkled her nose. "You smell funky."

"Okay, calm down. I'll tell you everything."

"Sorry, it was just such a mind-bender." She pressed a pillow against the wall on her bed and sat against it. I took Teagan's chair.

"Any news?" I asked.

Sage frowned and shook her head. "There's a media blitz going on, but nothing. It's like she disappeared into thin air too. Do you think…?"

"No." I cut her off. "What's happening to me is happening to me alone. Teagan is still in real danger, I'm afraid."

"What's happening to you?"

I proceeded to tell her the whole story. The further I got into it, especially the parts that were about an alternate her, the more her expression grew perplexed and stunned.

"World War Three?" she said. "That's what I smell?"

"And I've been wearing these clothes for a couple days."

"Where are Ryan's?"

"Radiation poison. I think they're still in the wash. You told me that the radiated items had to be washed several times."

"I told you?"

"Well, the other you."

She rubbed imaginary lines on her forehead. "It's so weird that there's a whole other set of us in other realms."

Then I told her about Blaine Tucker's nursery rhyme story.

"No way!" Sage blurted out.

"It could just be a coincidence, but it's the only lead we have right now. He told me about a cabin near here that his family used to go to when they wanted a break from the city."

"You think Teagan might be there?"

I shrugged a shoulder. "I don't know. It wouldn't hurt to check it out."

"I don't have a car, but I can borrow my brother's." Sage pulled out her phone. "Hey, Ben? Can I borrow your car?... I know, but transit is so slow and I have a doctor's appointment over an hour away... I don't know if I'm dying. That's why I need to borrow your car... No, I don't really think it's serious, just please, can I borrow it?"

She hung up and grinned. "Brothers can be such a pain."

I grinned back, hiding the sadness I had for the other Sage whose brother had died young. I didn't tell this Sage about that.

We drove through neighborhoods that were familiar to me but different. In this realm, the homes remained occupied, lawns mowed, kids bikes propped against walls. In my time, the *blue realm*, it was a ghost town overrun by weeds, the homes overwhelmed by weather and time. Broken glass and crumbling bricks. The only signs of life are wild. Maybe one house per street was claimed by squatters high on drugs. Which, ironically, was a step up from the bombed and burned-out version in the orange world.

My gaze was continually pulled to Sage's profile. Her dark hair hung in smooth chocolatey waves from under a white wool cap. She wore glasses with pink plastic frames and had a matching silk scarf wrapped around her neck. She looked pretty and vulnerable. So different from the GI Joe version of her from that morning.

Even though I'd only known this Sage for a short while, I was going to miss her when I left. I had to get back to my own time eventually. I'd arranged it with Tucker before I stepped into the chamber. He promised to give me twenty-four hours. I wanted to hang around here for a least a day to follow this lead. Then, well, I'd missed my midterms. I'd have to come up with a good excuse to explain my absence. Besides, even if I wanted to stay, and let's face it, this realm was tempting—better economy, cleaner environment, and, my eyes drifted back to Sage, *her*—there was already a Marlow Henry in this realm.

We'd left the city limits and were deep in a forested area of Michigan. The trees were thickly planted with multicolored leaves saturating the landscape. The road snaked around the rolling hills into a sparsely inhabited area. We hadn't passed a car coming from the other direction for some time.

Dark clouds had rolled in and drops began to splat on the windshield. Sage flicked on the wipers. *Scritch, scratch, scratch, scratch.*

"Are you sure this is the way?" Sage asked.

I double checked her GPS. "This is the address Blaine gave me. It's possible the cabin doesn't exist in this realm, though."

Sage slowed and squinted out the window. "There should be a driveway around here."

I leaned forward too, and helped her search. The rain rivulets made it difficult to see. Everything was covered in leaves. Trees and more trees. Then suddenly a break. I pointed. "There."

Sage slowed to almost a stop and turned onto a very narrow dirt road. "With the leaves and the rain it's hard to tell if it's been driven on lately."

The driveway opened up into a small field. A cabin sat in the middle. No lights. No sign of life.

"It's here and it must belong to the Tucker family," Sage said.

"Yeah." My chest grew heavy with disappointment. "I'm afraid the most we're going to accomplish here is to violate trespassing laws."

Sage twisted to look out the back window and began to reverse. "Stop," I said. "We're here. We might as well have a look around."

The rain picked up, forcing us to make a dash to the covered porch. The windows in front of us were ground level, but covered with drapes. I checked the door. Locked.

"There's nobody here," Sage said.

I was about to agree when I thought I heard something. Sage used her auto-starter to turn on the car.

"Shh," I said. "Turn that off."

She killed the engine. "What?"

"I think I heard something."

I knocked on the glass. There it was again. A faint call that sounded like "help."

Sage's eyes widened. "It's Teagan!"

Chapter 59

Marlow

YOU KNOW HOW, when you watch TV, and the cops kick in a locked door like it's a piece of cake? Yeah, not like that in real life. Fire spit up my shins as my foot connected with the door and I thought I put my hip out. I hobbled around like an insane person.

"Are you okay?" Sage asked, but she didn't waste any time seeing to my injuries. She skipped down the wooden steps and returned with a big rock. In two seconds flat, she had one of the living-room windows pounded out. Silence followed the sound of shattering glass. Thankfully, the pane was low and not too difficult to hop through without cutting a vein in the effort.

"Teagan!" Sage called.

"Sage? Sage!" We ran down a short dark hall toward her voice. I briefly took in the surroundings. The living room might have been cozy once upon a time, with a wood stove in the corner and an oversized couch and chair facing it. The floor was made of knotted pine, scuffed and worn. A throw rug lay under a marked-up coffee table riddled with empty pop bottles and an ashtray filled with butts.

A small kitchen had a few dirty dishes strewn along a chipped Formica countertop. A bad smell lingered in the air. Food maybe. Musk. Body odor.

A dead body.

"Oh my God," Sage said.

The bedroom was dim with the growing twilight. Enough light escaped a gauze-covered window to reveal Teagan. Her hair was brown now, and I almost didn't recognize her. Her wrists were tied to a headboard, and she lay nearly naked under a thin, white sheet. It was splattered with blood. Possibly belonging to the dead man who lay crumpled on the floor beside her. He'd succumbed to a gunshot wound to the chest.

Was he the rapist? He was fully clothed. And dead. With Teagan tied up, she couldn't have pulled the trigger.

Then who did?

Sage immediately began tugging on the ropes around one of Teagan's wrists. I rushed to free her other one.

"We're here now," Sage said. "We'll get you out of here." I heard the crack in her voice. It was hard to stay emotionally strong in a situation like this.

Once her arms were free, Teagan curled into a ball and wept on Sages lap. "I can't believe you found me."

Sage stroked her hair. "We did. And you're going to be okay. Where are your clothes?"

Teagan pointed to a dresser. "He put them in there."

I lifted a hand to show Sage I'd retrieve them.

"Who put them there, Teag?" Sage asked. "Who did this to you?"

"I don't know his name. I ran into him on campus once. He helped me pick up my books."

I pulled out what looked like workout clothes from the dresser and handed them to Sage.

"Do you know who the man on the floor is?" I asked.

Teagan stared at me like she saw me for the first time. "Averagegeek?"

I nodded. "Yeah."

Then her gaze went to the dead man. "The guy called him dad. Apparently he knows …knew my mother."

So that was the connection. Maybe that relationship had saved Teagan's life.

"Sage." I held out my hand. "Give me your phone. I'll call the police while you help Teagan dress."

I went into the hall to dial 911, but I couldn't get any reception. I had to go outside. I unlocked the front door and twisted open the dead bolt. I swung the door open wide and found myself staring at the end of a pistol pointed at my head.

"Hi, Blaine," I said.

Chapter 60

Marlow

"BACK UP," Blaine said coolly. His eyes were murky with hate. Or maybe fear. Probably both. He held the pistol with steady arms, his lips tugging slightly to one side. "You surprise me, Henry. I didn't think you had it in you."

He didn't know I wasn't the Marlow Henry from his world. Maybe that Marlow wouldn't be trembling as he stepped back into the room. *That* Marlow might own a gun and actually know how to use it. My mind quickly calculated all of the possible outcomes of the situation. None of them ended well for me or Sage or Teagan.

"Don't do anything stupid." He motioned with his free hand to a kitchen chair. "Sit down."

"You should turn yourself in," I said while complying.

"Shut up! You don't know what you're talking about. I can't go to jail."

Should've thought of that before you started raping and killing people, moron.

A full roll of duct tape rested on the counter. He tossed it at me. "Tape your legs to the chair, and make sure you make it tight."

I did as he said, taking as long as I possibly could. As far as Blaine knew, I was here alone and Teagan was still tied up in the bedroom. He didn't know about Sage. I'd spotted a door at the back of the hall. Hopefully it was a second way out.

"Who's the dead guy?" I asked. "Teagan's gone by the way."

"My worthless old man. And I assumed so," he answered smugly. "I doubt she'll get far, and I'm up for another chase."

"So what'd your dad do to you? You know, to make you hate him so much?"

My face stung with a sudden backhanded blow. "Shut up!"

My feet were tied and I waited for further instruction. I wasn't going to make his job easy.

"Put your hands behind your back."

When I hesitated, he shouted. "Now!"

I sighed and did as he said.

Blaine wrapped my wrists together tightly behind the chair, wrenching my shoulders back. "How'd you find me?" he asked. "No one knows about this place."

"You told me."

"Ha. I did not."

"You did. You told me about how you and your parents would come here to escape the pressures of the city."

Blaine had circled around in front of me by this point. He had the tape in his hand and I knew he was getting ready to paste a strip over my mouth. I had to keep him talking. "Your dad played chase and tickle games with you."

His scruffy jaw dropped and even in the dim lighting of the cabin I could see him grow white. "What did you say?"

"The gingerbread man. He sang it, and you ran."

His knees gave out and he lowered slowly to the floor. We were eye to eye now. "How do you know?"

"Is it true? Did he catch you?"

Blaine swallowed and spoke in a low monotone. "I screamed. I pleaded. He was always careful never to leave bruises above the neck. He always stopped shy of breaking my bones."

His eyes glistened, and I surprised myself by feeling a good amount of pity. He continued. "My mother was a drunk. She didn't stop him. I suffered at his hands for years until I got big enough to fight back. I vowed to kill him one day. And I did."

"I'm sorry."

"For what?"

"That this happened to you. Your father was sick. He needed help. And so do you. You don't have to be like him."

Blaine sprung to his feet, ripped off a piece of tape about four inches long and slapped it over my mouth.

"You don't know anything, so don't try to analyze me."

Both of our heads shot up at the sound of a car engine. Sage couldn't have called the cops because I'd taken her phone. Blaine grabbed his gun and ran outside. I heard the screech of wheels spinning in the gravel. I hopped and shuffled my chair across the floor so I could see out of the broken window. I just caught the taillights of Ben's car disappear. I was relieved that Sage and Teagan had gotten away. Not so crazy about being left behind in the company of a murderous psychopath, though.

Blaine jumped into the driver's side of his car. The engine refused to turn over. Only a pathetic click. He hopped out, slammed the door and swore. He lifted the hood and shook his head. I didn't know what Sage had done to disable his car, but kudos to her for her quick thinking.

Blaine stormed inside in a rage. His face was red like the devil's and he shoved me in his frustration. I toppled to the floor, and with no way to break my fall, hit my head with a whack. I wrestled to keep my breath even, with only my nose able to get air. Panic threatened to upend me.

Blaine rushed to the bedroom and from my vantage point on the floor, I saw him drag his father's body out the back. I wondered what he planned to do with it. Bury it? Burn it? Leave it to scavengers?

I wrenched at the tape around my wrists, but it was too tight to escape from, barely room for my blood to circulate. I was desperate to find a way out, but my situation seemed hopeless. In no time I heard Blaine's footsteps.

So, scavengers then.

He placed his gun on the table and lifted me back upright in the chair. My temple throbbed and I sensed a notable goose egg growing on the crown of my head. Blaine untied my feet, and I circled my ankles, working the blood back into my toes. It felt like my shoes were filled with red ants devouring my soles.

"Stand up," Blaine commanded. And I would have. Except for the cocking of a gun through the broken window.

"Put your hands up, Blaine Tucker!"

It wasn't Detective Kilroy. Sage Farrell stood framed by the window sill, legs parted, arms outstretched with both hands firmly gripping a gun. There was something very sexy about her and I wholeheartedly conceded to being rescued by her.

Blaine laughed. "I would, except, you see, I have my own gun." He must have grabbed it off the table just before Sage challenged him. He butted the barrel against my skull.

"Put yours down, or I'll blow off his head."

Sage hesitated for a moment, and my chest collapsed at seeing her fail so quickly after her attempt to rescue me. Why didn't she just keep driving to safety with Teagan."

Which made me think, where was Teagan?

In that instant, my question was answered. Blaine dropped his gun and cried out. I spun to see him gripping both sides of his neck. Teagan stood behind him with two dispensed epi pens in hand.

I had sense enough to kick Blaine's gun away. Sage swooped hers up off the floor.

"Blaine Tucker," she said. "Lay down and put your hands behind your head."

Blaine's body shuddered at the sudden overload of adrenaline and his knees buckled, bringing him face first to the floor with a thud. I pressed a knee into his back pinning him down and reached for his wrists, jerking them behind his back.

"Hand me the duct tape," I said to Sage.

"Where is it?"

"On the counter."

"I don't see it!"

I stretched to see the top of the kitchen counter, the last place I'd spotted the tape. My eyes scanned the wood floor.

"It's over there, against the wall." It must've rolled off the counter.

Sage handed me the tape, and I bound Blaine's wrists nice and tight and then I went to work on securing his ankles.

Sage and Teagan sat together on the couch. Sage had her arm around Teagan and she stroked her hair.

"It's over," she said in a comforting tone. "You're

going to be okay."

Blaine muttered thickly, "It's not over. It'll never be over."

Teagan gasped. I ripped off four inches of tape, and slapped it on Blaine's mouth. "Shut up, Tucker."

Once I was confident that Blaine was no longer a threat, I ushered the girls outside. "Wait in Ben's car. I'll try to get cell service."

Teagan looked pale and frail, and I could hardly believe she was the one who had subdued Blaine Tucker.

I patted her arm. "You were very brave in there."

She smiled weakly. "Thank you."

I jogged to the road through muck and fallen leaves with Sage's cell held over my head, praying for the bars to light up. The road was empty with the exception of a family of deer. They eyed me warily and then disappeared into the forest on the other side.

A quarter mile down the road, the bars lit up and I dialed 911.

Chapter 61

Marlow

TWENTY MINUTES LATER, three cop cars and two ambulances overwhelmed the yard. Blaine Tucker was arrested. His father's body was retrieved from a ravine behind the cabin. Teagan was treated and taken away by ambulance to the hospital where she was kept for observation overnight.

Sage and I were taken to the precinct and questioned further. Sage recounted once again how she and Teagan had subdued Blaine with her brother's gun, lawfully registered and carried in the glove compartment, and two epi pens, one near expiration. She told them that Ben had a peanut allergy and was always careful to get new epi pens before the old one expired.

The double shots to Blaine's neck first stunned him and then the rapid surge of adrenaline put him in an extreme stupor. The injections weren't life threatening, but it was enough to distract him from what he was doing at the moment and cloud his mind.

We eventually learned that the reason Blaine hadn't killed Teagan like he had Vanessa Rothman was because he wanted to use her to bait and taunt his father. Mr. Tucker had become obsessed with Mrs. Lake a few years earlier when they met at a social event. At first Mrs. Lake, having become disillusioned with her own marriage, had been enticed and seduced by an attractive and beguiling successful businessman. His attraction soon became obsessive and aggressive. He had threatened to harm her family if she defied him. It was unfortunate that Teagan had to suffer at the hands of the man's son before they could be free of them both.

The next day, Teagan's parents dropped her off at Sage's dorm to say good-bye. They waited protectively outside in their car after Teagan insisted she wanted to pack up her things alone. I sat on Sage's desk chair as she helped Teagan remove her artwork from the wall. They'd already filled Teagan's two suitcases with her clothes and sundry items, including all her art supplies. The police still had her laptop.

"I have mailing tubes for that," Teagan said, nodding to the hand-painted poster that Sage had rolled up. She held it while Sage tapped the poster inside. Sage's hand brushed against Teagan's and she held it.

"Are you going to be okay?" Sage asked.

Teagan ran a finger under one eye, capturing a

tear. "Eventually. Mom has arranged counseling. For all of us."

"What's next for you, Teagan?" I asked. "I mean, besides counseling."

She stroked her brunette hair, where the blue used to be. "I'm taking the rest of the semester off to figure it out." She sighed sadly. "I don't think I'll be coming back here."

I didn't blame her.

Sage and Teagan both let out a long breath when they realized that everything belonging to Teagan had been packed. There were two rolling suitcases, a couple large canvas bags and a box of artwork.

"Do you need help taking that out?" I asked.

"I think we're okay," Sage said. She grabbed both suitcases and Teagan had the bags over her shoulder and the box in her arms. I gathered they wanted to spend their last moments together on campus alone, without me.

Teagan placed the box down to give me a hug. "Averagegeek," she said. "You're not so average after all. Thanks for saving my life."

I smiled. "Any time."

She smiled back and considered me. "You look different without your glasses."

Teagan gathered up the box and the two of them left the room. I took the opportunity to study my face in the mirror. I did look different. Not better or worse just different.

Sage had a large variety of non-prescription lens glasses lying on her dresser. There was a pair with dark plastic rims that looked large enough to fit my face. I put them on.

It was strangely comforting. In a weird way, I missed my glasses. A part of me felt like I could hide behind them, which was ridiculous, since four inches of clear lenses could hardly conceal a man of my size.

It was a psychological hideout. Sage was right. People paid less attention to people with glasses. I'm not sure what it said about our society, but I actually didn't mind it.

I stepped in front of the window and watched as Teagan slipped into the backseat of her parents' car. She waved through the open window and blew kisses to Sage.

Sage blew them back. She didn't move from the curb until the Lake's car had disappeared around the corner.

I sat in her chair waiting for her to return. My eyes landed on the empty spots on the wall on Teagan's side of the room, ghostly shadows of where her art once hung.

Sage returned, gave me a short glance, then plopped face first on her bed, burying her nose in the pillow. Last night we were both so exhausted, emotionally and physically, we had fallen asleep within minutes of lying down, Sage on her bed and me in Teagan's.

Tonight was different.

Sage rolled over and stared at me. "Now what?"

"You mean, what to do with me? Am I right?"

"Not that I want to get rid of you," she said. She pulled herself up into a sitting position and hugged her pillow. "It's just, you're not actually a student here. There's another one of you out there. What's going to happen to you?"

A flash of light from outside caught my eye. "We might not have to worry about that for too long. I think my train has arrived."

Sage stared outside at the stirring wind and the rustle of leaves. A glow of dry lightning filled the sky.

"You can keep those," she said.

"Keep what?"

She pointed to her eyes and I remembered that I still had on a pair of her glasses. "Oh."

"To remember me by," she added.

I felt a grin creep up my face. "Thanks. I don't think I could forget you if I tried." I stood and took steps toward the door. "I should go. You take care, okay?"

Sage followed and wrapped her arms around me. She lay her head on my chest. "Thank you for helping me find
my best friend."

I patted her back. "You're welcome."

She kissed me gently on the cheek. A chaste kiss, but sweet. "Look me up when you get back."

"I will," I promised. Then I sprinted down the

hall, through the lounge and out the main doors. I stood under the lamppost that had just flickered on and waited.

I didn't have to wait for long.

Chapter 62

Marlow

THE SKY ABOVE was clear and blue. Once the electric tremors eased away, I took a moment to appreciate it. I was back in my world, warts and all. Litter traced the edges of the sidewalks, and the hedges weren't neatly trimmed. I breathed into the bottom of my soles, so relieved to be back. I headed toward my dorm.

Zed was in the guys lounge with his head stuck in the refrigerator. He pulled out a can of 7up and tugged on the metal tab. It burped with a fizzy sound, and Zed chugged it back. Then he spotted me. "Hey, there you are. I was about to send out a search party."

I had been gone for four days, the same amount of time most of the students had been gone for Thanksgiving. Seeing him slouching there as he let out a loud belch, I wanted to give him a big man hug, the kind with three slaps on the back. We hadn't been apart long enough to merit that kind of friendly expression, so I just said, "I stepped out for some air. How was your weekend?"

"Pretty boring. My younger brothers drove me crazy. Mom's turkey was great. I should've brought you some, though there was basically just the carcass left." He collapsed onto the couch and booted up the video game. "How about you? Were you bored out of your skull?"

"Uh, not exactly."

He rubbed his beard and glanced up at me. "Wanna play?"

"Sure." I settled in on the other end of the couch and picked up the controls. "Ready to get your butt kicked?"

⁓

Paul and Steve talked us into going out for a beer that evening. I was suffering some kind of jet lag due to my alternate universe travels and tried to beg off.

"Come on, Marlow," Paul said. "You've been sitting alone here all weekend. I know you're a geek, but you got us thinking you need therapy or something."

Maybe I did. Zed punched me in the arm. "We won't stay out late. One of us will get beaten up by eleven."

"I'm betting on Paul," Steve said.

"Yeah?" Paul said. "Wanna bet? I bet it's you."

Steve slapped the back of his head. "It'll be you, doofus."

Paul retaliated with a kick to Steve's rear end. "Who you calling a doofus?"

Zed's eyes never left the game. "My money's on both of them."

I laughed. "I'll bring first aid."

We ordered in three large meat-lovers pizzas. Afterward I showered and changed into fresh clothes. At moments I wondered if maybe I hadn't imagined the whole thing. But I could see the bar of soap in the shower. I could read the label on the shampoo bottle. My eyesight was proof that I hadn't gone crazy.

Despite the fact that I could see my reflection clearly in the mirror, I slipped on the glasses I'd gotten from Sage. Thinking of her made me smile. I was glad I had them, not just because they were a sweet reminder of her, but so the guys wouldn't ask questions. How would I explain my sudden ability to see?

Before we left, I took a moment to call my mom. "Sorry I didn't call earlier," I said.

My mom and I weren't exactly close, and most of that was due to my issues. I'd blamed her for my fatherless childhood. Our near-poverty existence. After learning of Blaine Tucker's disastrous father/son relationship, I realized maybe Mom had done me a favor.

"It's okay, son. I know you have a lot to do, but it is good to hear your voice."

She sounded old and lonely. "It'll be Christmas before you know it," I said. "You'll be sick of me by the time the holidays are over."

"I never get sick of you, Marlow. You know that. You're my baby."

"Yeah, Mom. I know."

The pub was one of many just on the outskirts of the campus grounds. It had a jukebox playing top forty, a couple pool tables, a bar and a seating area for beer drinkers and wing eaters.

I decided I deserved a beer and time to relax. No one to save. No new world to jump to. I could just be plain old boring Marlow Henry from the blue realm who was going to fail his first term because, despite the fact that he didn't go

home for Thanksgiving, he didn't show up for his exams and didn't get any essays written.

A gaggle of girls entered, and of course, all of us guys were immediately enthralled. My gaze landed on a dark-haired girl with coffee-colored eyes and my heart clogged in my throat. Sage Farrell.

She talked loudly, and her voice was slurred. She was obviously drunk.

She plugged the jukebox with quarters and started dancing. "Woo-hoo!" she yelled and waved at her gang of girls to join her.

I'd be lying if I said I could take my eyes off her. She was beautiful and alluring, sensual and vulnerable. I was at once completely thankful to Paul and Steve for dragging me out. Indebted in a way I'd never acknowledge to them.

The song changed to something slower, and Sage's moves slowed with it. Up to now she danced with other girls, but suddenly a male body was mixed in with the bunch. He nuzzled up to Sage and I was immediately alert. I could tell by her body language that she wasn't comfortable with his company. She kept turning her back to him, stepping away. He kept pressing close. Finally, she hip-checked him.

"Back off."

"Hey, I'm just dancing," he said. He didn't back off. I sat up straighter.

Sage made her way around the dance floor, stopping at the bar for another beer. She took it onto the dance floor. The music throbbed now with electronica. The guy kept his distance until she'd finished her drink, nearly dropping the empty glass in her effort to lay it on the bar. The guy pressed in behind her, as if he was trying to save her from spilling or something.

I tensed, moving to the edge of my seat prepared to pounce.

He moved her toward the door. She stumbled, trying to free herself from his grasp, but not quite clearheaded enough to do it.

That was it. I jumped to my feet. "Sage, there you are," I said. I nodded to the guy. "This is my sister. She called for a ride an hour ago and I just got here." The guy looked miffed, but concluded that it would be unwise to continue his pursuit. He huffed and disappeared.

Her gaze glazed over me. "You're not my brother." She sounded like she had marbles in her mouth.

"I know," I said. "But that guy is bad news."

"I hate bad guys," she said. "Are you a bad guy? A bad guy killed my best friend."

"No, I'm a good guy. Let me walk you home."

"Alone? I don't even know you."

It was true. She didn't know me. But I knew her better than she could imagine. "You're right not to accept my offer. I'll call you a cab."

She danced with her friends while I waited by the door, making sure no other guys made any unwanted advances. I called her over when the cab arrived. She got into it with two of her friends.

"Thanks." She stuck her head out the window. "I don't even know your name."

"Marlow."

"Thanks Marlow!" She finger waved, then sang out my name. "*Marlow, Marlow, Marlow.* Maybe I'll see you around!"

I smiled. Maybe.

The End

I hope you enjoyed reading GINGERBREAD MAN. Please consider leaving a review as they are very helpful to indie authors and also help readers find the books they love. If you want to make sure you don't miss any new release news or promo news sign up for my newsletter . For more info on my books or how to follow me on social media visit me at **leestraussbooks.com.**

LIFE IS BUT A DREAM

Dreams aren't real
Unless they are
And when someone wants to watch you drown
You better pay attention

Sage and Marlow are reunited in this second book of A Nursery Rhyme Suspense serial series. When Sage's dreams merge with Marlow's they know something strange is connecting them. But when the drowning dreams start to come true, Sage wonders if she can avoid her own death.

Life is but a Dream - Read on for the first chapter!

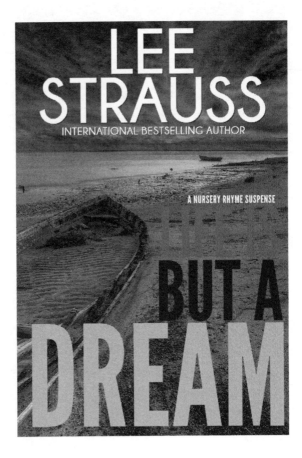

LIFE IS BUT A DREAM

When danger lurks in your sleep...

Chapter 1

Sage

SOMEONE WAS SITTING on my head. And blowing a trumpet in my ear. I groaned, stirring up a tidal wave of nausea. I sat up and the room spun, thrusting me onto my back. I wouldn't make it to the bathroom; I leaned over the edge of my bed and threw up on my black pumps.

I wiped my mouth on the shirt sleeve of my gray satin blouse, which I'd been wearing since the night before, and pinched my eyes shut, desperate for sleep to release me from my agony. Weighted darkness cloaked me and I slipped back into my dreams.

The air is cool and crisp, like late autumn. Leaves fall from the thinning branches. The world is an overexposed purple and green. My feet slip on the damp ground, and I grab the arm of the guy beside me. I don't see his face.

My chest tightens with fear, but I don't know of what. In front of us is an abandoned cabin, dark and sinister. Why are we here?

We're looking for something.

No. Someone.

We climb through a broken window and my pants snag on the jagged glass. My nose twitches at the smell of dust and mold and cigarette smoke.

Someone has been smoking here. Someone's here. We aren't safe! I grab the guy's arm again, this time seeing his face. Black-framed glasses over light green eyes, shaggy brown hair. His expression is serious. Somehow I know his name. Marlow.

We run down a dark hallway into a bedroom, and my heart leaps! A girl is tied to a bed. She's a brunette, but she has Teagan's face. Is it Teagan? My Teagan? Her eyes open and flash with recognition when she sees me.

"Sage?"

"Teagan! You're alive!"

Suddenly I'm in the hallway, walking toward the front door. I stare at my hand. I'm holding a cell phone, my cell phone, but it isn't my hand. It's large and masculine. I have a man's hand. I reach for the door, knowing what I have to do. I have to call 911. I have to get help. I open the door and yelp. A gun is pointed at my head.

My eyes sprung open. My heart beat frantically, thumping hard against my ribs. *Teagan*. When reality dawned, as it always did after a Teagan dream, a dark blanket of depression settled over me. It wasn't Teagan's body that slept soundly in the bed across the dorm room from mine. Teagan was gone. She was dead.

I squinted against the glow of morning light. An alarm went off and Nora's red head popped up from under thick covers. She tapped her phone, killing the siren, and yawned. Then her freckled nosed wrinkled.

"What's that awful smell?"

"I'm sorry," I said, feeling fresh embarrassment. "I threw up."

"In here?"

"I couldn't make it to the bathroom."

Nora turned on a light and a groan escaped my chapped lips.

"Well, are you going to clean that up?"

"Yes. I'm sorry," I said again. I was sorry. I'd become a drunken idiot since Teagan died.

"Sooner would be better than later," Nora said as she spritzed perfume into the room. She disappeared into the bathroom and I forced myself to sit up.

Nora O'Shea was my new roommate. We were in the same math and science program so we shared a lot of classes. Like me, she was focused and tidy, and she appreciated numbers and logic.

Lee Strauss

Teagan had been my best friend since grade school. She was an artist: messy, colorful and disorganised. She was nothing like me. And I missed her so much.

I heard the shower turn off, a signal that I had to start moving. After reaching for my glasses, my faves with bright purple frames, I managed to inch myself out of bed. I found an empty plastic grocery bag and gingerly picked up my pukey shoes and tossed them in. I stuck out my lower lip with regret. I really liked these shoes. I held the bag gingerly as I shuffled out of the room, down the hall and into the common lounge where I disposed of the bag in the garbage bin.

Nora exited the bathroom just as I got back, and I took a turn. I washed my hands then downed an extra-strength Tylenol with two glasses of water. I reached under the sink for a rag and the cleaning products, returned to my side of the room and started scrubbing the low-pile industrial carpet.

"Um," Nora started. "There's something I've been meaning to tell you."

I held my breath as I scrubbed my vomit out of the rug. "Yeah?"

"I've been hanging out with Jake."

My hand stopped and I looked up at her. "Teagan's Jake?"

"He's not Teagan's Jake. They broke up two weeks before she…"

"I know. It's just, I'm used to seeing him with her."

"That's why I haven't said anything before."

"So why are you saying anything now?"

"Because I think we're about to make it official."

I frowned.

"Sage, please understand. I really, really like him and he likes me. It's awful what happened to Teagan, but life goes on."

I inhaled deeply, but it wasn't enough to soothe the swelling pain in my chest.

"Look, if it makes it easier for you, we won't hang out when you're around."

I sighed again. "No. It's fine. You're free to date whomever you like."

"Thanks, Sage. I know the last four months have been hell for you."

Four months? Already? It felt like Teagan just left me last week.

Once the carpet was cleaned, I crawled back into bed and watched as Nora got ready to go out. She looked really cute in her jeans and trendy spring jacket. Her hair hung over her shoulder in a long, crimson braid.

She paused at the door. "Are you going to be okay?"

I nodded. "I'm fine. Are you meeting Jake?"

Her glossy lips pulled up into a smile. "Yeah."

"Say hi for me."

"I will."

I watched her go and it was like the sunshine left with her. The room suddenly grew dimmer and it threw me back into my dream. The cabin. Teagan. The guy. The gun.

I'd seen the guy before. He'd called a cab for me once, on my first drinking spree after Teagan died. He'd saved me from a potentially bad situation. I saw him around campus on occasion, but we never had reason to talk since then.

I wondered why I dreamed about him. What was the cabin all about? And why did Teagan sometimes have brown hair instead of her natural blond?

I was just glad they'd caught her killer. Some hotline tip. It wasn't the first time I'd dreamed about Teagan. That was normal. It also wasn't the first time I dreamed about Marlow, a guy I barely knew. In one apocalyptic dream, I power-hosed him in a decontamination shower. He was buck-naked.

In fact, he appeared in almost all the dreams I had about Teagan. At least the bad ones. Why? What was it about this guy? I wondered if I should look him up.

Books by Lee Strauss

The Perception Series
(dystopian/sci-fi/romance)
Ambition (short story prequel)
Perception (book 1)
Volition (book 2)
Contrition (book 3)

Playing with Matches (WW2
history/romance)
Playing with Matches
A Piece of Blue String (companion short story)

A Nursery Rhyme Suspense
(Romantic Suspense-mystery/sci-fi)
Gingerbread Man
Life is but a Dream
Hickory Dickory Dock

About the Author

Lee Strauss is the author of A Nursery Rhyme Suspense Series, The Perception Series (young adult dystopian), and young adult historical fiction. She is the married mother of four grown children, three boys and a girl, and divides her time between British Columbia, Canada and Dresden, Germany. When she's not writing or reading she likes to cycle, hike and practice yoga. She enjoys traveling (but not jet lag :0), soy lattes, red wine and dark chocolate.

Lee also writes younger YA fantasy as Elle Strauss.

For more info on books by Lee Strauss and her social media links visit **leestraussbooks.com**. To make sure you don't miss the next new release, be sure to sign up for her newsletter!

Acknowledgements

A big shout out to the fans of The Perception Series! Your enthusiasm encouraged me to keep writing in the science fiction/dystopian/romance genre. I hope you enjoy this new series, A Nursery Suspense.

I have to thank my husband Norm Strauss who helped me develop the initial idea as we walked the streets of London while there doing research for another book. Also to my son and daughter Jordan Strauss and Tasia Strauss along with Diana Balcaen, who helped me brainstorm plot.

Thanks so much to my beta readers, A. M. Offenwanger, Wendy Squire, Denise Jaden and Melinda Van Patter who always get the worse drafts, and to my faithful reviewers, especially Mandy Anderson of I Read Indie. Also to Steven Novak for another great set of covers and to Marie Jaskulka for editing.

As always, I am grateful to my friends and family for their love and support and to God who keeps me balanced and sane through all the craziness that is independent publishing.

Made in the USA
Charleston, SC
19 February 2016